RED MOON RISING

BILLIE SUE MOSIMAN

D1007022

DAW BOOKS, INC.

DONALD A. WOLLHEIM, FOUNDER

375 Hudson Street, New York, NY 10014

ELIZABETH R. WOLLHEIM

SHEILA E. GILBERT

PUBLISHERS

www.dawbooks.com

First Printing, February, 2001
2   3   4   5   6   7   8   9

DAW TRADEMARK REGISTERED
U.S. PAT. OFF. AND FOREIGN COUNTRIES
—MARCA REGISTRADA
HECHO EN U.S.A.

PRINTED IN THE U.S.A.

SHE WAS ALONE IN A TERRIBLE PLACE. . . .

It was a barren, scraggly wood where the moon was blood red, and there was no path, no starlight, no hope. She'd been here before, she knew, and thought it a dream. Mentor had rescued her, and in an insane way she had been momentarily furious with him.

Now she called his name, at first softly, "Mentor . . . Mentor," then louder, and louder, until she was screaming his name, frantic to find him or someone, anyone, to rescue her. The moon was melting now and oozing down the sky like thick red paint. When it touched the horizon, she knew something would happen, something unforeseen and quite fearsome. The trail lengthened, the trees pressed in on all sides, their bare limbs almost touching her, and she found she could not breathe. It was as if all the air had been sucked from this surreal universe, leaving her to suffocate, to fall to her knees gasping.

"We must turn back," came a voice.

"Mentor! Where are you? Why can't I see you? Get me out of here, please. Mentor, I can't breathe!"

Someone had her hand and was dragging her back the way she had come. She could not see who it was, but it didn't matter anyway; she was blacking out from lack of oxygen. A small voice in her mind whispered in a childlike singsong, "You're dead, you're dead, you're dead now, you're dead."

"Don't listen," Mentor said. "Get up, get to your feet, it's coming!"

This book is dedicated to my husband,
Lyle Duane Mosiman, for years of
unflagging love and support. He is the best
thing that ever happened to this writer.

I would like to thank Ed Gorman and
Martin Greenberg for their help with
this novel. Had it not been for them,
John Helfers, and my editor, Sheila Gilbert,
this work would not exist.

But first, on earth as vampire sent,
Thy corpse shall from its tomb be rent:
Then ghastly haunt thy native place,
And suck the blood of all thy race;
There from thy daughter, sister, wife,
At midnight drain the stream of life. . . .
Wet with thine own best blood shall drip
Thy gnashing tooth and haggard lip;
Then stalking to thy sullen grave
Go—and with the ghouls and afreets rave,
Till these in horror shrink away
From specter more accursed than they!
                    —Lord Byron,
                        The Giaour (1813)

1

It was an early Monday morning in March. Texas had come alive with drifts of bluebonnets and mild, warm days. Graduation was in another two months, and Della Joan Cambian could hardly wait to get to school.

It wasn't just that soon she'd have her diploma and *real* life could begin for her as a recognized adult in the world. She had a growing interest in Ryan Major, a new boy who had transferred from North Dallas a few weeks earlier.

Even though she always went lightly on makeup, often using none at all, today she decided to try a new shade of lipstick. What could it hurt? Besides, her color seemed to be off. Her natural olive complexion looked sallow. She tried opening the curtains on the windows in her room, letting in the morning light, and looking in the mirror again, but her skin still seemed to be some horrid shade of yellow-brown.

Applying the lipstick and hoping it would brighten her entire look, Dell paused when she saw the lesion on the back of her right forearm reflected in the mirror. She sat at her dressing table, stunned, her mother calling from the hall, warning that her primping would make her late for the school bus. Again.

Dell didn't answer her mother. She couldn't. Her arm was frozen, Cover Girl Burnt Sienna poised just a whisper from the mid-curve of her top lip. She blinked, slowly lowered her arm, and let the lipstick roll from her fingers. That's how her mother found her, staring like Narcissus at her own image.

"Dell, honey, what's the matter?"

In place of words, Dell raised her right arm until the mirror caught the pink festering oval of flesh. Her mother approached slowly and stared down into the mirrored reflection.

"Mom?"

Her mother reached out one hand as if she would touch the lesion, but her fingers danced in the air before disappearing from sight. "It's . . . it's just . . ."

"Mom? Will you look me over? Are there more? Are they everywhere?" Suddenly, Dell pushed back from the dressing table. In no time, she had her blue sweatshirt pulled high above and then over her head. As she lowered her arms to rip the shirt off, her mother caught and held her tightly. She was imprisoned by the sleeves, held in a position that afforded no movement.

"Don't, honey."

"Does it mean . . . ? Am I . . . ? Will I be like you now? Mom?" She felt tears well, and the room blurred. Over her mother's shoulder she could see her own face in the mirror. It was as if she had never really looked at herself before, as if who she saw reflected was a stranger. She was not just sallow. She was sick.

She could feel an irritation on her left shoulder. Now that she was concentrating on her body, she felt what might be another lesion on the back of her right knee. They were all over her, evidence of disease at work.

"Let me go, Mom."

Her mother released her, and she threw off the shirt and began turning and twisting to look over her body.

It was not as if she thought this day might never come. Of her immediate family, she was the last to contract the disease. They had all pretended it had skipped her. She might be spared. Others were. Her Aunt Celia hadn't ever gotten sick. Sometimes a few escaped their destiny. But very few.

The lesions indicated the beginning of a mutated form of a rare blood disease the medical community called porphyria. Next would come the terrible sensitivity to sunlight. Then her lips would feel paralyzed and betray her, so that she could not even smile. It would all pass swiftly. What took the real disease of porphyria decades to do to an afflicted human, the mutated virus would do to her within days.

The horror of it was enough to bear, more than enough to make her raving mad. But even worse was not knowing if she would turn into a Predator, a Craven, or a Natural, like those in her family. No one could predict the outcome of the process until the disease had run its course.

Once her mother let her go, Dell sagged onto the edge of her bed. She felt panic ruling her, causing her mind to race out of control. She hardly knew what to do. How was she to control an event that was rushing toward chaos, she asked herself. "There's no point in checking anymore," she said in a resigned voice. "I feel one on my shoulder and another behind my knee. I can sense things. If I can tell where they are without looking, then I'm sick, and that's all there is to it." She lay down on the unmade bed, pulling her legs up and hugging them. She still had on jeans and shoes, but she didn't care. She heard the school bus outside, heard it brake with a hiss, and after a minute, move on without her. She would miss a trig test and have to make it up. She wouldn't see Ryan today. Or all week. If she fell ill, how could she let her interest in him continue anyway? How could she have imagined she ever had a chance at a normal life?

"I'll call Mentor," her mother said, leaning down to pat her cheek the way she used to do when Dell was little and ran a fever.

Dell nodded, closing her eyes, trying not to think about it. Mentor came on house calls when summoned in a crisis. He had to be there for the young ones who were so devastated by the change. So it was true. Her mother knew it too. There could be no mistake if Mentor was sent for. This wasn't chicken pox or some other innocuous illness. It was not melanoma or another skin disease. It was the thing that stopped the human heart from beating. It was the monster that defied death and lived on within you, hungering and unholy.

That was the one true thing about the supernatural life she was about to enter—how unholy it truly was. It wasn't true, for example, that a vampire produced no reflected image. Her mother was proof enough to dispel that old myth. She looked in mirrors to apply makeup so that she would not appear to be so pale. It wasn't true that crosses or holy water affected them. In fact, most of the old myths about vampires were wrong—all made up, fictional, and totally inaccurate. Soon Dell would know from inside the reality of the vampire's life, what it was like to be the same as her parents and her brother.

Dell choked back a sob and turned her head into the pillow.

"I'll be right back," her mother said. "Don't worry. Don't cry. Please don't cry."

Dell heard her rush from the room like a draft of wind from an open window. When she wanted to, her mother could do miraculous things. True and real things. Move like shadow. Sleep standing up. Know her daughter's pain as her own. But she couldn't keep her from death. And she couldn't keep her from crying.

Not today.

* * *

While waiting for help, Dell's mother sat on her bedside and smoothed her brow. Dell kept her eyes tightly shut, trembling in increasing waves that shook her body. She felt faint and thought she was going to pass out. "Mom, I'm going to faint."

Her mother shushed her and leaned in close to kiss her cheek. "The family's coming," she said.

Dell teetered on the brink of consciousness, moving in and out, feeling first her mother's cool hand on her face and then not experiencing anything but a sense of loss. She wanted to ask for Aunt Celia, but she couldn't seem to speak. She was moving inexorably toward unconsciousness, but fought against it, afraid of what lay ahead. She never knew when her mother moved from her side or when Aunt Celia and her daughter, Carolyn, entered the room. She never knew when Mentor arrived. Her first realization that he was there was when he spoke, reaching her through the veil of unconsciousness that kept her wrapped solidly in its arms.

"What are you dreaming?" Mentor asked.

She could not see him, so he must be apart from it, helping her awaken. That's what Mentor did. That was his job. Helping.

She spun away from his voice and fell through dark space until she found herself in a strange surrounding. She was dreaming, she assumed. She saw something she had to tell Mentor about.

"I'm in a dark wood. And there's a red moon rising."

"Does it frighten you?"

"Yes!" She peered through leafless trees, tripped over exposed roots, moving always toward the red moon. Though she feared what it meant to her life, she was drawn against her will. She could sense there was something waiting out there, just beyond her field of vision. If she kept moving toward it, she would learn all she ever wanted to know about the world and how it worked.

"You can speak with the moon another time, Dell. Will you open your eyes now and visit with me? We have lessons and preparations."

She feared the moon, so luminous with blood, so majestic that it seemed to fill the sky with rays that turned the landscape scarlet. What did it mean for her? Yet waking to the reality of what she would become and how to move into that becoming was even more frightening. "No, I'll just stay here," she said, more careful now as she picked her way over brown tangled roots and through thick vines that shimmered and shivered as if malevolently alive. A limb with rough bark reached out and scraped her cheek, leaving a burning trail. She flung her arms at it, skipping aside and beginning to run now.

"Dell, it's time for you to return to us."

Time. Mentor knew everything. Mentor was as old as the hills in the hill country of Texas, he was older than any vampire she knew. He was older than dirt, as her grandfather would say. "Do I have to?" she asked. She took one more step through the barren forest, looked up at the startling sky, at the moon with a face like Death . . . and opened her eyes.

"I'm sorry," he said. "I didn't think it was healthy for you to stay in that place alone."

He had forced her out and awake. She found a blanket covering her bare arms. She was hot, suffocating, a sudden sheen of sweat popping from her brow. "How long did I sleep?"

"Not long. Less than an hour. Can I see the sores?"

She stretched out her arm and bent it at the elbow so that the lesion faced him.

"Are there more?"

"Two so far." She mentally searched her body and added, "No, there's a new one since Mom called you. Three more then, besides this one."

"How do you feel?" he asked.

She liked his eyes. Many of the Predators had shiny brown irises so dark they looked as black as the bottom of an oil drum. And since Mentor was technically a Predator—or had been at one time—she thought he would have eyes like that. Instead, his eyes were as warm and brown as coffee and kind, patient, knowing. There was no furtive agenda of harm hidden behind his eyes. He had come to help her.

She sat up, throwing off the blanket, uncaring that she sat before this old vampire in her bra. "Hot," she said, "burning up."

"It's fever. You'll be chilled in a few minutes and will need that blanket again."

Behind Mentor, she could see her family. Her father had his arm around her mother's shoulder. Her brother Eddie leaned against the wall, chewing on a fingernail. Then she saw Celia, her mother's sister, and her cousin Carolyn.

She reached out her arms and instantly Celia came to her side, leaning over the bed and hugging her. "Oh, I'm so sorry, baby. We're all here for you. Grandma and Grandpa are on the way."

Carolyn came around the other side of the bed and took one of Dell's hands and squeezed it. She was only a year younger than Dell, and all her life she'd faced this same event happening to her. So far, like her mother, she had not been infected.

Dell saw tears in her eyes. "Don't cry for me," she said, trying not to cry again herself. "I'm going to be all right. Won't I be all right, Mentor?"

He nodded at her, but he said nothing.

There was a rustle in the room and from behind her parents Dell saw her grandparents enter the room. The bedroom was crowded now with people, all of them watching her. Soon Dell's other aunts, uncles, and cousins would all file into the house, keeping vigil. Unable to fit into the bedroom, they would stand around the living room, walk in the yard, whisper her name to Heaven, and pray for her.

Her grandmother came to the bed. Celia moved aside, first kissing Dell on the cheek.

"Darling, we'll be waiting for you," Grandma said.

"I don't want to die!" Dell heard the panic in her own voice and saw the scared, startled look in her grandmother's eyes.

"You'll come back to us," Grandma said. She was in her eighties and vampire, a Natural, like all of Dell's family. "We'll wait here until that happens. When you open your eyes again, I'll be here."

The warmth of her grandmother's embrace gave Dell strength, but a trembling came over her nevertheless. She shivered uncontrollably. She heard Mentor ask everyone to stand back, and her grandmother let her go. Mentor scooted his chair closer to the bed.

"What does the moon dream mean?" Dell asked, feeling the outlines of the room shimmer and move in and out as if they were no more substantial than flimsy cloth.

He waved off the question of the dream. "Not important. We can talk about it later."

"What is important, then?"

"Your soul."

As the human girl she had been for nearly eighteen years, she might have scoffed at him. But as a changeling, she understood perfectly how serious it was to preserve the soul. If, in the midst of the change from death to life again, she lost all vestige of her mortal self, she might be condemned to wander the Earth like a fiendish nightmare bent on the annihilation of the human race.

"Help me, Mentor," she said, beginning to shake harder, holding her arms close to her body to warm her ribs.

He lifted the blanket and placed it gently around her shoulders. "That's what I'm here to do, Dell."

"I'm sick. I want to . . . die." She would die. Oh, yes, she would. But it would not be real dying, not a death of rest or peace, with her soul sleeping in the loving arms of her Creator. But die she would.

Mentor went down onto his knees and took both her trembling hands into his own. "In a few hours it will be dark, and you'll feel a little better. Until then we'll talk."

He looked so sad, she almost wanted to comfort him—except she had no emotional strength left to comfort even herself. "So cold," she said, teeth chattering. She felt as brittle as one of her mother's old china plates, her tongue sticking to the roof of her mouth. Her eyes felt dry, and she couldn't keep her knees from knocking together like nervous tambourines. The bed shook with her trembling. In a minute she might be fevered again. She would get sick and empty her stomach. She would pace the floor and stop to frantically feel for her heartbeat. Her little brother, Eddie, the only one she'd seen transform, had done that and it had broken her heart.

She would curse heaven and beg for hell, just as he had. She would claw the mattress and try to bury her face in the springs so that no one could see her private agony.

Tomorrow would be no better.

"You're wrong," Mentor said, brushing the hair from her eyes. "Tomorrow will be a little easier."

Dell was used to her family reading her mind, but they only did it when she said they could, respecting her privacy. "Don't do that," she said, breathless now, pushing at the blanket to get it away from contact with her burning skin. *Don't listen to my thoughts.*

"All right," he said. "If that's what you want."

Dell looked for her mother in the darkened room. *Mom, I need you!* Dell called to her silently.

Before Dell could blink, her mother was at her side, blowing on her skin, waving her hands around like windmills to cool her escalating temperature. "My baby," she crooned. "It's coming along, baby. Don't fight."

Mentor retreated to the dressing table chair he had pulled over to the bed. It was too small for his bulk, giving him the appearance of a creature on a perch. He sat in the shadows, his aging, craggy face hidden in darkness. Dell began to fear him until she caught the thought he projected to her. It was the very first time she had read anyone's thought at all, and she was glad it had come from Mentor. *We love you,* he said simply. *We're here for you. Don't be afraid. This is not the end.*

* * *

What Mentor had promised Dell was the truth. Dying this way was not the end. Becoming vampire was not the end. The end might never come for her, and there lay the problem for all of them, even himself. Especially himself. Though he had earned his respectful nickname more than a thousand years in the past, and though it had been his job to mentor, to help, and to guide new and desperate fledglings for as long as the memory of his race could remember, sometimes Mentor questioned not only his advice and the relevance of his role, but the very meaning of vampiric existence.

The wise men who had trained him in human psychology during the time of the ancients when there were so few of his kind could never have envisioned their teaching would have to sustain him throughout not one lifetime, but dozens of lifetimes. Certainly he had kept up with psychology and both the human and vampire spirits. He had augmented his education over progressive generations until finally, one day near the beginning of the new millennium in the year 2000, he turned away from scholarship and said to himself, "Enough. I can learn no more."

Yet even that was a lie he told to himself. He learned something new about spirit every time he was called upon to minister to someone as sick and miserable and dying as the girl now lying on her bed in a comalike trance. It was this challenge that kept him going, the task that drove away his own misery long enough so that he could reach out to vampire children such as Dell. What he had learned already from the girl was that teens today were just as earnest, needful, and as full of pure light as their predecessors had been.

Some parents had tried to tell him the young people were subversive, rebellious, uncontrollable, and sometimes conscienceless, as if born with deformed hearts. Mentor knew that was wrongheaded at the outset. But Dell Cambian was further proof. He could sense her true essence, and it was as uncontaminated by fraud, evil, and envy as a newborn babe's. Dell Cambian was worth saving, worth bringing into the Natural life. He would fight for her soul and show her how to fight for it. He would guide her to the other side and bring her back whole again.

Changed, of course, yes, changed. But whole and saved from the baser life of a Predator. Or, God forbid, the nonlife of a Craven.

Most of his kind believed that what one became—Natural, Predator, or Craven—had to do with the progression and mutation of the disease. For many years it was what he thought, too, but he came to realize it just was not so. Many of the Naturals had entered medical research trying to find an end to the disease. The first discovery they made was about the nature of the actual human death.

Mentor had been trying to spread the truth of the matter. The disease that made vampires, the mutation that killed and made men live again, did not determine a man's state of moral being. All it did was turn human into vampire. What sort of vampire one became had to do with the state of the soul. And how hard that soul fought for freedom from the prevailing darkness.

If the patient brought back too much of the darkness, he was Predator—vile, often depraved, without empathy, and truly heartless. A wicked creature. If the darkness brought back was less, the vampire suffered physical weaknesses, a faint hold on the world, and a depression that never relented. They were called the Craven. They were the cowardly and weak, useless to themselves and society. The Naturals brought back the least darkness from their encounter with death, and they were never as human as they once had been, but they *longed* to be, and that made all the difference.

"You must fight off the dark wood," Mentor whispered to the now comatose Dell. He projected his firm thought with the spoken words. He knew she could hear him on some level.

"Take her through it, Mentor," Dell's mother pleaded at his side. "Don't let her be lost to us."

Mentor looked up at the mother, a handsome woman with blonde hair and dark skin, her eyes shiny with tears. If she shed them they would be her blood and weaken her. He took her hand for a moment. She was as strong now as when he'd helped her through her own change. "Go and pray," he said.

"God doesn't listen to me. I prayed that neither of my children would ever get sick, and my prayers went unanswered."

"You merely prayed for the wrong result," Mentor said. "God does not bargain."

Dell's father approached the bed and behind him in the shadows came Eddie, Dell's younger sibling. The rest of the family gathered together in a corner of the room, standing close, holding a silent vigil. The elder Cambian said, "I would give my soul if this could be stopped."

Mentor knew his job included the family, not just Dell. He could not have any more mention of sacrifice. That simply created shame, when the sacrifice could not be given. Even now, he could see how the father's hands shook in rage and how the mother's face belied her pain, and even the boy child had bared his teeth, the incisors growing of their own accord, as if he might rip open a vein in his own arm and feed his sister to hurry her back to the world.

Mentor did not know if prayer helped, of if God even existed, but he encouraged his people to believe. Believing might create truth. It was written in Romans, in the Bible, "I am persuaded that neither death, nor life, nor angels, nor principalities, nor powers, nor things present, nor things to come, nor height, nor depth, nor any creature, shall be able to separate us from the love of God." If a man believed, then he always had God on his side.

"Go with your wife, take your son, and pray for Dell," he said, gesturing them away. He turned to the assemblage and commanded, "Leave us alone. Let me save what I can. We need to be alone for the journey."

When they'd left the room, Mentor placed his hands on each side of Dell's temples and turned her sweaty face toward him. He leaned in close. "I'm coming, Dell. I won't let you walk through the dark without me."

2

She was alone, dreadfully so. Not just alone as she had been at home before, when her parents were out and her brother not yet home from school. Not alone the way she'd felt one day at the mall with her friends when they shopped for clothes and she discovered that she hadn't any interest in fashion.

This time, she was alone in a terrible place, a reality she never had known existed. It was a barren, scraggly wood where the moon was an improbable blood red and there was no path, no starlight, no hope. She had been here recently, she knew, and thought it a dream. Mentor had brought her out and in an insane way she had been momentarily furious with him.

Now she called his name, at first softly, "Mentor . . . Mentor," then louder, and louder, until she was screaming his name, frantic to find him or someone, anyone, to rescue her. The moon, escaped from a Salvadore Dali painting, was melting now and oozing down the sky like thick red paint. When it touched the horizon, she knew something would happen, something unforeseen and quite fearsome. The trail lengthened, the trees pressed in on all sides, their bare limbs almost touching her, and she found she could not breathe. It was as if all the air had been sucked from this surreal universe, forgetting her, leaving her to suffocate, to fall to her knees gasping.

"We must turn back," came a voice.

"Mentor! Where are you? Why can't I see you? Get me out of here, please. Mentor, I can't breathe!" As she said it, it was true. She grabbed at her throat and opened her mouth fish-wide, sucking, finding nothing to breathe. *I'll die now*, she thought. *So this is how it happens? My lungs burst and fill with the blood-red moon.*

Someone had her hand and was dragging her back the way she had come. She could not see who it was, could not bend her neck and try to see behind her, but it didn't matter anyway; she was blacking out from lack of oxygen. Stars that had not been there before lit the Dali sky, flaring just at the back of her brain. She thought her mouth was working, gaping, and she was still struggling, but a small voice in her mind whispered in a childlike singsong, "You're dead, you're dead, you're dead now, you're dead."

"Don't listen," Mentor said, and she knew the voice belonged to him. "It's not really the truth. Only listen to what I tell you, Dell. Try to get to your feet."

Get to her feet. She had always been obedient, at least almost always. But how could she stand if she could not catch her breath? She gasped and tried to turn her head so he could see for himself that she was losing the battle.

"Up! Get up, get to your feet, it's coming!"

She wanted desperately to comply. *Something* was coming, and maybe if she could ascertain what exactly that was, she would be motivated to climb to her feet, air or no air in her poor scalding lungs. Whatever it was it had produced panic in Mentor's voice. He jerked at her arm, and she flipped over onto her back. It was then she could see the thing that frightened Mentor so.

Her mind raged against it.

"Dell, you must help yourself. If you don't get up and move, all is lost."

He must be a Predator, but more bloodthirsty than
any she had known on Earth. He stood so tall his
cape blocked the bloody sky and the moon's melting
curves seemed to be red wings attached to his back.
He swept down toward them from a hill, his face set
against any plea for mercy.

Suddenly the world filled with his thunderous
voice. "In order to wreak revenge, you must come
with me!"

No, I can't, she thought, *I won't.*

"Don't listen to him," Mentor said, drawing her
away from the approaching demon.

"I will give you the power of a god," boomed the
Predator's voice. "You will be ruler over the Earth,
if only you'll come with me."

And I will kill and take innocent life the way you
do, she thought. *No, no, that's not what I want.*

Dell found the last bit of air in the bottom of her
burning lungs and drew strength from it. She scrambled to her feet and, turning her back to the maraud-
ing creature, clutched Mentor's hand. They ran
swiftly, barely touching the ground, and she knew
Mentor was supernaturally speeding them away.
They moved so fast past the blackened trees that the
trunks were but a blur to the right and left of her.
The light glowed red all around and from out of the
clouds it dripped like liquid to cover the earth. Mentor led her into the clouds, which were more mist
than anything else, the moisture cool against her
skin. If she were dead and being pursued by a de-
vouring vampire, then she must find some way
through this death dream and back to her parents
where they might lay her to rest. She would not be
taken.

The clouds parted, and Dell stood alongside Mentor at the edge of a great cliff. Below she could see
for miles, and across a chasm there appeared to be
numerous dark-mouthed caves yawning.

"Come back to me," screamed the creature at their

backs. "Be one of my children. I will give you all the power of the universe."

"Hold tight to me," Mentor said. "Don't listen to his promises."

She clutched at his hand. Suddenly, Mentor stepped off the cliff and pulled her with him into clear space above the canyons. Behind her, she thought she could hear the frenzied footsteps of the Giant Predator, thought she could smell his fetid breath at her neck. She would not look back, never would she look back. And she would not look down, knowing if she did she might collapse and lose touch with Mentor, to fall forever into oblivion.

They crossed the chasm through thin air, air that was without air, and settled on the lip of a cave opening. Mentor drew her inside.

She did collapse now, falling to her knees in a near faint. She realized with a shock that she had not taken a breath since she first heard Mentor's voice back in the red forest. Could she speak, without air in her lungs to voice the words?

"I . . . I . . ."

"Yes," he said, sitting beside her on the cold, damp earth of the cave floor. "You can speak. And you have no need of air here. This is the place where the soul lives once the body's heart has stopped beating."

"I don't believe all this. Am I dead?" She clutched at her chest, feeling for a heartbeat.

"The disease has taken you away, Dell."

"Dead, then?" She had her hand flat against her rib cage, and there was silence beneath it.

He nodded. He reached out and touched her face tenderly. "Don't be afraid. You'll live again."

"And breathe again? Just like my parents and Eddie?"

"Yes, like them. But you must understand you will never need breath again. You'll have to learn to breathe only to pass through the world without arousing suspicion."

"It took them hours to learn how to breathe again. It was awful watching Eddie like that."

"I'm afraid that's part of the learning process."

"What was that . . . that thing back in the woods? I know he was evil, but what was he?" she asked.

Mentor gazed over the gorge to the far side and the red, misty clouds there. It was as if he could see through it to the heart of the haunted woods. There was no sign of the large Predator. "It was The Maker. He isn't the only one. There's one more."

"The maker of Predators? That's what I saw?"

"Yes."

"And if I hadn't run, he'd have made me one, too?" She knew the answer, but she had to ask it.

"Yes."

Dell thought it over. "And the other one . . . somewhere in this place is a Craven Maker?" She shivered at the thought of the Craven and what it might be like to meet the one who made them all. They weren't as scary or ferocious as the Predators, but their lives on Earth were full of suffering and loneliness, which seemed to her just as horrible a fate.

"This cave," he said, "is the place of the Mistress."

"Then why did you bring me . . . ?"

She never got to finish her question. From out of the vast darkness at the back of the cave came a shuffling sound, and into the red light spilling from the chasm into the mouth of the cave came a creature that could stir pity in the hardest soul.

She was ancient, far older than Mentor, Dell knew it from the depths in her eyes. Down those blank corridors lay a million years of anguish. She was stooped and dressed in tattered layers of soiled white cloth. She shuffled rather than walked, and her mouth hung open on empty gums, her chin almost touching her chest.

Dell pushed back along the ground, heading for the void. "Get her away from me," she cried, flailing her arms to ward off the presence. "Oh, dear God, save me."

Mentor was again at her side and said quietly, "This time you do not run away. The Predator would have made you one of his had he caught you, but the Craven one comes as a supplicant. She begs your sympathy and asks you to join her. You must find a way to deny the request."

Dell turned wild eyes to Mentor. "Can't you help me?"

"I am helping you. It was your own will that propelled you away from the red moon. It must be your will to turn away from the Craven's cave. Use me as your staff, lean on me when you feel weak."

Dell hardly understood what was being asked of her. She faced the apparition. The devastation, the blasted landscape hidden behind the blank eyes made her weep. Tears ran down her cheeks unchecked. She nearly reached out to take the ancient woman's frail hand. But she felt Mentor strong next to her and knew she could not do it or she would be giving permission. She would return to herself in the real world weak and nearly blind, hiding from the sun, unwilling to walk free ever again among humanity. If she gave in now, she would forever be tormented and tortured by illness and despair.

"If you are mine," said the Craven, "you will never kill. Others will care for you. You will seek the darkness that comforts. You will leave behind comradeship of mankind so that you won't envy him. All things of the world will fade away and mean little to you."

She looked full on the ancient's face and said, "I know you've suffered an eternity and you want me to go with you, but I can't. You have to understand. I can't go with you."

"Forgive her," Mentor instructed.

"I forgive you for hoping to spirit me away and make me a part of your suffering," she said meaning every word.

The Craven Maker sighed and it was harder to bear than if she had wept and begged. It was the sigh of a loneliness that had gone on forever without abating.

Dell felt herself weakening, making a move forward as if to embrace the old sick woman, but resolve held her back. She bowed her head and shook it slowly from side to side. "I can't help you," she said. "I can't spend the rest of my time in sorrow and sickness, never to see the light of day, never to be close to humans again. I would rather be dead in my grave." She didn't know where the words were coming from to explain her position and to deny the old woman satisfaction. It was as if she had aged fifty years in only a few hours since the onset of the mutated disease.

The Mistress turned slowly and padded back into the black hole of the cave until they could not even hear her footsteps.

Dell turned into Mentor's arms. "Can I go home now? Please, help me find my way."

Mentor lifted her into his arms and ascended from the mouth of the cave, over the deep chasm, above the red clouds, beyond the haunted forest, and past the sagging blood moon. When again Dell opened her eyes, she was in her bed, in her own bedroom, holding onto Mentor's strong hands.

She tried to breathe and couldn't. She tried to cry and couldn't. She wanted to speak and nothing came from her lips.

"Now you learn how to be a Natural," he said. "The first step is to relax into your body and get to know it again. You have passed the hardest tests of all."

Dell gazed down at herself. Someone had changed her clothes and dressed her in a long granny nightgown. She tried to remember it. Maybe she'd gotten it for Christmas or Aunt Celia had given it to her for her birthday. She was closest to her Aunt Celia of all her aunts, but she had to admit Aunt Celia always gave her old-fashioned things that a girl her age privately shunned. Carolyn often complained that her mother belonged in another age, one of long dresses to the ankles and button-up shoes.

It was not only the gown she did not recognize. She found herself alien. A cold hard body. With a working brain. No air in her lungs. No beating of a live heart in her chest. It all seemed unholy. Why must she go on with knowledge of life when she was not alive?

It was enough to drive her mad.

* * *

Life among the undead had been nearly as normal as for someone who lived with a human family. Dell remembered early memories that lay in her distant past like shiny shards of mirrors reflecting bits of her childhood. When she was almost five, living in the daydream that children dreamed, she recalled a sunny spring day with her mother. Her brother was a newborn, lying in a bassinet in the living room while her mother attended to her regimen of household cleaning. The blinds were drawn against the bright light that threatened to spill around the edges of the windows. She remembered the dark drapes printed with large green leaves, the marching-soldier columns of plastic blinds, and the light peeking around all the edges with a golden aura.

Dell stood at the corner of an Early American maple coffee table, clutching a baby doll, her attention switching from the brightly outlined windows to her mother's swift movements with a dust cloth. Suddenly her mother lifted off her feet and was first near the top of the television and then in a blink she was across the room, without ever touching the floor, and dusting a tall bookshelf full of porcelain ladies in frilly dresses.

It was not at all startling. She had seen her mother do strange things before and thought nothing of it. If her mother could levitate and fly through the air, if she could move like a tornado, or if she could appear and disappear in a twinkling, then that is just how the world was arranged. Surely all mothers could do the same.

Another mirrored memory was of her father on a hot summer day. He stood in the backyard turning hamburger patties on a grill. Mom had gone indoors to make a pitcher of lemonade. The scent of the searing meat made Dell's mouth water. She was so hungry that her stomach growled. She had noticed that only she and Eddie ever ate hamburgers. Her parents carried on a conversation as their children ate and didn't even have a plate setting before them. None of that mattered, of course, just so long as she got her own fat hamburger with the juices squeezing into the bun and the mayo and ketchup dripping over the sides.

Eddie found the old crepe myrtle at the back of the privacy fence and began to climb it, the brown peeling bark of the limbs flaking off in his small hands. Dell must have been seven and Eddie almost three. Dell watched him from the swing set where she pushed herself back and forth lazily. She could have told her father that Eddie was doing something he shouldn't, but she was curious to see if her brother could make the climb she had been making for some time already. If he could, then they might have races up the tree to see which one reached the top first. But only if he didn't fall now, didn't prove he was too little for the game.

Eddie made it to the very top of the old tree before his father noticed. Dell turned her head at her father's cry. "Eddie! Get down from there."

Eddie, startled, lost his hold, gazing out in his dumbfounded way from between the pendulous white blooms, and began to plummet.

That was when her father sped across the lawn in a blur, in a motion that was inhuman, and leaped into the air, catching his son in mid-fall.

"Wow," Dell recalled whispering below her breath. "Gee."

When Dell was a few years older, she understood that her parents' abilities might be above and beyond normal parental behavior. No one else could do what they did. Not a single soul. Children climbed trees and fell, no rescuers in sight. Mothers dusted in a thoroughly mundane way, slowly, on two feet. Most refrigerators held more food and no blood bags. Parents ate the same food as their children.

When Eddie got sick and began to change, her parents sat Dell down and explained everything. The blood, the swiftness of movement, the appearing and disappearing acts, the way they were never ill, not even with a cold, not even with a fever. They told her why they might be caught standing in the hall or the kitchen, napping. When Eddie got sick, Dell faced the numbing truth. Her family wasn't really human anymore. And she was about to lose her brother, too.

Eddie was twelve when he got sick. The disease came on rapidly and waylaid him one winter afternoon when he was lying on the sofa reading comics. It was Dell who found him prostrate, sweating, unconscious. His body was covered with sores and his lips were pulled tightly back from his teeth so that he looked as if he were in great pain. One look at him spurred Dell to the telephone to call her mother at work. "Mom, Mom, come quick, Eddie's dying."

While her father took care of Eddie, Dell's mother sat with her at the kitchen breakfast counter and told her what was happening. And what *might* happen to her one day. They carried the genes for a terrible disease that merely crippled and killed humans, but in them it caused death and then life again, but a life that changed their very molecular structure and made them hunger for blood. There was no escape and no cure. A group of Naturals were working on a cure, but it seemed they were making no headway yet.

Now it was Dell's turn to change, to become what she'd hoped never to be. It was an affliction that had plagued their kind, those who carried the deformed genes, for more than four thousand years. As she lay on her bed in the long gown, unable to handle her fate, unable to move or speak, her eyes staring into Mentor's at her bedside, she wondered if she had the courage for this. How had little Eddie been able to accept it? How had her parents, aunts, uncles, and grandparents? Why hadn't they all long since found a way to die rather than live this way?

She could see Mentor sitting nearby, gazing at her. She tried to blink to let him know she was cognizant of him. Her eyelids came down halfway, then went up again.

"I know you're there. I can hear your thoughts. I didn't ask permission, so I hope it's all right."

She blinked just halfway again.

How do I ever act human again? she asked him in her thoughts. *How do any of you stand this?*

"We live because we must, Dell, and so will you. There's a place in the world for us or we wouldn't be here. You'll learn to be yourself again. Your human self. You'll learn it so well, you'll be a natural at it." He smiled at the play on the word they used for those who continued on as if human.

Dell rolled her eyes back into her head and fiercely tried to sit up. She couldn't even lift her head from the pillow. She sent messages to her legs to try to make them rise and they ignored her, lying like dead, fallen trees on the bed.

Oh, God, she would never learn how to walk again, to talk, to brush her hair, and to do her trig assignments. She would never learn to smile or laugh or . . . hope.

"Oh, yes, you will," Mentor said. "It just takes time and faith. You're not someone who will give up. I know you aren't."

She didn't know that herself. Mentor might know more than she, but she wanted very much to shout in his face that he was wrong, he was totally wrong. She could give up if she wanted to and this felt like a time to want to. The alternative—to learn to live again—seemed impossible.

3

Charles Upton lay in his bed propped up on half a dozen pillows. His butler—a real one trained in London and transported to Houston, Texas by Upton's private jet—had left the room moments before to instruct the cook to prepare Charles his usual breakfast—a poached egg and dry toast. Butter—any kind of grease—nauseated him.

On the bedside table rested a wood and ivory-inlaid tray filled with a stack of unopened mail. Charles looked at it with a wary eye, as if it contained bombs or poison glue on the envelope seals. He would rather not handle the mail. Not today. Not any day. He should talk to David about rerouting the mail from his penthouse atop Upton Towers to the offices below so that David could sort through it. Daily tasks had become too much trouble to deal with anymore.

Anyhow, none of it was personal mail. His family had all deserted him when he'd gotten ill. They thought it was contagious or something, or they just couldn't stomach the sight of him. If he'd ever married and had children, maybe he would have someone at his side now who cared. But then he doubted it. Women always betrayed you and took the money and ran. Children failed all your expectations and took your money and ran, too. He realized he pretty much hated women and children.

He glanced across the large silvery-gray carpeted bedroom, decorated in an ornate Louis-the-Fifteenth style, to the gilt mirror over a writing desk. If he were to make the effort to get out of bed and sit at the desk, he would see his terrible image staring back at him. Well, he'd make the effort, by God! He wasn't so crippled yet that he had to lie in his bed like a dying man.

He threw back the covers and swung his legs to the floor. He carefully pushed up with both his arms, putting weight on his legs, and felt stronger right away. He walked to the mirror over the desk and stood there without any assistance, staring at his reflection.

Maybe soon he'd have all mirrors taken from the penthouse. He wasn't sure he could stand to look at himself anymore.

The disease struck when he was in his mid-forties. Now, at sixty-eight, it had progressed to where he could not go out in public without being stared at. Just entering the elevator and running into one of his Upton employees on the descent to the Tower lobby could mean confronting the truth: he was a monster.

His butler and cook, his doctors, and his partner, David, were used to his appearance. Everyone else in the world would be horrified, and it would show instantly on their faces. That was the reason two years ago he'd given over the public running of his oil and shipping empire to David. How long would it have taken his competitors to find ways to sabotage his business interests if the world ever found out he was so ill and so . . . deformed? Two weeks, max.

The doctors had even begun referring to him, in private (or what they thought was private, because Charles had once inadvertently overheard them), as The Old Vampire.

Vampire! How dare they. He'd fired them immediately, threatening to have their practices sued for millions. He then carried through with a suit for defamation. Not that he'd win, but it gave him satisfaction to haul his doctors into courtrooms. He had had to find other doctors as replacements, of course, who behind closed doors probably joked about him in the same way. Doctors couldn't help him any longer anyway, if ever they could. He kept finding sores on his body that would not heal despite having been prescribed every known antibiotic on and off the market. His flesh was riddled with oozing, red, open wounds. He had bandages on both arms where the sores were the worst, and there was a patch across the back of his neck that, without covering, would stain his pillows.

He went closer to the mirror and stared deeply into his own eyes. His gaze was strong and determined, but the shell that housed the eyes was deteriorating rapidly. He began to glare at his own teeth, his stiff lips that were pulled back from the gums, and he snarled like an animal, cursing mentally the thing he had become.

His eyes and his skin had become ultrasensitive to sunlight, so he stayed indoors and hid behind drawn drapes. They told him his body would be harmed if he were out in the sun for any length of time. As if it weren't already! The bottom half of his face had slowly grown rigid and his lips had pulled back into a rictus that made him look like a decayed mummy. His thin hair fell out in tufts, and scalded-looking spots covered the pink skin on his skull.

Charles snarled once more before returning to the bed and plopping down on the side of the mattress. He clenched one fist. Raised it above the covers and let it fall. Raised it again, higher, and hit the bed with a solid thump. He would like to pound something more than the mattress. If he could get his hands around the throat of God, he'd strangle him and bring him to his knees. He'd pound him into oblivion for this curse placed upon him.

Porphyria they called it. "The Old Vampire," they called him, because he was pale and his teeth showed like glistening wet fangs. And as he aged and retreated from the world, his thirst for revenge grew like a strange, alien wildflower in a fertilized pasture.

Charles reached to the opened book lying on the covers. He lifted the leather volume carefully, smoothing the cream-colored pages. He squinted his eyes and began to read about the legend of the vampire. At first, his reading in this area had just been something to do, a diversion to keep his mind off his infirmities. He had researched the vampire myth to keep his mind busy. Since even his doctors referred to him as one of those creatures, perhaps he could find something within the literature to use to frighten them with. It was one more instance of an old, sick man reaching for a straw, he knew that, but he thought it would be grand to know enough about the myth to play into it when around the specialists who handled his case.

You want a vampire, he thought. *I will give you a vampire.*

After a few months of reading, however, his reason for reading about vampires began to change. Revenge against the medical community went by the wayside. He slowly began to discover traces of what might be truth tucked away in articles and books about vampires. In among the ridiculous fiction, he began to notice bits and pieces of reports in some more scholarly tomes that left him wondering. In one such article, published in a respected journal, he found reports of a "real" vampire who had been discovered. He flipped through the book in his hand until he found the page that contained the reprint.

A True Vampire Story

How It All Began . . .

This is the story of Arnod Paole, one of the few vampire histories that has been sufficiently documented over the years to lend it historical validity. In the spring of 1727, Arnod Paole returned home from the military to settle in his hometown of Meduegna, near Belgrade. He bought some land, built a home, and began work as a farmer. After a short time, he married a local girl. Her father's land bordered his, and would be a fine addition, so the two were wed. Paole confided to his wife that he was haunted by nightmares. He dreamed that he would die early. In the military, he had been in Greece. Local beliefs there included myths about how the dead came back to haunt the living. They came back in the form of revenants or vampires. While in Greece, and hearing those tales, Paole believed he had been visited by an undead being. Afterward, he hunted down the unholy grave, on the advice of locals. He burned the corpse. However, what he'd done seemed so horrible to him, so frightening, he had to flee Greece. He resigned from the military and went home.

Soon after marrying, Paole fell from a hayloft, and was brought, comatose, back to his home. Within a few days, and without regaining consciousness, he died and was buried in the town cemetery. A month later reports began to filter through the townspeople claiming Paole had been seen. Some said they'd seen him in their own homes, wandering like a ghost. Some weeks after those reports, many of the people who had seen Paole in their homes died under inexplicable circumstances. This caused the town fathers to sign a petition to exhume Arnod Paole. They must make sure he was dead.

Two military officers, two army surgeons, and a local priest were called to the task. Upon opening the coffin they found Paole, but there was no decomposition of the body. He had new skin and nails, the old ones having fallen away. And on the corpse's lips they saw wet, fresh blood. They decided they must drive a stake through the body. They swore that when they did it, Paole screamed and fresh blood spilled out. Then they scattered garlic around the remains, and around each of the graves where Paole had sent his newest victims.

All was quiet until 1732, when more inexplicable deaths began to occur. This time, the whole town went to the graveyard. What they found was written up in books over time, the reports given by three army surgeons, cosigned by a lieutenant colonel, and a sublieutenant. Eleven disinterred corpses showed the same traits as the Paole corpse had earlier. No decomposition, new skin grown, fresh blood in the body. There was never an explanation for the second instance of vampirism, although one theory was that Paole had feasted on local cattle as well as people during his walking dead phase. Perhaps, they said, when the cows were killed for meat, the vampire qualities were consumed and came alive in anyone who ate the meat. It was the only conclusion they could find.

Charles closed the volume and rested it on his knees. The evidence was sketchy, but it did point toward the possibility there might be something to the old myth. If he'd only found this one piece of truth, he might have dismissed it as hyperbole, as fancy, but he kept turning up more and more information in his studies that claimed there were, in the past and, even today, real vampires. People who had died and were yet not dead. People who lived on as immortals.

He had brought it up to David on a recent visit. David had scoffed at first, thinking probably that his partner had finally lost his mind to the disease. When he'd seen Charles was serious, he rearranged his face and said quietly, "Is this what you believe?"

"I don't know what I believe," Charles had responded, tossing aside the book from which he'd quoted. Then he calmed himself and stared at David. "But what if it's true?"

David had hunched his shoulders as if to say, Well, what if it *is*?

Charles knew he'd get nowhere with David. David was a brilliant businessman, shrewd and quite competent, a diplomat with the foreign offices, a super salesman of their oil tankers, but he was no scientist.

He lacked imagination. He wasn't open to anything he could not put his hands on and know was real. He hadn't an idea about cell regeneration or the damning effects the porphyria was having on Charles' body. He couldn't imagine how desperate a man could become when the world shunned him and he was shut off from view, hiding behind closed doors and drawn drapes. He didn't know that a man needed . . . hope. However small and illogical it might seem to others, Charles was grasping for the hope he might survive his debilitating and fatal disease. Some way. Any way. Even if it meant turning to old myths and beginning to believe they might hold the secret of life for him.

Because Charles could not personally get out and investigate this idea, he would need someone healthy, trained in the sciences, and motivated to search and seek out the truth in Charles' stead. He needed a man dedicated to the hunt. But where could he be found and how could he be motivated? Money would accomplish both tasks. Money had always been the best weapon of all. There was not a man on the planet he could not manipulate through money. He fervently believed that.

Charles let the book rest on his lap. He closed his eyes, and in his mind he played his favorite imaginary scene. He was taken and made into a vampire. He thought it might be painful, but he was prepared for that after years of living with pain. After his change, he lived forever, ruling over his growing global empire with all the ruthlessness that had brought him his great fortune. He had the strength for lovers again and left them strewn in his wake, begging for him. He took over corporations, crushing his competitors, running them into the ground. He was impervious to disease and to the grave. He became a god, worshiped and feared by millions. In the end of this fantasy, in a future where technology had changed the face of everyday life and countries were brought under his thumb, he ruled the world.

When he opened his eyes, he tried to temper his fantastic visions by hitting himself over the head with reality.

He was sick and dying. He was old. He couldn't even run his own business anymore.

And he would not live forever. In fact, his doctors did not give him long. A year or two, if that.

George, his butler, knocked softly on the bedroom door before entering with the serving tray. Charles looked at him, a man in his prime living out his life as a servant, and he hated him. He couldn't stomach peasants. The subservient made him want to retch. The world was full of them! And it was men like him who gave them all jobs and a means to survive. Without the money from billionaires like him supporting the structure of world economies, all the servants and peasants would die away.

He snatched the tray from George's hands and jerked his head toward the door to dismiss him. He would *not* say thank you. He would not admit that he was dependent on the other man's generosity.

He ought to fire the man and find someone older and slower and with less reason to smirk behind his back. Not that he ever caught George smirking, but if he ever did . . .

Raising the silver coffee server to pour a cup of coffee, Charles caught a brief, distorted reflection of his own face. He set down the server quickly and glanced away from it. The rounded surface of the silver had contorted his face even more. Oh, he was a monster, a monster in his body and mind, and some days he did not want to be reminded of it. Some days that knowledge was enough to send rage pumping through his heart like a shot of adrenaline.

He balanced the tray on his knees and clenched one fist. He raised it and began to pound the bed. Slowly, carefully, so as not to tip over the tray, methodically and relentlessly he hit the bed again and again and again.

4

In time, Mentor would explain to Dell that the disease itself was responsible for the presence of vampires upon the Earth, but that the choice of what kind of vampire one became was spiritual. Supernatural. The disease that took human cells and caused them to mutate into those of a vampire had nothing to do with the nature of the being who was finally created. He had once tried telling this secret to a young person before he entered the dream, before he died, but it caused such horror and revulsion, Mentor decided it was best to let the dying patient learn all that he must within the confines of the change itself. Warning or explaining did not seem to do the good he had hoped it would. He realized finally that one cannot explain away the supernatural, cannot warn about the dangers of the spirit.

Over the years Mentor had studied the writings of scientists and biologists hoping to understand how the body could be overtaken and killed, yet made to live again as something altogether new. All other diseases ravaged the body, consuming and defeating it until the soul fled from it forever. In contrast, the mutated disease of porphyria deformed the body and took it to the brink of death, but at the last moment the cells revived, becoming new cells that were neither human nor animal. However, the human soul was left to struggle on, the mind remaining, the

memories intact. And on that brink of death was
where the soul determined what path it would follow. Closed off from heaven and blocked from the
gates of hell, the soul had but three choices. It could
embrace evil fully and become a Predator vampire,
seeking to take down humans in order to survive. It
could fall back to the weakest link of vampiric existence and hide from man as a Craven. Or it could
muster the strength to live on in human society,
learning to hide away its supernatural powers in
order to go forward into history as if truly human
still.

This last path was the hardest. A Predator lived
by night, slept by day, and had no use for a conscience. A Craven merely passed as a diseased
human, handicapped by sunlight, sick all the time,
lost forever in the despair of loneliness behind drawn
shades, dependent on the charity of Predators to supply them with life-sustaining blood. But a Natural!
He chose to walk in the day, converse and interact
with humans as one of them, keeping secret the
stillness of his heart and the cruelty of immortality.
Naturals worked hard to earn enough money not
only to live as humans lived, but to pay the Predators
for the blood they needed. They were not killers like
the Predators. They hoped never to take life.

Dell's parents worked very hard, harder perhaps
than most humans. Her mother was a payroll accountant at a car dealership in Dallas. She often
worked Saturdays, needing the overtime pay. Dell's
father was a software engineer, fighting for pay-
grade updates, and cost of living allowances. Everyone in Dell's family worked long hours, some of
them working two jobs, and never complaining about
it for they wanted, most of all, to live in the world
naturally.

At various times some of the Naturals thought
about setting up their own blood banks, cutting the
Predators out of the loop, but the supply chain had
been set up this way from the beginning and the

Predators were not eager to give up the power and profit they enjoyed. Rather than go to war with them to win control of the blood banks, the Naturals bowed to tradition and continued buying from the Predators. Working and working and buying.

It was not true that the blood went into their stomachs as had the food they'd eaten as human beings. The digestive system never worked in the same way again after the moment of death. All vampires took blood through their fangs, which sped that warm blood, alive with living cells, throughout their blood system, reviving them, keeping their skin supple, brains functioning, and their muscles hard. Though they never aged again, they were able to keep the body functioning for a normal human lifespan of seventy to a hundred years. Then they had to migrate to another body, preferably a youthful one.

The body, though supplied with living blood, was still no more than a physical specimen. As the years moved past, the wear and tear on that physical form eventually caused the inner organs to fail, one by one, just as they did in humans.

Mentor had lived in so many bodies he hardly recognized his own face when he saw it reflected from a mirror. In fact, the body he possessed now was elderly. He would have to migrate in the next few years.

He mused on the first time he had had to change bodies. There were but hundreds of his kind then, a new race, and not many of them had realized they had to or could change from one human shell to another. Mentor was one of the first, sitting alone one night in a cold, drafty castle high up in the Swiss mountains. He had hidden himself away from the world. His wife, a human, had died in Scotland, a country he'd fled. Like his wife's, his own body was aged and decrepit. He just wanted to be alone and forgotten, if possible. He had reverted to his predatory ways once his wife had passed. He swept down from the mountain retreat into nearby villages, taking

humans at will, leaving behind drained corpses. He
had no more care for humans and their world. They
were frail and they died so easily, just as his wife
had.

Misery and grief tore at him, robbing him of the
humanity he'd been able to forge as a beloved
husband.

Then one night he'd been on the prowl, sweeping
in with a blizzard into a village, moving swiftly
toward fresh blood. He smelled it on the icy wind.
He following the scent, his hunger like a siren call
in his veins.

He found the human, a young man trudging
through hip-deep snowdrifts toward a lighted pub.
Mentor appeared before him out of nowhere, halting
his progress.

The human, frightened out of his wits, began to
stutter and tried to run away. Mentor caught him by
the coat collar and hauled him down to the ground.
Just as he was ripping into his victim's neck, something began to happen. The blood suffusing Mentor's
body seemed to stop along the way and coagulate in
dry, dead veins. The heart inside his chest would not
revive to life, the veins, arteries, and capillaries began
to break and splatter the new warm infusion of blood
throughout the old body. He was hemorrhaging all
inside from hundreds of tiny spigots of broken
vessels.

Mentor's human form was so worn out the veins
and arteries had lost all elasticity. They were shutting
down or bursting all along the pathways from neck
to limbs.

Mentor fell back from the young dying man in the
snowdrift and gasped, blood dripping from his fangs
to spot the pristine snow. He knew what was the
matter. He had intimate knowledge of the inner
workings of his human body. He could feel the old
arterial system failing. He looked about wildly, the
light from the pub a yellow beacon. But he could not
go there. He could not be saved by medicine or a

surgeon, no more than an ancient human could be saved. He fell onto his back next to the young man and stared up into the frenzy of the white blowing blizzard.

Where will I go, he wondered? *What will happen to me now? Will I be allowed to die and meet with my beloved?*

Even as he asked himself these questions, he knew the answers. He would not die, but the body he inhabited was going to. If he stayed in it much longer he would be trapped, a living spirit inside a body that no longer functioned in any way. He'd be a prisoner in the flesh. They would come from the pub and find him, pronounce him dead, and bury him.

He felt like shouting out his grief and horror at the snowy sky. He had to get out of the old, decayed body with the burst veins and the hemorrhaging system. He turned on his side to the young man who lay in the snow, his arms thrown out at his sides. The young man was already dying. Mentor reached over and slipped his old hand beneath the other man's thick wool coat. He slipped it beneath the rough shirt and to the man's chest. He felt for the heart. It beat erratically and the breathing was shallow.

Mentor lay that way, his hand on the man's chest, waiting. He closed his eyes and began to will himself away from his own dying form. The young man's veins were strong and they would carry blood, even after his spirit left the body. The young man would be a perfect vehicle.

All Mentor had to do was wait for the moment of death for them both and find a way to make the switch.

How? How was he to do it? Why had it come to this, what manner of supreme being would have devised such a terrible plot for his kind?

He forced his whole being into an introspective trance where he seemed to pull and tug at his spirit that was attached so steadfastly to the old body. He did not know if it would work or how it worked. He only had faith that it would. He could not imagine lying in the dead old body in a casket for the rest of eternity, trapped by earth, brother to the darkness.

Beneath his hand he felt the other man's heart cease, the breathing end. Now was the time.

He tugged harder, blasting with all his might against the structure of the inner body, pushing against the still heart, the deflated lungs, willing with all his might and soul to be set free.

The chaotic fury of his will sent out a message that reached a vampire older yet than Mentor. This being used the name Balatan, and he, too, had come to the mountains of Switzerland to hide away and live a quiet life for his own personal reasons. Mentor had known of him, but they'd never met, both preferring their self-enforced solitude. They frequented different villages, careful not to compete for territory.

Within minutes, the Predator was at Mentor's side in the swirling snow. Mentor could no longer open his eyes or move his limbs. He sensed the being nearby and called to him frantically. *What do I do? Save me!*

Balatan seemed to enter Mentor's destroyed body in order to help him release himself from the boundaries of the flesh. Mentor felt him like a shawl over the shoulders. His spirit was cold as an ice floe and dark as the bottom of a mine. He screamed at him, "Let go! Step into the void, and I will guide you to the other body!"

Mentor did as he was told, insane with fear and the thought of the grave's entrapment. He pushed harder and harder, willing himself loose from the tendons, muscles, and flabby flesh, tearing himself from the dead meat that had been his body since the day he was born.

He screamed mentally, crying out in horror and despair, beating against the material body with every ounce of his consciousness. Suddenly he found himself free, light as the air, and Balatan had hold of him, jerking him up and away from the snow. Once loose from the old man he had become, Mentor could see the body below him, and he almost rushed back to it, longing for the familiarity of that flesh and bone.

Balatan shouted, "No!" and pushed him this time, sending his spirit flying down toward the young man's form on the snow.

Mentor flung out his invisible self, making it as wide as a blanket, and it hit the dead young man's body like a wave crashing from high. He fell for what seemed like ages through darkness, and then he opened eyes on a new world.

Balatan hovered over him in the air, dressed all in black wool. "Welcome to your new body."

Mentor blinked. He moved one hand, crushing a fistful of snow, and feeling how cold it was. He managed to sit up and look down at his hands. They were young hands, unmarried by life, the knuckles smooth and the skin tight. He looked up at Balatan and realized he had disappeared.

So this is how it is done, Mentor thought, rejoicing. *We do not have to lie in old bodies trapped in a graveyard. We move into another body and use it instead.* He doubted he could have done it without Balatan's help, but he wasn't sure. He expected he would have struggled for as long as it took in order to wrench himself free. Balatan had surely shortcutted the process, however, and one day he would thank him.

The switch left him momentarily confused, so that it took him some time to get to his feet and stumble away into the night. He was hungry and deprived of blood. His old body had taken most of what made the new body function.

Before the night was over, Mentor had taken a second victim, a drunk from the pub who had wandered out to relieve himself in the snow. The killing revived Mentor's youthful body and he was able then to get back to his empty castle where he could sit by a fire and think over what it all meant. A vampire had supernatural powers, some he realized he hadn't yet discovered. One of them was the ability to take a new home.

* * *

Mentor tried to explain things to Dell. Dell's aunt, Celia Widen, sat nearby. Celia held onto Dell's hand and now and again patted it. Mentor said, "The Cravens and Naturals, just like the Predators, also need fresh blood, but their fangs only go into blood bags, not into the flesh of humankind. Without new blood with living cells, a vampire perishes. His veins collapse, the arteries shrink, the heart shrivels. Finally, the muscles atrophy, the brain softens in the skull, and the skin dries to crusty leather. I know this is graphic, but you have to understand everything." He paused to see how she was taking the information. She did not look as horrified as he expected. Probably because she knew some of this already.

He continued, "It's a horrible thing to see a vampire die of starvation. It's a torturously slow process. Only lack of blood or fire can end a vampire's life. If he loses a limb, his cells grew a new one. If he's injured, the cells renew the flesh. As for crosses and holy water and the silly ropes of garlic necklaces—well, that's merely myth and superstition. There are far worse obstacles to contend with than Stoker could have ever imagined for his infamous Count Dracula."

Dell smiled.

"Deprive a vampire of new blood and he'll eventually dry to dust and be gone. Burn him in an inferno and his cells have no chance to renew and will turn to cinder. Otherwise, our kind, or at least our minds and souls, are impervious to the effects of aging, death, and destruction."

As Mentor sat at Dell's bedside, he knew she struggled to come back into the world as a new being. That struggle was almost as difficult as facing her death or choosing which path her soul should follow. He imparted his strength to her, pulsing waves out from his own strong body to surround her, in the same way a supernatural human healer cured the ill by radiating energy through his hands. Soon he would have to leave. Already he had telepathically received pleas for his assistance from others going through the same process as Dell, and he must be there to guide them. The cries were piteous and urgent. *Save me. Help me. Find me and take me from the arms of destruction.*

Mentor turned his attention fully back to Dell and saw she was trying to tell him something. He opened the channel and listened to her thoughts. *You can go,* she told him. *I'll be all right. Aunt Celia will see about me.*

"Yes," he told her, "you will. You will be fine now. You'll find a way to rise and walk again. Your parents and your brother love you and want you with them. This is the dawning of your new life."

One single tear fell from her eyes. Mentor reached out and plucked it from her cheek with his finger. It was her blood. He tasted it to discover if she could make the journey without a transfusion. He found it metallic and cold, but with enough red cells to keep her going until she was strong enough to drink on her own.

"I have to go away for a while," he said aloud. "You know why. There are always others who need me. But I'll be back. We'll set up sessions once you're on your feet. You'll go back to school and resume your life. For a while, you will come to me every day and I'll teach you what you need to know to survive."

Thank you, she said, and he could feel her struggling to lift her hand to him. He patted her shoulder and stood.

"I'm happy to be of service," he said, smiling warmly. "Good-bye, Celia." She nodded her head at him.

He was about to turn away and leave when he heard Dell's thoughts scrambling after him, seeking an answer to a question. He leaned down and stared into her open eyes. "What is it? What do you need to know so desperately?"

What are you? What are you, Mentor?

He knew she meant what sort of vampire was he. He glanced at Celia. She knew almost everything of the vampire life though she was not one. He looked back down at his charge.

"I am not a god," he said. "I know that's what you're thinking. That I must be a god to know so much and to have the ability to enter death's arms with you. But, my dear, I am merely old and experienced. It's been my duty to do this for hundreds of years. And I am . . . technically . . . a Predator." He could see the surprise and fear mingling in her eyes. Again he patted her shoulder and said, "Reformed. A reformed Predator. I've lived so many thousands of years that I've gone beyond evil and crossed over into understanding. I can kill—easily—and decide not to. At least most of the time." He knew guilt had crept into his eyes and he turned away so she wouldn't see. "I take my blood as you will, artificially, not from the living flesh. Most of the time." He was incapable of telling a lie.

He knew her mind was eased, though she could not possibly understand how many hundreds of years he had fought to free himself from the thirst to kill. She could not imagine the pain he had endured and the willpower he had exerted in order to change himself from one of the greatest and most powerful leaders of the Predators into a creature who had sworn to help others along the passage. Nor could she ever fathom why, even now, he would kill when it meant preserving the secret of their clan or when a Predator could not be restrained and threatened to give them all away by his wanton acts of murder.

Like shifting shadow, he moved from the room.

He would say good-bye to her family, assure them she was coming along, and exhort them to help her until his return.

The calls for help thrummed through his brain from the dying. Dozens of voices called to him. He must hurry. He must save some of them from choosing the wrong path.

It was his duty. His job. His reason to exist.

5

Dell watched Mentor leave and immediately fell into a panic. Her throat closed as if it were a sock being twisted and wrung by strong hands. Her mind would not behave or obey, falling first into despair at her predicament then leaping toward joy at the mere thought of living forever with her family at her side. She must get control of her seesawing emotions. They swayed through her—swinging pendulums of fear, hope, disgust, and loathing, self-pity, and sudden elation. She was in danger of losing her mind.

She had heard of that happening before during the change. The result was permanent madness. An insanity that never relented. Predators hunted those who went mad and put them down. They were caught out in the open, away from anyone who might help them, and set on fire. While they burned in agony, a ring of Predators watched, showing no mercy, laughing, swearing at the dying one and condemning him to utter darkness.

She must not let go of her mind. She must not let this defeat her. More than anything she wanted to live. She was too young to go mad and find herself hunted and killed. She had hardly even begun her life yet. Even if she had to live as a vampire, she meant to do it.

She felt Aunt Celia squeeze her hand. She tried to

squeeze it back but couldn't. From the corner of her eyes she saw someone enter the room. It was Eddie. He was fourteen now, though he had stopped growing at twelve. He was a big boy who had nearly reached his adult height when the change had happened. Soon, of course, he would have to leave the family and go away. The school authorities, teachers, neighbors, and his friends would finally realize he had not changed over the years, had not grown, had not physically aged in any way.

Nevertheless, inside the body the cells aged, like those of the cloned sheep, Dolly—who looked younger than her clone, but was actually aging quickly. In each vampiric cell the march of time continued and wore the youthful-looking body completely out. The heart tired of working, the kidneys failed, the liver and lungs and stomach all surrendered in the end to the march of time.

Eddie would be sent to live with relatives in another state. Her parents would make trips to see him, but for all practical purposes, Eddie would be lost to them. He would become a wanderer, moving from clan to clan, from family to family, in order to keep secret the fact he never aged. One day the trips her parents made to see him would grow less frequent until finally Eddie would be entirely on his own in the world. It was hardest on the ones who changed when so young. They couldn't really have a normal life with humans unless they kept on the move.

Since the change came on now when she was seventeen, almost eighteen, she would be able to remain at home for some time, aging her face over the years with skillfully applied makeup and disguising her young body with more mature choices in clothes.

"Dell?" Eddie's voice was soft and young, his voice having never changed. In the dark room, without seeing him, he could be any age, from five to twelve.

"She can't talk yet," Celia said.

"I know, but she can talk to me in here." Eddie pointed to his head.

"Do you want me to leave?"

"You don't have to."

Celia gave Dell a kiss and stood, disengaging her hand from Dell's. "I'll see about your mother. I'll be back, Dell."

Once Celia had left the room, Eddie again called Dell's name. She wanted to answer him, but still couldn't control her vocal cords. She sent out her thoughts to him instead. *Hi, Eddie. This is a terrible thing, isn't it? I never knew it was so bad for you.*

"Aww, you couldn't know. No one knows until you go through it."

She kept silent, not knowing what thought to project.

"Dell? Maybe I can help. It just takes practice to do everything again, that's all. I know how hard it is. It's kind of like . . . well, like relaxation techniques, only turned on their heads. You know how you can hypnotize yourself?"

No, I don't.

"Well, you lie down and begin at your feet, relaxing your toes first, then the arch of your foot, then the ankle, and on up the body all the way to your brain. It relaxes people who get all stressed out." He grinned, and she loved him so much at that moment she wanted to leap from the bed and hug him tight. He looked so young, but he'd already lived two successful years in his new life. He was just a kid. A boy. Her little brother. And a very wise vampire already.

"Anyway, what you do is send thoughts down to your toes, just as if you were going into relaxation, but instead of telling your toes to relax, you tell them to wake up. Get it? Wake up, Toes!"

If she could have laughed, it would have been a big, openmouthed true laugh. She laughed instead in her mind at how seriously her brother had said, "Wake up, Toes!"

"Once you have the toes awake, you move up the

foot to the ankle, to the calves of your legs, to your knees, thighs, abdomen, chest, arms, and finally to your neck and head. If you'll try, I know you can do it. That's how Mentor taught me how to move again."

Mentor had to go away.

"I know. That's why I'm here telling you stuff. Just concentrate on your toes, okay? Tell them they belong to you and you mean for them to work right again. You just can't get *anywhere* without toes."

She saw his grin widen and knew he was trying for humor to urge her along in an easy way. Never mind that this was the most serious of endeavors. Never mind that it would determine whether or not she could ever return to the world again.

"Go ahead," he said, leaning over the bed to throw back the hem of her gown. He stared at her toes like a surgeon waiting to see if his operation had left her paralyzed or if she would recover feeling in her extremities. "Go on, move them. Think, Dell, put your spine into it. Think about moving your toes, then we'll get your feet moving. You've got to do this. It's the only way."

She knew he would not leave her alone unless she showed some sign of progress. She focused on her feet. She narrowed in on just the tips of her toes, imagining where they were, the dark copper nail polish she had used on them the day before, the way her second toe was longer than her big toe. There, she could visualize them now. Not bad feet, as feet went. Not too large, the skin smooth and tan from a summer swimming at the area pool.

She could move them if she wanted, that's what Eddie was saying. If she *really* wanted to move them, she could. It was all within reach. She had to exert her will for the first time in her life. She'd do it, she knew she could.

Move, she commanded.

She visualized first stretching and then clenching her toes. If they would move, she could consider herself on the road back to life. She must make them obey.

Move.

"That's it!" Eddie yelled, "it's working, you're doing it, I knew you could do it!"

MOVE.

Stretch. Clench.

MOVE!

Wriggle. She wanted them to wriggle, she wanted her toes to go crazy, she wanted them to dance like individual ballet stars. She wanted to do so well that Eddie would jump right out of his skin he'd be so happy for her.

She thought she could feel them moving now.

"Your ankles, concentrate, Dell. Twist your feet around from the ankle. You can do it. You have to do it, it's just a little more effort, a little more."

Dell saw her parents come into the room. They quietly approached the bed, and Eddie turned to them, grinning like a monkey. "She's coming back," he fairly shouted. "Dell's moving her feet."

Her mother brushed a hand across her cold brow. Dell could not yet blink, so she was able to see the fine lines in her mother's palm. It struck her now for the first time that her mother had borne both her children before the disease struck. Neither her mother nor her father had been a vampire yet. They'd taken an awful chance having children, knowing that later they might fall ill and both their offspring after them. How could her mother have had the courage to have a family? How had they ever made that decision?

Dell's father knelt beside the bed and took her lax hand into his own. "Come on, baby. Eddie's right. You have to move, or there will be marks on your skin where the blood has settled. They'll last a long time. You won't be able to go anywhere people can see you for a very long time. You have life. Now you have to animate the body before it's too late."

Dell tried, Lord have mercy, she was trying. She

let go of all thoughts except those centered on her feet and legs. She visualized moving up her body, commanding it to respond, just as Eddie had told her to do. She felt her calves clench then relax. She felt her thighs tighten and loosen. She felt her stomach contract then expand, as if she'd taken a breath all the way down to her belly. She felt her chest walls push apart, and then her throat opened by only the will of her thought processes. Next she concentrated on her lips, her tongue, her vocal cords. Finally, her nose, ears, eyes, eyebrows. She could sense every individual hair on her head, from root to hair end.

She blinked. The sensation was so strange that she thought she might cry. She was not dead! She was no more dead than a baby just born kicking and screaming from the womb. She might have been dead, but no more.

She lived!

Her mother grabbed her around the shoulders and hugged her and kissed her cheeks. Her father held tight to her hand. Eddie was all over the room, walking up the wall like a spider, doing flips off the ceiling, whooping like a crane.

Out of reflex, Dell sucked in a breath. She knew she didn't need it, not really, though it would keep her blood fresher longer. That first breath burned like lava pouring into her Arctic lungs. She coughed and hacked, pushing herself up on one elbow to lean over the side of the bed, feeling sick.

If Eddie would stop laughing and clapping long enough, she'd send him one last thought communication. But he was celebrating too hard to pay attention to her. Instead, after a couple of false starts, she said in a hoarse voice she did not recognize, "Thanks, Ed . . . Eddie, could . . . couldn't have done it . . . without you."

6

Dell had now moved her limbs and gained control once again of her body. She thought she felt different since her heart had stopped beating and she was now officially vampire. She felt, for the most part, cold. She could not keep her teeth from chattering.

Her mother had wrapped her in a blanket and sat beside her on the bed.

"When will I warm up, Mom?"

"Honey, the blood will make you warm."

Dell's father had gone to the kitchen to retrieve a blood bag for his daughter. The taking of the blood was the next step in her change, they had told her. Without it, she would eventually fall back into unconsciousness.

"I'm not sure I can do it," she said. "I don't think I can . . . drink blood, Mom."

"It's not drinking," her mother said. "You'll see, be patient."

Eddie sat in the chair Mentor had occupied earlier. He seemed happy just to see his sister talking and moving. Dell noticed he hadn't any advice about what she faced in the next few minutes.

Dell's father came into the room, carefully transporting the transparent plastic bag of human hemoglobin. Each bag cost the Cambians a dear price. They worked hard to afford the blood and treated it with great respect. For as long as Dell could remember they had never dropped a bag or punctured it accidentally. Blood had never been spilled in their home.

She had always assumed that her parents and Eddie partook of the blood late in the night because she rarely saw one of them taking a bag from the fridge. She had also assumed that they drank it, so it was a mild surprise to her to learn they did not.

"All right," her father said, holding the bag at the height of his chest. "Stand up, Dell. I'll show you how."

She stood, but averted her gaze from the blood bag. The bags had always seemed horrible to her. How could anyone think of touching them? They sat in a covered white cardboard box on the top shelf of the refrigerator. The box was always there and always contained at least a few bags, but more often it was crammed full. She had thought of the blood as insulin for diabetics. Now it was medicine to keep her family healthy.

"Look at me, Dell."

She forced her eyes to his. "I don't think I can do this, Daddy."

"Baby, you have to. The thirst hasn't come on you yet, but after this it will, and it'll be easier for you. But if we don't get this into you soon, you won't be able to move around and talk to us much longer."

Dell sighed. She again glanced away from her father and into the corners of the room as if she could find an alternative there. She had no urge to taste blood, could not bring herself to imagine it in her mouth or on her tongue. The very thought made her want to gag. But her father was waiting, they were all waiting. She looked at her father again and found her resolve. "Okay, what should I do?"

"You see that there's a pocket of air here at the top of the bag? That's the area you're going to pierce. The rest will happen naturally. I'll hold this for you and help you position it so it will drain. Next time you'll be able to do it alone."

"But how do I . . . ?"

"Put your mouth here," he said, indicating a spot at the top of the blood bag. "When you do, close your eyes. Don't think of anything. It'll be all right, trust me."

She approached closer and eyed the bag. He held it out to her carefully, and she moved her lips toward it. *Don't think about it,* she told herself. *They say you must do this, so just screw up your courage and do it.*

Her lips came into contact with the cold plastic. She tasted condensed water drops that warmed in her mouth. She had her teeth around the top corner of the bag and closed her eyes. She'd never be able to do this. She'd never be able to rip through the thick plastic to get at the dark ruby liquid inside.

Suddenly her body spasmed and she felt her father's hand holding onto her shoulder to keep her in place. She heard, as at a distance, her mother's soothing voice, but she didn't know what she was saying. She heard Eddie urging her on, saying what he'd said to get her to concentrate on moving her toes. "You can do it," he was saying again. "C'mon, Dell, you can do it."

There was a sensation of movement behind her top lip, as if hard sticks had been shoved against her incisors and straight into her gums. It didn't hurt very much, but she reacted against it, trying to pull away from contact with the bag. She heard her father's voice command her to. *"Be still, stay."*

The strange sensation grew, and she moved her tongue away from the side of the bag to feel her top teeth. She felt her incisors, now long and pointed, like miniature daggers. Her tongue flicked away swiftly and fear filled her. Fangs! They had grown of their own accord, without her intervention or thought. How had it happened?

As soon as the sensation of growth in her mouth ceased, the fear fled, and a deep feeling of desire overwhelmed her. Her olfactory senses sharpened, and she could smell the scent of the blood right through the plastic. Now it was like the scent of delicate perfume.

She was about to open her eyes and pull back when something inside her forced her teeth down around the top of the bag, her fangs easily piercing the plastic. She knew her father was lifting the bag now, tipping the contents up so that her fangs could get at it.

She had to do nothing of her own will but obey the strong call spiraling through her to partake. At this point she knew she could not pull back from the thing her body yearned for most in all the world. The blood spilled over her incisors, chilling them, and she could feel the coldness sweep through tiny openings in her fangs. The blood swept through hollows and into small veins in the roof of her mouth, moved rapidly into larger veins at the back of her head, and coursed down through her neck into her blood system. It moved like cold snakes entering her body.

She knew it as life. She sensed how alive the blood was, how new, fresh, and sustaining. She thought she could feel it mingling with her own pooled, coagulating dead blood, reviving it. Her brain exploded with ecstasy, and her body quivered with electric currents of pleasure. She lost herself in the rush of feeling that came on the heels of the commingling going on from her head to her feet.

Without warning, someone placed a hand to her forehead and forced her back. Her mouth released the bag with a sucking noise that sounded as loud as timber falling and her eyelids flew open. She felt droplets of blood slide down from her upper lip and felt her incisors retract of their own volition, pushing back up into the recesses of her gums with a shriek of pain that caused her to bring her hands to her face.

She wanted more! Why were they depriving her?

She wasn't finished, though she could see the bag was emptied. She needed another one, and another.

"There, there," her father said, lowering the empty blood bag to his side. "Sit down, Dell. Let it work the magic."

Her mother led her back to the bed and she sat, stunned and mindless except for the desire for *more*. It was not blood, but life. She felt no revulsion toward it now. In fact, she wanted it as much as she'd ever wanted food or drink since the day she was born.

It was as if tiny sparks had ignited in her brain and her neurons were firing off cannons. She felt invincible, able to conquer anyone and anything; she felt as if she might fly.

"Stay calm," her mother said, brushing back the hair at her temple. "This will pass soon and you'll feel like yourself again."

Oh, God, why hadn't they told her that becoming one of them would give her this much strength and vitality? Why hadn't they been happier for her when she had called to her mother to show her the sores that indicated she was going to become one of them? How had they kept this gift from her for so long, kept it all to themselves, leaving her weak and prone to death or accident in her frail human form?

"It's pretty cool, huh, Dell?" Eddie asked. He jiggled around on the chair like a younger child unable to keep still.

"Hush, Eddie," her mother said.

"But Mom, it's *immortality*. It's a great event. She'll have those feelings over and over again forever, and we ought to tell her."

She blinked and gave herself over to the renewal taking place in her body. She'd never felt so alive, so healthy, so fine and wonderful as this ever in her life. And all it took was blood, sweet blood, blood with living cells that brought her to life with such force she knew if she were ever denied the sensation,

she would roar like a lion and take down armies
with her bare hands.

"Oh, Jesus," she said softly. "I have to move about.
Mom, let me go."

She shook off her mother's touch and rose from
the bed in one swift motion that a mortal wouldn't
have been able to see. She sped to the door of her
room, down the hall and into the kitchen. She felt
her parents and grandparents gathering at her back.
She saw Celia bending over at the sink, washing a
cup and saucer, and her scent was strongly human
and female. At the kitchen table sat Carolyn, looking
up from a sandwich in her hands, startled to see her
cousin out of bed.

Dell could sense everything, every movement
around her, every thought. There was a fly behind
the curtain at the window, buzzing, seeking exit. The
tiled floor protested mightily as her feet stepped
across it. The compressor on the refrigerator
hummed like an aircraft readying for takeoff. Outside
the walls she could hear a dog snuffling along the
sidewalk, birds taking wing or landing with a flutter
on tree limbs. In the house next door she sensed their
neighbor as she searched for keys to the car, mut-
tering below her breath at how memory always
failed her.

The world was open and furious with sound and
sensation. Dust motes filled the sunny windows,
twirling like universes. Water sang in the pipes
below the sink. She could even hear the whine of
electricity that whipped down the wire in the walls
to the outlets, feeding the appliances. Life! Life everywhere, in every atom, all of it weaker and without a
tenth of the power she knew she possessed.

She turned around and stood immobile, eyes wide
in surprise at the world she'd been allowed to enter.
"It's marvelous," she whispered. "It's heaven. Why
didn't you tell me? Why did you let me fear it so
long?"

"You should come back to bed," Grandma said.

Her mother spoke to her silently, by thought waves. *It's not all heavenly, Dell. We have to be careful.*

Dell could not believe her, chose not to believe her. She was in love with all things, living and inanimate. She understood instinctively their compositions and the life they had once lived, as in the case of wood and plastic and vinyl, or were living at the moment, such as the blood and the food in the refrigerator, the animals outside, the neighbors in the houses surrounding her own. This intimate knowledge and understanding of the world was like a tremendous power surge and it made her giddy.

She could fly, she knew she could. She could walk up the wall to the ceiling, as Eddie had done. She could crush iron and bend steel and make things move with just the power of her will. She could . . . she could do more, she knew, but wasn't sure yet exactly what. But something stupendous, something she'd never even imagined yet.

Her parents came to her and each took one of her arms, as if to restrain her. "Come back to your room," her mother said.

"Yes, do as your mother says, dear." Grandma stepped out of the way so Dell could be led across the kitchen.

"Why? I feel fine, I feel great! I don't need to go to bed. I don't ever want to sleep again!"

Dell's two paternal uncles came to the doorway and stared at her. Boyd and Daniel had come all the way from San Antonio at their brother's urging, and now they gave her looks that spoke silently of love and understanding. Behind them she caught glimpses of their wives, her aunts. All of them vampire. All had undergone this same event in their lives and they knew both her agony and her newfound thrill of joy.

It seemed nearly everyone in the family had arrived at the house and now they were all watching her, commanding her to do as they bid.

"Mentor is on his way," her father said, leading

her into the hall as Boyd and Daniel and their wives moved silently back into the living room. "There's more to this than the initial sense of power. There's also . . . danger."

She let them lead her back to the room, though she knew if she caught them by surprise, she could have shaken her parents off like pesky insects. She felt the strength in her arms rippling through her and imagined how easily she could heft cars and small buildings and blocks of stone.

In some ways she realized she was acting like someone hopped up on a narcotic. She'd seen kids at school act if as they were superhuman, as if they owned the planet. They were deluded, of course, and she knew she was not, but she was still behaving like a drug addict nearing euphoric frenzy. She must listen to her parents, her family. She must sit and wait for Mentor to tell her what she could and could not do. There were secrets that had not yet been revealed to her, that's what her mother was trying to say.

But it was going to be hard to do as she was told. It was going to take all her willpower to keep from running out of the house and throwing up her hands to the sky to thank heaven for her new life.

"Okay," she said, "Okay, I'll relax. I'll try, really."

She felt her mother's hand tense on her upper arm and knew that she was worried about her. She turned her attention to her father and found his mind also gnawing at worry like a termite on fresh wood.

"Not me," Eddie said at her back, where he trailed them down the hallway. "I'm not worried one little bit."

Dell smiled, and remembering, moved her tongue to her incisors to feel for them. Now she knew the blood was not drunk. It was not like food that had to go through the digestive system to be turned into energy. It went straight into her veins and arteries, straight into her heart and brain, renewing all the organs to their original healthy living states. It made her live again. It was the means to survival.

And she would do anything for it. Anything.

* * *

Mentor used the door as a human would, though it was within his power to migrate through solid objects. He always forced himself to be as natural as the Naturals when possible. To understand their anxieties and problems, he had to have intimate knowledge of their lives and to do that, he must live and act as they did. There were times he lived as the Predators, too, using his abilities to their fullest, and now and again he lived as the Cravens, shutting himself up in the house, drawing the curtains, letting his mind die down to a weak signal. To be of service, he had to know intimately the inner workings of the different clans' emotional lives.

He did not bother to knock, knowing those inside would know he was there. He stepped across one of the Cravens lying at the foot of the door, head pillowed on outthrust arm, staring up at him with wide eyes. "You should get up and out of the way in order to help yourself," he said casually as he left that one behind.

Mentor's "patient," the vampire he had been summoned to help, was toward the back of the house in one of the last bedrooms. The vampire was a Craven named Dolan, and it was rumored Dolan was on a suicidal rampage. Any act of undue aggression, even one involving only the self, Mentor tried to stop. Unfortunately, Dolan meant to do harm to others of his kind before destroying himself. And that was not going to happen. It was against all moral law to destroy your own kind unless there was just cause.

Mentor stepped into the room and said to Dolan, "I've come to stop you."

Dolan was an old vampire, crouched in the corner, his back to the door. He had both arms over his head and was shivering as if he were cold. Mentor said, "Don't try to make me feel sorry for you. That's not going to work. What you're planning to do is against our law. I can't stop you from ending your life. But I will stop you from taking anyone with you. Do you understand?"

Dolan turned slowly to face Mentor. There was no telling how many lifetimes he had lived, but they were many. His face reflected a soul gouged with ruts and roads that made him look a thousand years old. Like Mentor, he had chosen an older male body to inhabit, but it was in his eyes that his true age showed.

He bared his teeth now to show Mentor he was willing to fight. Mentor said, "I will take you down if I have to. But listen to me, I would rather you talk this out."

"Why should I talk to you?" said Dolan. "You're only here to stop me from doing what I want to do. I think I would rather fight you and die in the trying. At least there might be some honor in that."

"And what would you know about honor?" asked Mentor. "Do you think it's honorable to wish to take others with you?"

"They all want to die anyway. I'd be doing them a favor. Why must you always interfere? Who gave you the right to intervene? You're not God Almighty."

"No, I'm not. But I've earned the right to intervene and you know that. Believe me, you're not taking any of the others in this house with you."

"Oh, good Christ! Have you seen them? What about the one by the door, did you see him? Do you really think he wants to live?"

"Maybe he doesn't want to live, but that's up to him, not you."

"Listen to me! Why aren't you listening, Mentor? Have you ever been a Craven? Do you know what it's like to be powerless and to live in the darkness forever? Have you ever begged for death?"

Mentor recalled the times when he'd gone into seclusion, living as a Craven, feeding on hopelessness. "We've all begged for death. But if we give it to ourselves, we pay with our souls."

"That's totally incomprehensible to me. I don't believe it. There is no punishment worse than what I've already suffered."

Mentor shrugged. "You may be right, but you won't find out until you're gone and then it's too late. I can't let you make that decision for others."

Dolan swooped from the floor, enraged and ready to do battle. It was only then that Mentor smelled smoke and saw a cloud of it coming from the corner where the old vampire had been stooping, his back to the room. He'd set a fire. He meant to burn the place down. He meant the fire to consume them all.

One second before Dolan reached his throat, Mentor stepped aside and then rushed forward to the corner. He waved his hand, concentrating mightily on the molecules in the room's air, and created a damp cloak of mist that put out the fire. He then turned swiftly and struck Dolan on the side of his head, knocking him to the floor. "If I have to," he said, "if you force me to it—I will have you put into chains. You'll never be free again. You know I speak the truth."

Dolan bellowed in frustration.

Mentor continued, "If you want to do away with yourself, that's fine with me. That's entirely up to you. But you will not, do you hear me, *you will not* take anyone else with you."

Dolan fell to his knees, head hanging. In a small voice he said, "You have to help me. Mentor, you have to help me. I can't go on this way."

Mentor checked the fire to be sure it was out before stepping close to his patient. "That's all you had to do," he said. "All you had to do was ask. Now stand up and come with me."

As he escorted Dolan out of the house, he noticed the Craven who had been on the floor was gone now, probably locked in his room, living out his fate with whatever strength he had left. Mentor sensed many more of the Cravens hiding in other rooms, cringing from the disturbance they'd sensed going on in the house. At least he had saved them from an untimely demise.

It was dark outside, so Dolan could be led back to Mentor's house, as the Craven could not bear sunlight. At home, Mentor would place Dolan into a specially built basement room where he could rest and be instructed on how to live out the rest of his life. If he set fire to himself when Mentor was gone, then at least something had been done to try to save him first.

Mentor did not save them all. In fact, he saved relatively few once they had decided to do away with themselves. But he was charged to have mercy. It was his job to deal with the despairing. It had never been promised that he would always triumph.

As he hustled the old vampire along the street, pools of iridescence shining through an early evening fog, the streetlights made the two of them appear to be a couple of old friends going home from work. If only it were so, thought Mentor. *If only we were human again, friends out having a drink, and on our way home.*

He shook his head sadly. *No wonder so many of us want to die. And the wonder lies in the fact that so many of us go on.*

"Tell me what brought you to this impasse," Mentor said.

In a chastened voice the old vampire said, "Is confession good for the soul, then?"

Mentor saw an alleycat dart across the sidewalk and behind a garbage can with a bulging lid. He felt its hunger and experienced a sense of kinship with it. "You don't have to confess to anything. You just have to talk about your feelings."

The tale began, haltingly at first, with long pauses. As they walked the silent street, Dolan shying from the beams of headlights from an occasional car, the story unfolded. It was not that different from others Mentor had heard, but nevertheless he paid strict attention. Dew fell from the fog and soaked their shoulders and gathered like silver jewels in their hair.

Dolan talked, he wept softly, and Mentor listened carefully without responding, guiding the old one closer and closer to safety. Near his home, Mentor heard the silent plea reach him from the Cambian family. Dell, the new vampire, had taken blood and was in a state of ecstasy. She was listening to her parents, staying put in her home, but they feared she might break free from them into the night.

Mentor hurried Dolan into the house, down into the basement, and asked him to hold out his wrists.

Dolan stared at the handcuffs made of solid steel. He laughed. "Do you really think they will hold me if I want to go? I possess more strength than it may appear."

Mentor slapped the cuffs on him anyway, fastening them tight. "Of course they can't hold you. But they might make you think before you fight your way out of them. I have to leave for a while. You'll be on your own for a few hours. It's up to you, Dolan. What happens now is up to your own conscience. But if you do free yourself, and if you return to that house where the others lie helpless, I swear I will be on you in a millisecond."

Dolan slumped to the floor, hanging his cuffed hands over his upright knees. "I'll wait for you to come back."

"Good."

"I won't set fire to your house."

"Even better." Mentor smiled and turned for the stairs.

"Mentor?"

"Yes?" He paused on the bottom step, his hand on the rail.

"I don't know how you do this. I don't know how

you keep going year after year when there are so many of us who need you."

Mentor went up the stairs. At the landing before the door he said, "If I didn't do it, I'd be like you are now. I'd turn myself to ash." He heard the old vampire's low growl of a laugh as he shut the door behind him and locked it with dead bolts. He didn't think what he'd admitted to was a laughing matter. But laughter was better than tears, so he forgave his houseguest, moved to the front door, and left him behind in the darkness of solitude.

7

Dr. Alan Star had been working on Charles Upton's case for nearly a year. Upton's porphyria was unrelenting, taking the old man in one of the most horrible ways anyone could meet his end. The disease being quite rare, this was only the second case Alan had attended in his career as a specialist in blood diseases. The first one had been a woman in Birmingham, Alabama, where Alan had finished his residency. Maggie. She had been elderly like Upton, and finally untreatable, dying in the hospital while Alan sat by her side, watching and agonizing. Maggie of the bright eyes, dimming into stillness. Yet there had been no reproach there for him that he hadn't done all that he could.

Alan hated to lose a patient. All doctors were wretched when it happened, but Alan truly counted a loss as a personal failure. With all the modern drugs and technology at his disposal, he couldn't believe something hadn't been found yet to counteract the finality of many blood diseases. Yes, people died; it was to be expected. Some came to him as a last resort, already too far gone to save. But that didn't matter. As a blood specialist, when Alan couldn't change the course of a disease or at least alleviate the worst symptoms, he felt devastated. He knew he wasn't responsible—he always did everything he could to prevent a death. Yet the few losses he'd suffered haunted him. They were never far from his mind.

So when Charles Upton requested to see Alan at his penthouse, Alan found the time to make it. Perhaps it was best to talk to the old man and give him the bad news—that there was little that could be done now—in person, in his own home.

It surprised Alan when he was let into the extravagant apartment and ushered by a man in uniform into Upton's private bedroom. On the edge of the bed sat the old man in the last stages of his disease, but he was brimming with energy and excitement. He stood and greeted Alan, shaking his hand before resuming his place on the bed.

Most people had trouble even looking at Upton. The disease had deformed his face, caused hair to grow in tufts on the backs of his hands and in spots on his upper arms, and then there were the open sores covered by bandages. Upton was so swathed with white wrappings that he looked like a torn-up accident victim.

"Dr. Star! What a lucky last name you have. Has it given you any trouble?"

Alan wasn't quite sure what Upton meant. Had his name given him trouble? As in grade school when kids could be unusually cruel?

"Uh . . . I don't think so," he said cautiously.

"Never mind, come and sit down. I have a proposition to put to you."

Alan sat in an imported French ivory-and-gold chair that he guessed might be worth more than a Porsche. Money had never humbled him, but this kind of money, out of all proportion to common incomes, could daunt anyone.

What Upton had just said intrigued him. Everyone knew Charles Upton had more money than God. Most of Alan's colleagues knew Alan sought capital for a new research center for blood diseases. Maybe Upton had found that out, and was about to finance his dream. Maybe today was not the best of times to give the bad news to the old man. It could wait . . . at least a little while. Upton's demise wasn't imminent. Yet.

"What proposition is that, sir?" Alan asked.

"What do you know about the vampire legend?"

The first thing that popped into Alan's mind was, *Oh, my God, he's lost his mind.* It was possible the disease had affected his thought processes. Vampires, for Pete's sake!

He cleared his throat and looked at his shoes on the beautiful carpet. They needed cleaning, his shoes. Actually, they needed throwing away. He should buy a pair of new shoes occasionally, it certainly wouldn't be a sin. He'd worn these leather loafers for years only because they were comfortable and he hated to break in a new pair.

"Well?" Charles said, squirming on the edge of the bed. "Are you deaf?"

Alan looked up. He was being rude, and it was irritating the old man. He'd talk about anything, he supposed. He had a little time before his patient rounds at the hospital. "No, I was just thinking. I don't suppose I know very much at all about vampire legends. I've never gone in for horror."

"I hear you are looking for someone to back you for a new research center," the old man said, seemingly changing the subject.

Alan brightened. "Oh, yes, I certainly am. Porphyria, for instance—if we had a facility where we could run more tests and try out more combinations of drug treatments, do experiments on DNA . . ."

Upton waved him off and he let the sentence die. He frowned in confusion.

Upton said, "I have no illusions that I am going to live long enough to benefit from your research, Dr. Star."

"But . . ."

"Yet I have a real proposition for you, regardless. How would you like to have that research center, paid for, free and clear? All the latest equipment money can buy, staff, a modern facility in the heart of this city?"

Alan didn't know how to respond. Was he hearing the man correctly? Was he being offered all that, just out of the blue, out of the kindness of the old billionaire's heart? It couldn't be. There were always strings. This was Earth, not Mars. Millions of dollars were not invested without some kind of return.

He thought his best bet in this instance was to reply calmly and carefully, just as if he were offered this kind of thing every day. "I would love to have that, sir. It would mean the world to me."

"Well, that's what I'm offering. Naturally, I want something from you. You're not a stupid man. If you were, I wouldn't have called you and made the offer. I've done my own . . . research. You're one of the brightest physicians in the state. Just because you can't cure me doesn't mean I don't understand how brilliant you are."

"Thank you, sir." Alan realized he didn't have to tell Upton he was losing the battle with porphyria. The man knew he was dying. He knew there would never be a cure in time. So what could he want from him?

"I asked you what you knew about vampires. The legend of the vampire?"

Alan nodded, wondering what that had to do with the offer of a research center.

"I guess you've heard some of the other doctors who have been on my case refer to me as 'The Old Vampire.' Don't deny it. I heard them, so I know you must have."

"That was an unfortunate . . ."

"I don't want your sympathy, Doctor, and there's no point apologizing for those idiots. I'm trying to get you to understand where I'm going with the vampire thing."

"Yes, sir." Now he was thoroughly confused. He knew Upton had fired and sued his last doctors for referring to him as a vampire in a rather cruel, mocking way in what they thought was privacy. But what . . . ?

"I want you to know, first of all, that this disease has not affected my mind," Upton said.

Alan thought that might be debatable, but he kept his peace.

"Secondly, I want you to know that, though I was furious with my last doctors and I have a lawsuit pending against them for defamation of my good name, I've come to look at myself as they must have. I know I look like a monster. I know that with my distorted face I could shame a special effects master. I'm not fooling myself. I'm sick, disgusting to look at, and dying. But what if . . ." He paused and Alan straightened in his chair. Upton was being honest with him and though he didn't know where he was going with his confession, it was intriguing to see a man so beset by fate find a way to face the truth about his condition.

Upton continued, "I'll just blurt it out. I've done some study into the vampire legends, and some of them seem to indicate that it isn't all a myth. There might have been people who lived after death. Who came back to life. I know it's fantastic, but . . . what if it's true? How many medical marvels do we enjoy today that would have seemed fantastic to us fifty years ago? Twenty years ago! And if there were vampires, real vampires in the past, what if there are real ones living and moving around among us today?"

Alan was flabbergasted. He hadn't expected this. Not anything like this. Though Upton claimed to be in his right mind, all indications were he was suffering from psychosis. The thought of his dream research center coming true faded like bright cloth left for a month under the hot Texas sun. He couldn't take money from a madman. He couldn't use him that way.

"I see how you're looking at me," Upton said, scowling. "You think I've lost it. Well, think again, Dr. Star. I'm as sane as you are. I did not live sixty-

eight years and amass the fortune I have today by
being a flake."

"But, Mr. Upton, we're talking about fictional creatures, horror movie actors, not reality."

"What if you're wrong?"

Alan tried to consider it, but every time he tried
to think about fictional vampires as real he wanted
to burst out laughing. That would be worse than
rude; that would get him booted out of the apartment. "If I'm wrong?" he said.

"Here's the deal. I don't have time to waste trying
to convince you of anything. I've read the literature.
You haven't. I'm going to send along what I have
with you; my man's got it packaged and waiting in
the other room. Take your time reading it. Meanwhile, here's what I propose. You'll have nothing to
lose and a great deal to gain. No one has to know
anything about all this, not a soul. Not my partner
in my business, not my butler, no one. It's strictly
between you and me."

"What do you want from me?"

"I want you to search out and find me a vampire.
I want the thing brought to me. I want it to give me
my life back. I refuse to die."

There it was. On the table. A dead man's hand,
aces and eights. Alan flinched in surprise and tried
to compose his face. He couldn't look at the old man
again. He stared at the floor. His shoes needed cleaning at the very least if he wasn't going to replace
them.

"Dr. Star?"

Alan glanced up.

"You may think me insane if you like. That's your
prerogative. What I'm offering is simple. I'll write
you a check to cover any kind of medical facility you
want. I don't care if it costs four million or forty
million." He waved his hand to dismiss the spending
of money that very soon would mean nothing to him.
"In fact, once you start work for me on this, I'll fund
the buying of the land and have construction begin

right away. You pick the architect, and I'll write him a check. All I ask is that you do as I say. You search, put on an *honest* search for me. If I die before you find a vampire, I'll leave enough in my will for you to finish your research center. You're not going to lose on this. No one will ever know why I have given you the money. Your reputation as a doctor of medicine will remain pristine.

"But I will demand your complete loyalty and will expect you to devote yourself to what I ask."

"But my patients . . ."

"Let me be perfectly honest with you, Alan. I know this means you have to take time off from your real work. I know this might take more time than you want. But I don't have any choice in this matter. If you share your time with me and the hospital, you may never find what I need. I'm asking a great favor. I'm willing to pay for it. When this is over, you can return to your work, all the richer."

"But I don't know how I'd start. I mean, where would I look? Don't you need an investigator instead? Someone professional, who knows what to do?"

"Except for me and my partner, David, I'd say you're one of the smartest, most intelligent men in the state of Texas. I wouldn't have come to you if you hadn't been. You'll find a way to do this. You're not a private investigator, but you have a wonderful mind. You know how to research problems, it's your business. You know how to track down symptoms and diseases. Turn those traits to tracking down a living vampire, and I expect you'll turn up something. In fact, I believe it to the tune of forty million, if that's what it takes."

Alan sat biting down on his tongue. He couldn't say no, and he couldn't say yes. If he said no, there went his dream in a puff of smoke. He'd never again find someone willing to build him a research center, and if he tried to do it on his own he would be a very old man before he got the money and the credit.

If he said yes, he'd be saying yes to a crazy project that made no real sense. He'd be playing into the psychosis of a desperate, dying man.

"I don't know if I can do this, sir. I want to help you, but since I don't believe there are such creatures as vampires, it would be immoral of me to say that I could try to find one in order to get the funding I need."

"That's what I thought you would say. I'm glad you said it because it proves you're an honest man. Now let's forget it and move on. Take the literature home and read it. Call me in a couple of days and tell me what you think then. Tell me I'm insane then. Tell me you don't believe it could be true. If there is one speck of hope, I'm willing to gamble. After all, Doctor, I'm dying. I have nothing to lose and a new life if I win. So will you read the works and call me? Say you'll do that much. It costs you nothing but a little of your time."

Alan felt sorry for him. He was touched by the old man's fervor and incredible life force. He thought that money might save him, that myth might be made reality, that he might find a way to beat death. He hoped never to meet a man as desperate as this again.

"All right, I'll read it," he said, pity overwhelming his good sense.

"And you'll call me afterward?"

"Yes. But I really can't promise to do this, Mr. Upton."

"Just think it over. Think about the people you could save if you have a research center to work on discoveries that would cure them. Think about the future, Dr. Star. Think about children who get porphyria and what they are going to have to face. Do it for them."

It was certainly tempting. Upton had no close relatives he cared for and his money, when he was gone, would do little good in the world. Why not just take some of it now and use it to help mankind? But he'd be lying to himself and to Upton to get it, wouldn't he? Well, he'd read the old man's papers and books. He'd do what he promised.

"I'll read the material," he repeated.

"Thank you. I think after you see what I've found, you'll be convinced enough to pursue this for me. Even if you aren't convinced . . . forty million dollars could do a lot of good."

Alan was alone in the private elevator that took him to the lobby of the Upton building. In his hands he carried two heavy polyester satchels of books. What could the old man have found? How could he possibly have sold himself this bill of goods?

Out on the sunny street in his car, turning toward the hospital where he was due for a consultation, Alan glanced at the bags of books taking up the passenger seat. This was crazy. This was really daft.

But he'd do it. Upton knew how much he longed to do research, to man his own facility, to coordinate a staff of qualified researchers to help him unearth the remaining questions in hematology.

He would at least look at the books. As daft as it might be, he wouldn't be able to help himself.

Vampires, he thought. *Oh, God.*

8

Dell spent hours with Mentor listening to his advice. Sometimes her mind wandered, and she focused on the sounds outside the house. Sometimes she heard sounds *inside* the house, too. A June bug trapped at the window in the kitchen. A lone roach, antennae wriggling, on the floor beneath the refrigerator. The electricity in the wires inside the walls—that bothered her the most. It was like a background hum in her ears that wouldn't go away.

Nevertheless, she picked up most of what Mentor said to her and took it to heart. She could not try out her newfound supernatural powers that involved great physical strength right away. She could not show her exuberance in front of humans as they'd think she'd gone mad or was suffering from manic attacks. She could not ever let anyone know what had happened. She could not begin to act differently around her friends. She could not let them know she could read their thoughts if she wanted.

There were so many things she was supposed to *not* do that she wondered exactly what she *could* do.

"You can go on living your life as you always have," Mentor said, intercepting her thought. "A human lifetime is a gift."

"That's going to be nearly impossible. Living like I did before," she said, thinking of eating hamburgers and fries, slurping down milkshakes, going to football games and dances and to the mall to shop with her friends.

"It will in the beginning. But after a few weeks, you'll adjust."

"The funny thing is," she said, "I thought I'd feel . . . dead. I thought I'd hate being this way and I'd want to . . . die for real. I didn't know I'd feel so alive and thrilled about it."

"This feeling might pass, Dell," he warned. "There will be times when you'll feel just the opposite. Times when life will be unbearable."

"It's hard to believe that."

"It is now, but you'll have to trust me. Our emotions tend to swing widely, leaving us hanging on stars or dropped into the lowest pit. You'll call for me if that happens, won't you? When you think you can't go on?"

"Yes, of course, I will," she said.

"Good. Then tomorrow or the next day you will need to return to school. As a Natural, you're going to take up your old life and carry on. The sun will not harm you, the night and darkness will not call to you. You've chosen the path that allows you the greatest freedom in this world."

"I won't . . ." She could hardly say it. She tried again. "I won't try to . . . harm anyone, will I? I mean, I won't be like a Predator, will I?" Already she yearned for one of the blood-filled bags in the refrigerator. It was like a thirst that never ended. Her throat was as parched as a mesquite tree in a dry plain in the middle of a West Texas summer.

Mentor took his time answering. He was probably listening to her thoughts, weighing her need. Finally he said, "I can't promise that you'll never be tempted. At times, all of us fight the urge to just take what we want when we want it. It's so easy that way, you see. It's something you'll have to wrestle with and overcome."

"Your conscience is strong, Dell. Your humanity still resides inside you. Murder isn't something your mind will accept, though your hunger might grow strong. But there will be times when hunger overpowers the heart and your mind may get confused. It's at those times you'll be most vulnerable to committing an act against man. If you ever give in, even once, the next time will be easier. *So you must never give in.* Do you understand? Never, no matter what provocation or how weak you think you are or how great your need for sustenance."

"I didn't really think that would ever happen," she said sadly. "And this urge will be there all of my life?"

"I'm afraid so. It's the nature of our affliction. Unfortunately, it's part of being vampire, any kind of vampire."

She thought long and hard about what Mentor had said once he left. A horrible thought occurred to her. She called her mother into her room and shut the door.

"Mom, I have to ask you something."

"Anything, darling."

"Mentor told me I'd have urges now and then to drink blood from a human."

"That urge will come less often as you live this life."

"Well, what I wanted to ask is . . ." She wasn't sure she actually wanted to know, but she had to ask. "I wanted to know if you or Daddy ever wanted to drink from Eddie or me before we . . . we got sick."

Her mother's face registered surprise, and then she smiled. "Oh, only about once a week. No big deal."

Dell laughed, realizing her mother was teasing her. "No, really, Mom. Were you ever tempted that way?"

"No."

"Never?"

"Never. You're my flesh and my blood. Your father and I would have set ourselves on fire before we'd bring harm to you."

Dell breathed a sigh of relief. She didn't know how she would have handled the thought that her parents had hungered for her. "Okay, thanks, Mom. I didn't think you did, but I had to find out."

Her mother gave her a hug and opened the door. She paused on the threshold. "Do you think you're up for school tomorrow?"

"I can try. I guess if I feel out of sorts once I get there, I can call you at work and come home."

"That's my girl! I'm sure you'll be fine. The faster you get back into your normal routine, the better off you'll be. Remember, you graduate this year. And at the top of your class!"

Dell smiled as her mother left the room. Her mother loved and appreciated her. She was proud of all her accomplishments.

Restless now, Dell went to her dressing table and sat down before the mirror. She didn't look different. The sores that had erupted so rapidly were now healed, not even leaving scars. She was tan and fit, a girl verging on womanhood, and the only change she could detect was the look in her eyes. That look was one of knowledge and sadness. She knew now of death and of living on after death as a new being. Would her friends and classmates notice her eyes? Would they suspect she was different? Maybe she could wear sunglasses for a while, like some of the weird kids in school. She could say she had a sty. Or pink eye. Everyone hated getting pink eye.

She wouldn't know how her friends would react to her, though, until she went back to school and faced them.

"I can do this," she said aloud, turning away from the mirror and the dead look in her eyes. "I can live again."

*   *   *

It took Dell two more days before she was ready to face the world outside her home. During that time, with her parents at work and Eddie at school, she wandered the empty house and tried to stay away from the transfusion bags in the refrigerator. Given her deep hunger, she thought she could down them all at once. The idea made her laugh, but the sudden sound of laughter in the quiet house gave her pause. She rubbed the back of her neck where the hair there had crept up. To ease her mind into trance, she tried to watch television. *Think nothing and nothing will matter,* she told herself, hunting down the remote where her little brother had stashed it between the sofa cushions.

Usually TV talk shows could turn her into a mindless vegetable, but it didn't work this time. She watched *Jerry Springer,* horrified at the guests as most Americans were, and remembered she'd heard her parents talking about a Predator in Fort Worth, Texas, who got himself booked on there one time to discuss the vampire "legend." Mentor was called in to squelch the renegade, for it was bandied about among the Predator community that the vampire doing the show was disgruntled and mentally unstable. He promised the Springer show that he would show his fangs and even take a victim under the watchful eye of the camera, if they wanted. A willing victim, if they could find one.

Secrecy was everything to vampires. Without it, they weren't safe. Rarely did anyone get out of hand and try to give the secret to the media. Mentor went to the renegade and discussed his upcoming television appearance. He judged the vampire to be clearly unreliable, his mind teetering on the brink of insanity, and had taken him away for his own good, and the good of all vampires everywhere. The Springer people booked wannabe vampires instead.

Dell's parents did not know where the renegade was taken, but they understood there *was* a place, a monastery run by vampire monks somewhere in another part of the world. Was it Asia? The far reaches of China? There someone could be kept prisoner until well, or if it was judged he would never be well again, rumor had it the prisoner was bound forever. There was no alternative.

Dell hoped the talk show hopeful hadn't been destroyed or imprisoned for the rest of his vampire life. She did not want to think about what it might be like to be held prisoner by powerful supernatural monks, but burning the renegade for turning to the media seemed to her too harsh a judgment. Go on *Jerry Springer* and die for it. She almost laughed aloud again, thinking cynically that some of the guests ought to have that option.

Maybe she would ask Mentor what had happened to the renegade vampire. . . .

Turning off the TV, she wandered the rooms again, peeking through the drawn curtains at the postage-stamp-sized front yard. Their house looked similar to all the other houses on the street in the suburb. Brick, three bedrooms, two baths, two-car garage. Decidedly middle class. Which was about all her parents could afford, given that a majority of their income went to Predators for the blood.

They had lived in the house since she was born. Their neighbors knew them enough to speak to. Some neighbors had moved in and moved out again, their incomes taking them to more sophisticated habitats. The ones who stayed kept to themselves, so that a family of vampires could live unnoticed by curious humans.

Two of Dell's friends lived on the same street; she'd grown up with them. They had spent nights at one another's houses, had backyard barbecues together, played dolls under the shade of the crape myrtle. She had gone swimming with them at the neighborhood pool, discussed boys with them, and traded clothes.

Knowing her so well, would they ever guess she had changed? She couldn't let that happen. They'd never known about Eddie or her parents. Why should she think they'd discover her secret? No one believed in vampires anyway. It was the stuff of movies and books and TV shows. Quite a popular myth in entertainment now and again, but that made the reality of them even more fantastic. If Hollywood made them up, how could they be real? Impossible.

And some of the movies! They made her family laugh. They made them fall off their chairs laughing. What idiot had done those scripts, what nincompoop had written those books, they asked one another?

Dell had just rented an old video about vampires starring James Woods, one of her favorite actors. Even *he* could not make the inane dialogue come out as real—and if he couldn't, no one could. It was that bad. In the movie it was all the Catholic Church's fault there were vampires. An exorcism in the 1600s had gone badly. Hah! If only that was what it was. How easily the mistake could have been rectified. Near the end of the movie, with Jimmy Woods ransacking a vampire town with his trusty steel bow-and-arrow contraption, the arrow connected to a steel cord hooked to a Jeep to haul vampires out into the sun to burn, Dell got up and savagely turned off the VCR. This kind of thing made her angry. It made vampires look . . . like . . . animals. Rabid animals that had to be put out of their misery.

She wished that one day she could tell Hollywood how it really was, how difficult it was to maintain a normal existence, how heartbreaking it was to know you were cut off from mankind, how the prospect of living for many lifetimes over drained the soul of pity and hope. Not that they would believe her or that she would ever really want to tell them. No. She would not want Mentor tracking *her* down, taking her off to some dreary old monastery.

So her friends had their heads full of stupid movie ideas of what vampires should be and would never be looking for someone like her anyway. There was no reason for her closest friends to even have the thought that she was something other than human.

It would be the same as believing she was an alien from outer space, hatched from an egg.

Unless she did something really stupid, no one would ever know.

Then again, if she didn't learn how to breathe properly, she was going to be in one hell of a lot of trouble, she thought, realizing she hadn't taken a breath in minutes.

She sucked in air and let it out as she walked the house, room to room. If she ran, she would have to exert her will and pretend she was breathless. If someone were to accidentally knock her down or if she fell—which she supposed she probably wouldn't, ever again, unless it was to fool someone, she would have to pretend she'd lost her breath. She must recall how she'd breathed naturally for seventeen years, unconsciously, and get into the habit of it all over again.

On the second day she thought she had mastered breathing so that it came more naturally to her. It was funny how the air tasted. It was as if the little sacs in her lungs had taste buds and relayed them to her brain, the same as her tongue did. The air in the living room sometimes recalled the taste and scent of popcorn left over from human guests. Sometimes it tasted of the tweed fabric on the sofas and sometimes it just seemed it was a room full of dust despite the fact that her mother was a neat housekeeper. The air in her bedroom was made up of distinct scents of lipstick and foundation powder and deodorant and peach toilet water. The bathroom—she tried to stay out of the bathroom. It tasted downright foul, with old, stale scents coming up from the drains of the tub and sink. Those particular bodily functions had ceased along with the end of her intake of food and drink. Pure blood did not produce waste. The bathrooms now were just places where they bathed and shaved.

On her second day home alone when Eddie got off the school bus, Dell met him at the door. He threw down his schoolbooks on the sofa and made for the kitchen. He never had to study anymore. His memory was phenomenal. All he had to do was glance over pages and they were committed forever to memory. That was a change Dell was looking forward to. Now perhaps she'd truly *understand* chemistry. She would soon tackle her father's computer, go on the Internet, and study the online encyclopedias. She'd end up acing her tests. She'd have more knowledge than a college grad. She wouldn't even need to go to college, except for the sheepskin she might want to show the world so they'd believe she was educated.

She followed Eddie to the kitchen, watched him take a bag from the white cardboard box, and loft it higher than his face. He hadn't even said hello to her yet.

"You get really hungry at school, don't you?" she asked.

"Mmmm." He had his fangs in the bag, but he cut his gaze to her.

"Isn't it funny? It feels almost like when we were human and needed to eat food."

He nodded.

"But it's not really food, the blood. It just keeps us vibrant, gives us our energy back. It doesn't even go into our stomachs. And the hunger isn't centered there, is it? It's like . . . all over our bodies . . . or mostly in our brains. Like if our brains had teeth, they would crawl out to search for blood." The thought gave her a shiver. It made her think of zombie movies. More dumb stuff from Hollywood. She rubbed her arms.

"Mmmm."

He finished draining the bag and, with his foot, hit the garbage pail pedal. He dropped the bag inside. They were very careful to double bag their garbage for pickup. They didn't want some garbage man breaking open one of the bags all over the street, strewing dozens of plastic transfusion bags that were slick with rotting blood.

Eddie turned to her. "Is that what you do all day here, think about how everything's different?"

"Well, yeah, I guess I do. What did you think about?"

"Scaling Mount Everest."

"No joke?"

He laughed, passing her by, heading for his room. "Yeah, it's a joke. I don't remember what I thought about. Girls, maybe."

She had to remember he'd changed two years before, so he was fourteen now even though he didn't look it. He was definitely in the girl stage. Some things stayed the same.

"I have some questions," she said, following on his heels.

He plopped down on his twin-sized bed, swinging his feet up, and put his hands behind his head, staring at the ceiling. "Shoot."

"You mentioned girls. You think about girls a lot, I guess. What are you going to do about it?"

"About what?" He hadn't taken his gaze off the ceiling, as if her questions might have their answers written there.

"About girls. Are you going to date? Have a girlfriend?"

He closed his eyes and didn't respond for several seconds. Finally, he said, "Mentor discussed that with me. He'll get around to it with you, too."

"Tell me what he said."

"I think he should tell you. Or what's the point of having Mentor?"

"Eddie!"

He opened his eyes and looked at her. "What?"

"Tell me," she said impatiently.

He shrugged. "You can't get involved . . . uh . . . romantically . . . with humans."

She had been afraid of that. Ryan Major's face floated into her mind. The boy who had just transferred to her school and who, before she'd changed, she had been hoping to find a way to meet. He didn't even know her yet. And now he probably never would. Some other girl, a cheerleader no doubt, would snag his attention and Dell would be lonely. All of her life! All of her many lives!

She sank down onto the side of her brother's bed. He moved his legs over to make room for her. "Do our kind ever fall in love? With another vampire, maybe?"

"I don't know."

"So we go through all the years to come without . . . without loving anyone?"

"Mentor didn't say that."

"I guess he wouldn't. I mean, Mom and Dad fell in love."

"Yeah, but they met before they changed," Eddie said carefully.

"Well? What did Mentor say? It isn't like our emotions died. How do we keep from, well, from falling in love?"

"You need to ask Mentor."

"I'm asking you!" She hit one of his legs with her fist. How come he was still a pesky kid brother? She wished he was thirty and smart.

"Well, I'm *not* thirty," he said, reading her mind. "But I am smart." He grinned widely. "Mentor said . . ." He paused.

She hit him again with her fist to jostle him.

"Stop it! That hurts. He said it's like the hunger. You don't want to ever kill someone, right?"

"Right. He told me that. How I might have to fight off the urge."

"You do the same thing about boys."

"I have to fight off falling in love?"

"Something like that."

"That's horrible! Mom and Dad found one another, and Grandma and Grandpa. Even Uncle Boyd and Uncle Daniel."

"I think they were *all* human and together before . . ." Eddie said.

"Oh. But Mom and Dad knew they might become vampire."

"Now you have the gist of it," Eddie said.

"But if they'd already changed, they would still have gotten together, right?"

"I guess."

"You're saying then that I just have to stay away from humans. My only choice is someone like me."

"Ask Mentor."

Dell gave up. She rose from the bed and stomped out of the room to show her displeasure. She didn't want to talk about love and boys and marriage anyway. It had just come to her, that's all. What did he think, that she cared?

Eddie was sitting on the living room sofa holding his book bag when she entered the room.

"I wish you'd stop that." She meant how he appeared somewhere else all of a sudden. She'd left him on his bed and yet here he was in the living room.

"I can't help it if I can move instantaneously and you can't."

"I can't *yet*."

He grinned at her and unzipped his bag. "Give me a minute to flip through my history notes. I have a test tomorrow."

She found the remote and turned on the TV. "I hate TV," she said, feeling petulant and wanting to criticize everything around her.

"Then don't watch it."

She saw him open a notebook and begin turning the pages rapidly. In less than two minutes he closed it again and stuffed it back into the book bag.

She studiously ignored him. So what if she couldn't do anything with her powers yet? So what if there was no point in trying to talk to Ryan Major? She flipped the channel changer, going through various HBO cable channels. All the movies were either action flicks or romantic comedies. She was not in the mood for either.

"You're seriously pissed, aren't you?" Eddie asked.

She changed the channel again.

"Look, there's more to it than what I said. You'll just have to talk to Mentor about these things."

"Okay!" She mashed the channel changing button hard and saw the CNN news come on. She left it there, watching pictures of a flood in Ohio.

"No point in getting mad at me. It's not my idea. I'm left out in the cold, too, you know."

Dell reconsidered. Her temper, like every other emotion, seemed set on a hair trigger. "I'm sorry. I know it's not your fault. All this takes getting used to, that's all."

"Not all of it sucks," he said. Then he laughed. "Sucks. Get it?"

She couldn't smile. Eddie's jokes weren't all that good to begin with.

"Anyway, take it easy, Weezy. Things will work out."

Weezy. That almost made her laugh. He liked to be playful with her, rhyming a name for her with whatever he was saying at the moment. She expected some day he'd get to say, "There's a hitch, Bitch."

"What are you smiling at?" he asked, glancing at the flood waters on the TV screen.

"Nothing." She was surprised he hadn't read her mind.

"Want to play Monopoly?" he asked.

"You always beat me. You always get the hotels first."

"Chess?"

"Not now. I always get checkmated."

"Well, I'm going out. Tell Mom and Dad I've already eaten."

She watched him go, this time the normal way, one step at a time. She heard the front door shut. She was left with CNN and a reporter in hip boots and a yellow rain slicker.

She couldn't wait to get back to school.

9

The first day back at school Dell was as nervous as a goose stranded in the center of a freeway. Cheyenne, one of her friends from her neighborhood, was waiting for her at the front entrance before classes started. "I tried to call, but your mom said you were in bed. What's up?"

Dell was careful not to look her in the eyes. She said, "Oh, the usual, you know, cramps and stuff."

"Oh, yeah, that. Maybe you need hormone shots."

Surprised, Dell said, "Why would I need that?"

"Well, that's what my mom would say. She said she saw it on some TV show about girls who get bad cramps. Hormones are all screwed up. A couple shots—boom!—everything back to normal."

"Sounds drastic to me." In fact, she wondered about that. Would she menstruate? For what reason? She'd never have children if she could never have a boyfriend. Oh, God, she couldn't ask Mentor about that. She'd have to talk to her mother. She sighed aloud, and Cheyenne looked over at her.

"You all right?"

"I'm fine. Just a little tired."

They walked under a cool portico out of the hot spring sun, and then through the entrance doors into the building. School would end in three weeks, thank God. She didn't know if she could stand being indoors even that long. The long dark hallway illuminated by overhead fluorescent lights was oppressive to her, and the sounds of the lockers banging open and shut sounded like an orchestra's percussion section had gone cymbal-mad.

"You have your sunglasses on."

Dell touched the nosepiece. "They're almost clear. My eyes are bothering me."

"Listen, my mom said you could go blind if you have a seeing problem and you don't go to the optometrist."

"Come on, Cheyenne. You know how your mom is." Cheyenne's mom had been pushing odd cures and potions on her daughter's friends since they were in first grade together. Dell opened her locker and took out the books for her first class, English with Mr. Dupree.

Cheyenne nodded as she waited by Dell's locker. Her attention had strayed down the hallway where she looked for Bobby, her boyfriend. He sometimes walked her to her own locker where they could sneak a quick kiss behind the locker door. Dell envied her now more than ever. She didn't have to think in order to breathe. She would get married and have someone to love her forever. And she had a head of luxuriant short black hair that rivaled the darkest night. Dell's own wild, slightly kinky red-blonde hair was like a bright beacon signaling rocky shoals ahead whereas Cheyenne's hair was sexy and sleek.

Cheyenne didn't see Bobby yet, so she turned back to Dell, who was moving down the hall shoulder to shoulder with the other kids. She caught up with her. "My mom, yeah, my mom's got a cure for everything and that cure means doctors, new treatments, herbal therapy, or vinegar. Did I tell you she thinks vinegar is heaven's elixir? She takes two tablespoons of the stuff every morning. Never mind what I said. You look good in those sunglasses anyway. If you had on black clothes, you could almost be one of Loder's gang."

"Heaven preserve us!" Dell exclaimed, laughing.

Loder's group were outcasts in the predominately white, Christian, middle class Lyndon B. Johnson High. They wore only black, were into leather—even in this heat—always kept on their sunglasses, and she'd even heard some of them had split off into their own little cult and were into vampirism. She shuddered. She could show them vampire! She could bring a Predator into class that would make them cower and wet their seats.

She had a great loathing for kids who pretended they were searching for death and immortality. They were wayward children, totally disillusioned and, not only that, but they were silly. Black clothes and sunglasses weren't going to make them live forever. It was just . . . crazy. It was just . . . sad.

"Mr. Dupree's gonna notice, though," Cheyenne was saying. They both shared Dupree's first period. He wasn't a bad teacher, but he was pompous as hell. He made the kids who dressed strangely his scapegoats, quoting Byron and teasing them about being displaced in history by a few hundred years. "You should be over in seventeenth-century England at some castle," he often said in his booming voice and pointing at one kid or another. "Frolicking through stone halls and tossing plum seeds into a cold, dead hearth."

"Let him," Dell said, turning into Dupree's room. "He doesn't scare me."

As it happened, Dupree glanced only once at Dell in her seat in the middle of the classroom, blinked, then looked away. Dell had tried a little mind coaxing. She sent the message to him telepathically: *Sunglasses are normal wear. Some students hate the glare off the windows. Keep your business to yourself.* It surprised and amazed her that it worked.

It must have worked. He didn't even ridicule Brady or Chignon, the two kids in her class dressed today in tattered black jeans and shirts. He stuck to the program, talking about Texas literature—which was lame, in his opinion—and Southwestern authors in general. Their assignment was to read Larry King's *Best Little Whorehouse In Texas*, the play. Dell knew she could finish it in under five minutes and besides, she liked the assignment. She'd even been to La-Grange and seen the old tumbledown whorehouse when she was a little girl on a short vacation with her parents.

The day went fine except during History where she sat just one seat in front of Ryan Major. She felt him staring at the back of her neck until she turned around, her index finger going to the centerpiece of her sunglasses. She knew he could see her eyes. But it wasn't her eyes he was interested in. When she turned she watched his gaze fall from her face to her chest. She turned back around immediately and if she could have blushed, she would have. Was he looking at her breasts or had she accidentally stopped breathing? What if she'd forgotten to take breaths? Oh, God, what could he think if she had?

She tried to calm herself. She knew if she wanted, she could peek into his mind. Her history teacher was boring anyway, making the past so dry and brittle no one listened to him. Should she really pry into people's minds? Was it fair?

To hell with fair. She'd been granted supernatural powers and decades on Earth to use them. It would be stupid to ignore her abilities. She wanted to test them.

She narrowed her eyes to slits and turned inward. She visualized Ryan behind her. His forest-green pullover T-shirt, his new denim jeans, his hands crossed on his desk, a class ring on his right hand from North Dallas. Although he would graduate now from Lyndon B. Johnson, his ring would be from the other school. It must be hard for him to change schools that way, right at the end. She imagined his face, his eyes on her back as she carefully breathed. *Easy, easy*, she told herself. *Slip in easy so he won't know.*

And then she was there, reading his thoughts, not

shocked by how jumbled they were. Her parents had explained about that. How it wasn't as easy to read people as she thought. The brain, they said, was a storm of activity and thoughts were like snowflakes in a blizzard, flying everywhere, each snowflake a connecting thought to another until the ground of the brain was covered with hills and valleys of thoughts layered and packed down like snow in drifts.

She heard Ryan's thoughts as if they were being whispered in her ear. She got a snippet of this and one of that. She was not gifted enough in mind reading to be able to follow the several streams of thoughts in their completeness. She caught tail ends and bits and pieces. . . . *wonder if it's satin . . . long hair, I like long hair, why do most girls cut off their hair anyway? . . . she's so still . . . like a statue . . . breathing so gently . . . wait, is she even breathing? . . .*

He had wondered if her blouse was made of satin. Silk, she could have told him. She'd given up her usual sweatshirt and jeans today in favor of a sky-blue silk blouse and a short tropical-printed skirt. She was a different person. She felt like dressing differently now.

He liked her hair long. She resisted an urge to slide her hand behind her neck and lift her hair up to let it fall. She knew it would catch the light and shine if she did that. Her hair, as unmanageable as it was, was almost metallic, like crinkled gold foil, when caught in a certain light.

Though she could read what he was thinking, she knew it was morally irresponsible to act on that knowledge for personal gain or ego. So she did not reach out and lift her hair for his benefit. For a full two minutes. Then, smiling, feeling happy she had the power to play with people even if it was not exactly fair, she reached back and lifted her long hair, letting it fall softly across her shoulders and cascade down her back again. That would get his attention.

And he had wondered why she was so still and if he'd really noticed she wasn't breathing for a time.

God!

She *had* lapsed in her breathing. How dangerous it was out here in the public view where she must be completely human and normal again. She must not let that happen again. This one time Ryan (and anyone else behind her who might have noticed) would put it down to their imaginations. She *must* be breathing, they just couldn't see her doing it, that's all. But if she made this mistake very often, someone somewhere, maybe even Ryan, would call attention to it, or even ask her outright—Why aren't you breathing? How can you not breathe?

She tumbled away from contact with Ryan's mind and concentrated only on her breathing. She took a deep breath, in fact, and let it out in a little quiet *whoosh*. There. Let him see that. Let him not wonder and puzzle over things that were none of his business.

Dell smiled again, and bit the inside of her lip. At least he was interested enough in her to be staring. He had noticed her. Probably only because she sat in front of him, but still . . . he liked her hair. He had wondered what her shirt was made of.

Then darkness surrounded her thoughts and she fell into a deep depression while her history teacher's voice droned in the background and the seconds ticked off on the schoolhouse clock on the wall above his head. It didn't matter if Ryan noticed her or not. He shouldn't, really. And she shouldn't care. They had no future, not even as friends.

Chancellor, her history teacher, was saying something about a myth concerning living forever, about eternity. She came to suddenly, focusing on his words. They had been studying the myths of primitive South American and African tribes for the past week. She guessed his recital now had something to do with it.

Chancellor said, "The Namibian people tell their children about the hare and the moon to teach a lesson about the afterlife. The hare asked the moon if the moon would ever die. The moon said that he rose each night without fail and the hare could live forever, too, if only he believed. The hare said that he could not believe in the eternal, he had seen too many of his kind die, sometimes horrible deaths, and they did not rise again to live.

"The moon told the hare that even though his fellow hares did not appear to be alive, nevertheless, they lived; no one could see them, that was all. Like when the moon disappeared in the daylight—it had not gone forever, but only for a time. The hare said he could not believe in eternity and so he guessed he would really die, no matter what the moon said. The Namibian parents told their children this story and it was the reason why animals and men appeared to die now and not live again. But the moon was eternal, riding the sky forever, because he believed that he would. And despite the way it looked, men and animals also lived on, invisible, but eternal."

Chancellor ended the story and asked for a show of hands from any students who knew of other myths of eternal life held by primitive people.

Dell, touched by the story of the Namibians, lowered her head and thought it all out. The myth was right. That's what her teacher did not know. Not only was the moon eternal, but all that lived beneath it, even the hares. And some of the eternal life walked among the living as if alive, too, and no one was the wiser. She was now an eternal creature, but even if she'd remained human and died human, she would have only been invisible, and not gone forever.

When the bell rang, indicating the end of class, Dell gathered her books and headed for the door, the thoughts of the Namibian tale still puzzling her. She felt someone tap her on the shoulder in the hall and she turned.

"Hi," he said. "My name's Ryan. You're Della?"

"Just Dell," she said. "My mom named me after a singer she liked." A lump rose in her throat to prevent her from speaking anymore. She'd had a few

boyfriends, nothing serious, but she could not remember being this attracted or tongue-tied. *Ridiculous,* she told herself. *Stop being so damn ridiculous.*

Despite her own growing sense of foolishness, she
sent out an intense thought that she knew would be
embedded in his mind. *Dell's special. Dell's the one
for me.* She couldn't help herself. She found him so
attractive she felt she had to make sure he thought
of her in the same way.

She said, clearing her throat first, "You're from
North Dallas? How do you like it here?"

He fell into an easy walk at her side. "I like it just
fine," he said. "Particularly all the different kinds of
kids here. It's like being in another world." He gestured mildly toward some of the kids dressed in
black walking in front of them.

Dell glanced over at him to see if he was for real.
He liked the outcasts? He thought them cool? Kids
who were only making their lives harder and cutting
themselves off from whole groups of people?

"Really?" she said. Then she laughed, thinking
how odd *she* was. "Well, we have a lot of different
kinds of kids here, that's for sure."

"Does Mr. Chancellor always talk about rabbits
and the moon?"

"Oh, he goes off on these tangents now and again.
It's the only time I listen to him."

"I can see why." He grinned. "The rest of the time
he's pretty dull."

"You noticed, huh?" She smiled at him.

They parted ways when she turned into her next
classroom and his own class was in another wing of
the school. "Nice to meet you, Dell," he said, as he
sprinted away in order to beat the bell.

She stood watching him go and thought to herself,
Yeah, nice to meet you, too. Now she knew for sure he
liked her. So what was she going to do about that,
beyond the thought she'd implanted? What could
she do?

She could hardly wait for her meeting with Mentor

after school. She was to go to his house every day
where he would train and guide her until she was
ready to go on her own. The first thing she would
ask was about a vampire's personal life. Her respon-
sibility to humans and her interaction with them. She
really needed guidance. She hoped there was no
strict rule against relationships with humans, especially since she would be walking and living among
them. She envisioned a dreary thousand-year life
without them.

* * *

The first thing that struck Dell on entering Mentor's house was how dark it was. He must have read
her mind for he said, "I can turn on the lights if
you'd like." He hit a switch that caused an overhead
light to come on, though she noticed it was a small,
sparkly chandelier holding three small bulbs. It gave
out a weak glow that hardly chased the dark away.
Shadows retreated, but not far, cringing in the corners of the room.

"No, the light doesn't bother me," he said as if
she'd asked him a question. He motioned for her to
sit on a sofa near the fireplace. "I've become accustomed to the dark. The sunlight won't bother you for
long either. You'll be able to dispose of those soon."

Dell removed her sunglasses, folding the stems
carefully and placing them in her lap. "I went back
to school today."

"How did it go?" He sounded cheerful as he settled into an opposite sofa, stuffing a pillow behind
his back.

"Okay, I guess. One of my best friends asked why
I was wearing the sunglasses, but no one else seemed
to care. Lots of kids wear them in school."

"Do they?"

"Yeah, sure. Kids into . . . well, alternative thinking, you might say. You know."

He smiled indulgently. "Well, contrary to common

belief, I don't really know everything, Dell. I haven't been inside a high school in quite a few years."

She shrugged. "Okay, well, there's some kids who are outside the mainstream. They keep to themselves, they wear different kinds of clothes to distinguish them from others. They wear heavy eye makeup and sunglasses all day. Some of them . . ." she paused, wondering how he would take this, ". . . some of them want to be vampires." She hurried on, seeing his eyebrows raise, "They're just all disillusioned, kind of like the hippies in the Sixties, I guess. The Establishment sucks, that sort of thing. The really sad ones cut themselves on their arms. I don't know if it's for the pain, like they like it . . ." She shrugged. ". . . and sometimes they let others drink their blood, but it looks pretty dangerous to me. Some of them get their teeth filed down. Stuff like that. I always wanted to take them aside and tell them they shouldn't want to act that way. They should love walking in the sunlight and take good care of their bodies. They shouldn't want to live forever on nothing but blood; it's not natural."

She didn't know she'd thought all these things until she just now confessed them to Mentor. It was as if he drew things out of her, her deepest and most private thoughts. It could be a trick, but she suspected it was not. She was simply comfortable with him and knew he had her best interests at heart. She guessed that this was how people felt when they went to shrinks and talked openly about their problems.

That he did not know about the pretend-vampires at her school did not surprise her. Though they had been in the news now and then, most people just tried to pretend they didn't exist. She'd heard about a case where a "vampire" boy in the Northeast lost touch with reality and murdered his parents while they slept. He had self-inflicted cuts all over his arms, and he said vampirism gave him "freedom." She didn't think Mentor paid really close attention to what was going on in society, especially among the youth.

Mentor shifted uneasily on the sofa, stuffing the pillow at his back again. He said, "I didn't know some of your contemporaries were heading in that direction. Like you, I think that's a dangerous road to take. I suppose, because of the way the vampire is romanticized in American entertainment, it would be only natural for the disenchanted to rush toward the unknown, to seek it out, and to make it their own. The young have a way of finding something they think is new to believe in."

"What was that noise?" Dell asked abruptly, sitting forward on the sofa. It was from down below, in his basement, a terrible moaning. All her nerve ends began to tingle, and it was as if her brain came alert, red lights blinking in all corners of her mind as it checked for danger.

"Would you like to see for yourself?" He rose and took her hand. He led her to the kitchen and the basement door.

"No one I know in Texas has a basement," she said, fascinated.

"This was constructed especially for me. I felt it would come in handy. In rainy seasons it weeps a little, but otherwise it seems to do well."

She followed him down the narrow stairs into the soft gloom. There was a small lamp on an old wooden table along the wall facing the stairs, but it illuminated little. The place was damp and cool and smelled like wet metal. She sensed a being in the basement and knew he was their kind, but she was curious as to what he was doing in Mentor's basement and wondered at the despairing moan she'd heard.

Mentor stepped aside at the bottom of the stairs and put his arm around her shoulder. She looked over at the pitiful creature chained to the concrete wall. He lifted his head and opened his eyes. "Do you have to chain her, too?" he asked.

"No, she just wanted to know what the noise was about. How are you today, Dolan?"

"I'm almost ready to go home."

"I'm happy to hear that."

Inquisitive, Dell turned her head toward Mentor, wondering what this was all about.

Reading her mind, Mentor said, "Dolan here almost did away with himself and the whole house of Cravens where he was living. I have talked him out of those desperate actions. Haven't I, Dolan?"

"Yes, Master."

Dell laughed, hearing the sarcastic mockery in the other man's voice. He was mimicking Dr. Frankenstein's toady. "So you've changed your mind because you're chained here?"

He gave her a silent stare before responding. "Mentor's given me some time to think it over."

"This is sort of a 'safe' place," Mentor explained. "If Dolan wished, he could free himself from the chains, and he could get out of this basement, too. By not exerting his will and by staying quietly alone to contemplate the sin he had wished to commit, he has come to a new understanding."

"Don't let him fool you," Dolan said. "It would take *tremendous* willpower to free myself, and he knows I'm too weak to do it. But he's still right. I have allowed the imprisonment, and I work out my problems in solitude."

Upstairs again, the basement door bolted, they took their seats across from one another on the twin sofas.

"What did his moaning mean?" she asked.

"It probably escaped him when he realized there were two of us free here, upstairs."

"I felt sorry for him."

Mentor nodded knowingly. His eyes reflected his own pity. "Killing is only allowed to the Predators, because it's in their nature and can't be gotten out of them. But a Craven who decides to kill himself and others who have not asked him to do so, is an aberration. He needed help, that's all. But now let's talk abut you."

Dell looked away. So many questions were on her mind. Which one should she ask first? "Will I ever feel natural again?"

"You will. Yes, you will. It takes time."

"I met a boy today . . ."

"Human?"

"Yes. I think he may be interested in me. I was interested first, before . . . before this happened." She meant her death in the natural world. She waved her arm around herself as if she were an organic model that had been hand built. "What I want to know is . . ."

She didn't finish her sentence and was quiet for so long that he prompted her. "Yes?"

"Well, what I want to know is can I have a boyfriend? I know it sounds stupid to you. Juvenile." She looked down, embarrassed. "But I'm seventeen, Mentor. I haven't changed so much that I don't care about . . . people."

"Can you have a human boyfriend, you mean?"

She glanced away again, knowing the answer was going to be negative and wishing she'd never asked it. She said in a soft voice, "Can I ever have someone to love?"

Mentor scooted forward on the sofa and rested his hands between his knees. In his old body with his Albert Einstein gray, unruly hair, he was hardly intimidating, but she drew herself to attention under his heavy stare.

"No one can stop you from getting involved with humans," he said. At her look of surprise, he continued, "Naturals live side by side with them. It happens often that the close proximity creates a bond. You must know what the drawbacks are?"

"I know some of them," she said. She thought about it a moment and realized the greatest drawback. "Humans die."

He sat back. "Just so. Humans die. If we really

want to, we can give our diseased cells to one of them, changing him into one of us, but that's so rarely done that it's almost nonexistent. Giving someone this kind of life is too monumental a decision to make without any concern or thought. You understand that, don't you? We don't really have the right to grant eternal life. When we do it, we also grant eternal agony."

Yes, she understood. Look at what she was going through and how many years she would continue to go through it. She nodded her head in agreement. It was an immoral act to make the disease spread to the uninfected that way. If they all were to do it, the entire world's population one day would be only vampire, and then they would all truly die.

"So," Mentor said, "no one can stop you from being involved with your young man. But you must think where it will lead. Or not lead. He is not like you. If you've any heart, you won't wish to make him like you. As he ages, you won't—not on the surface. When you must migrate to a new body, the way we all have to when the old ones wear out, will he love that body, too? When he reaches the end of his days, will you be able to stand by him and watch him leave you alone again and lonely?"

She shook her head and felt the tears well in her eyes. Mentor knew she had already thought of her future. He knew she was not simply asking about having a high school sweetheart, but a partner, a mate. Maybe not Ryan, but someone.

When she wiped the tears away, she was disgusted to see her own blood smeared on her knuckles. Mentor leaned forward and handed her a handkerchief. She wiped her hands in a frenzy and tried not to cry.

"This is a cruel life, then," she said in a broken voice. "I knew that, but I . . . didn't really understand it."

She heard the vampire in the basement moaning, and she drew in her shoulders.

"We are as chained as he is," she said, wiping at

her cheeks and eyes with the handkerchief, frantically cleaning away the blood.

Mentor's voice was soft as he said, "That is why
I'm here, Dell. To help you find a way to move
through the days while dragging all the chains behind you."

She had her eyes shut, the handkerchief over them
and she thought, *I don't know if you can do that, Mentor. I don't know how any of us stand it.*

10

Dr. Alan Star had finished reading the marked volumes, magazines, and photocopied articles Charles Upton had given him to study. He sat in his apartment, the papers scattered all around him, his feet propped on the coffee table. He ate from a can of pork and beans with a spoon.

He knew it was an odd habit he'd gotten into, but sometimes he couldn't face the idea of walking into the kitchen to cook a meal for one. On those days he simply chose a can from the cabinet, whether it was a can of corn, beans, hominy, tuna—whatever—and sat in the living room eating from the can with a spoon. It filled his belly, dispelled the hunger until he could go out to buy a meal. Why dirty a dish?

As he spooned the beans into his mouth, he thought over some of the stories he'd been reading. Only to a dying man would the tales seem to have some semblance of reality. Okay, there was a case or two where graves of the dead were dug up and the corpse was missing. And there were eyewitness accounts testifying to seeing those who had died walking through a town. But the stories did not take place in modern society, in today's world. They happened in Yugoslavia or Cuba or Haiti, where the people were already steeped in superstition. Didn't Upton notice that?

Also, there was some research into the Haiti zombielike incidents, where the dead seemed to return, that showed witch doctors used a potion that included poison from the blow fish. Given in correct dosage it could make a man appear dead. Within twenty-four hours the witch doctor dug up the grave of the victim, revived him, and used him for a slave.

None of these later theories explaining how a dead man might walk again were found in Upton's papers.

So what was Alan going to say to Upton, that was the question? Could he really live with himself if he took the money and spent his days hunting down a . . . vampire?

He grimaced, feeling the slimy chunk of fat in his mouth that was invariably found in cans of pork and beans. He spit it back into the can and set it on the coffee table. Andy Warhol had become famous painting cans of Campbell Soup. It was no mystery to Alan that the cans were not of pork and beans. Jesus, next time he'd lay off the beans and choose good old whole golden corn kernels. Corn never had mysterious meat in it.

He stared at the books and papers at his feet. He sighed and began to gather them and put them back into the bag. He had an appointment with Upton at three o'clock. He'd have to make a decision by then. He would have to wrestle with his conscience and decide which choice did the least harm. He wished now he'd never been on the staff tending Charles Upton and that he was not one of the leading experts in Upton's disease.

Alan rose, took the can and spoon to the kitchen and set it alongside a row of empty cans on the counter. His mouth twisted in distaste. He had to stop eating like this. If anyone saw the mess he'd made, they wouldn't believe it.

He turned away and strode to the bathroom, where he turned on the shower. He had two hours to bathe, dress, and make his way to Upton Towers. He had two hours to determine just how far he would go to build his research center.

As he stripped, he knew already what he had to do. Being honest with himself, he admitted he had known all along, even before reading Upton's research.

He would let the man hire him to track down vampires. He would make a true and thorough search. He would not stint on that search, nor would he let his own prejudices and disbelief deter him. He would bring to the hunt all of his critical faculties and lessons learned.

If Upton wanted a vampire hunter, then he had just hired one.

Stepping into the shower, Alan smiled. The thing was, he could never tell anyone about this. Never. Oh, God, not a word. It was a secret worse than his eating habits.

* * *

Charles Upton could see through Dr. Star's guise. Just like Upton's partner, David, the man did not believe.

Upton dismissed the thought. It didn't matter what Star believed. What mattered was that Upton had convinced him to search for a living vampire, even if it took him to Europe, even if it took him the rest of Upton's life. Which would not be so long, Upton thought ruefully, so it wasn't that great a sacrifice. *I'm a real bastard*, he thought. *I take advantage of people who want my money. Of course, hasn't that been the way throughout all my life?*

"I'll make sure the hospital won't give you any trouble about time off," Upton said.

"I appreciate that, Mr. Upton."

"I know how you care about your patients. If any of them really need you, you have my permission to halt the search in order to see about them."

"Thank you, sir."

"Can't you call me Charles?" Upton tried to smile,

but his paralyzed lips would not move for him. He hoped the smile reached his eyes instead.

"Okay, I'll try, Charles."

"There, that wasn't so bad, was it? Well then, our business is concluded. I'll have my will updated and a copy sent to you immediately. I'll also send a contract that states our arrangement, and will deposit ten million dollars in a special operating account. I'll have my partner begin negotiations for land in the downtown area and soon we'll have a construction crew on the site. He's used to me giving millions to charity. I have to, for tax purposes, and if nothing else, David understands taxes. Do you have a name for your new facility?"

"Not yet, sir. Uh . . . Charles."

"All in good time, I'm sure. Meanwhile I'll let you get started on your work. If you need to hire anyone, just give me a call, and I'll handle it for you. If you need transportation anywhere, I'll have a flight booked. Any expenses you incur on my behalf will be completely covered."

When Alan did not respond, Upton eyed him carefully. "Look, I know what you must think. I know this is going to be hard for you. I know I must look like a man who has gone insane. But ask yourself this. What harm will it do? If your search turns up nothing, then that's it, isn't it? You still get your center. I'm the only one who can lose. I take all the risk."

"I know," Alan said.

"All right, then, let's shake on it. Let it begin. If there is such a thing as immortality, let's find it." He held out his old gnarled hand where new sores had erupted. The doctor took it unflinchingly, and shook with him.

Upton watched him leave the bedroom before he drew the bag of books and papers close to him. He unzipped the bag and drew out one of the books, turning to the page with the folded corner.

It gave him hope to read about the possibility of life after death, no matter how farfetched, no matter how superstitious and crazy and unsubstantiated. He thought the possibility of real vampires walking the Earth no more a fantasy than the one held by millions of a God in heaven and a final reckoning of the soul.

* * *

Alan rode down in the Towers' private penthouse elevator with his hands locked together behind his back. He'd done it. He'd taken the step that men of science would have scoffed at. He was Upton's vampire detective. If he tried to sell this to Hollywood, they'd lap it up, but if it ever got out to his colleagues, he'd be laughed out of the Houston medical community. His reputation and his practice would die on the vine.

He shook his head as the doors of the elevator opened and he stepped into the shiny, black marble lobby of his benefactor's building. He hardly knew where to start. He had to find out who was going to cover his patients, and come up with a story that they would believe. Even with Upton intervening for him, there would be questions. Then he would consult the notes he'd taken on the articles he'd read. Where would he have to go? Who would he have to see in order to convince the old man there was no such thing as vampires? Would he ever convince him?

Probably not. Probably whatever he came across would be dismissed out of hand. This was the wildest goose chase any sane doctor had ever undertaken, and he would have to carry around the guilt of his greed and weakness for a very long time.

As he made his way into the underground garage and over to his car, he felt a knot tightening in his stomach. It was the beans he'd eaten, he guessed.

Or it could be the decision he'd made.

* * *

When Alan got back to his office, he found a message from Bette Kinyo on the answering machine. It was not unusual for Bette Kinyo to give him a friendly call just to say hello. Alan Star thought the call that afternoon was just such a greeting.

"Bette! How the hell are you? Been to any good medical conventions lately?" He and Bette had gone to medical school together and dated a few times before drifting apart. Neither of them was ready to get into a serious relationship, mainly because both were headed in different directions in their careers. Bette did not want to practice medicine so much as she wanted to stick with her microscopes in a laboratory. Now she headed up a Dallas lab where they did HIV testing on blood supplies for the city. Alan, on the other hand, wanted nothing more than to practice and save lives in that close, hands-on environment occurring between a patient and doctor.

"Hello, Alan. You know the last convention I attended was with you in Austin. Listen, I called to check out something." She sounded pensive.

"Okay, shoot. I'm hurt you're not calling to ask me out, but shoot anyway." He smiled into the phone. Why had he let this woman get away from him? She was smart, hell, brilliant in her field. And he loved her small face with the dark Oriental sparkling eyes. At every convention they attended, usually at least twice a year, they took a room together in the hotel and renewed their affair. When the convention ended, they went their separate ways, back to Dallas and to Houston, with phone calls their only contact. It was a strange system for sometime lovers, though he had to admit she brightened his life considerably when he was around her periodically.

"Alan, you know I have a record of all the blood supplies in the city, right?"

"Sure." What could this be about, he wondered?

"Well, for some months I've been concerned. One of the banks, the Strand-Catel, has been low on blood about once a month for as far back as I've been testing. I just never noticed it before."

"Low?" His brow furrowed.

"Not dangerously low, I mean they can supply the hospitals if they have to, but I began to notice huge shipments from Strand-Catel going out of the city. They're shipped to Houston, El Paso, San Antonio, even down to Del Rio."

"So maybe they supply other places, not just Dallas, what's wrong with that?"

"Well, that's it. I looked into it and those cities have plenty of banks, enough to cover their own needs unless . . ."

"What?"

"Well, unless those cities have emergencies. You know, hurricanes, a deadly virus outbreak like *e Coli*, or major highway accidents."

"Well, I haven't noticed Houston needing any extra blood."

"That's just it, Alan. There haven't *been* any emergencies needing supplies for the people who live there. I just don't get it."

It was then that the light bulb went off in Alan's head. He shook himself mentally, trying to rid his mind of the nonsense. Blood. Vampires. Missing blood, blood shipped out of a central location to cities that were not in need. Unless . . . But that was fantasy.

"Alan?"

"I'm sorry, yeah, go ahead."

"So that's why I'm calling. Your hospital hasn't sent a request for blood supplies from this Dallas outfit?"

"I don't know, but I can find out."

"Would you do that for me? I just can't figure out what's going on. These shipments go out untested, and that's totally against regulations. I'm hoping the labs in those cities are doing their jobs. It worries me, that's all. I looked up the records after I noticed the pattern and this has been going on for a long time, Alan. A very long time. Years, in fact."

"Any other blood bank doing the same thing?"

"No, just Strand-Catel. That's why I didn't catch on for so long."

"Okay, sure, I'll find out something for you, Bette. I'll do some sleuthing." He knew she could hear the humor in his voice because she laughed. She didn't know he wasn't kidding. His real job now was looking into things that had to do with the use and care of blood.

* * *

In a supply room next to the doctor's lounge where Alan Star was taking his call from Bette, a Natural by the name of Hank sat listening to the conversation. He could hear both parties easily through walls and phone wires. He had accidentally picked up the thought "vampire" from Dr. Star when walking down the hall earlier and had followed him. Doctors did not generally go around thinking about vampires. It intrigued Hank enough that he stuck near Star most of the day. Every now and then he tried to carefully tiptoe into the doctor's thoughts, hoping to find out more details.

Now he heard the woman share her suspicions about Strand-Catel. Hank would have to alert Ross, the Dallas Predator who owned that particular blood bank.

Leigh, a female lab research assistant and also a Natural, spoke aloud. "This could interfere with our research."

Hank knew that. It was an ominous turn of events, certainly. "Nothing's going to stop us," he said, trying to sound confident. Early on, Ross, the Predator with the most power in the Southwest, had tried to stop them from getting into research. If there was a cure found, he'd be out of business. He didn't like any one of the Naturals thinking they might one day do something about the disease. If the Naturals stopped needing blood to survive, there went Ross' control right out the front door.

Hank didn't like Ross worth a damn. He might have gone to war with him had it not been for Mentor's plea for peace among the clans. If truth were told, Hank relished the thought he was going to be the one to tell Ross of the Dallas investigation by Kinyo. He'd love to hear him roar, that's what he'd really love.

Hank, Leigh, and another Natural, Dr. Shamoi, a molecular scientist and world-famous hematologist, had been medical researchers for many years, looking for a cure for the disease that turned them into vampires. They'd gone along quite well in the hospital system that employed Dr. Star. Often left to their own devices, they spent every spare moment delving into the molecular level of blood, trying to discover just what it was that changed porphyria from a human killer into a mutated disease that had afflicted their clans ever since 2000 B.C. If they could find the trigger mechanism, perhaps they could cure themselves—or at least offer the cure to those who wanted it. Some of them, Hank reflected, would never want to give up the supernatural life. More power to them, that was his position. But for the rest of them, like himself, who longed for a normal life again, a cure would be a glorious discovery.

Leigh said, "What are we going to do, Hank?"

"I'll talk with Ross. Go back to the lab and don't worry about Dr. Star. He's a nonbeliever. He won't get anywhere."

"And the woman in Dallas?"

Hank hesitated. He didn't have enough information to say anything about the woman. "Maybe Mentor can see about her."

Leigh, looking relieved, left the stuffy supply room for the lab. Hank leaned against the shelves and closed his eyes. Tonight after his shift he'd call Ross, and Mentor, too. No point in sending out a telepathic alarm at this point. He'd only get everyone riled up and have them descending on his hospital, further delaying important work.

And *who*, he wondered, was Upton? He had no first name, no other clue to the fellow's existence. All he knew from the tidbits he'd gleaned from Star's brain was that Upton had employed him. *Christ*, he thought, *if it isn't one thing, it's ten dozen more.*

11

Once Mentor let Dolan go, the house settled into a slow, numbing buzz of lethargy. There were always the unseen life-forms in a house. Cockroaches, spiders, silverfish, scorpions, flies, beetles, termites, mosquitoes. All of them flying just at the edge of the house seeking entry or crawling around inside or beneath it. Mentor counted these unseen creatures as his friends. They shut out the larger noises that filtered in through the walls from outside. If he let them, the sounds—of their little tapping feet, their wriggling antennae, the crackling of the beetles' hard shells—focused him in a way silence could never do.

Dolan had been contrite. "I won't do it again," he said.

"If you have to do it, do it only to yourself," Mentor advised.

Dolan gave him a puzzled look. "You're saying you won't try to stop me if I just want to destroy myself."

"Not after this, Dolan, no. If after these days on your own in my basement, where you were alone with your own conscience, you decide you can't go on, well . . . I won't interfere a second time."

"I heard that about you."

Mentor unlocked the front door before turning back. "What did you hear?"

"That there're no second chances."

Mentor shrugged. "I plead guilty."

"But it hurts you, doesn't it? I mean if I fall down. If I kill myself. You'll blame yourself."

"I don't think I want to answer that question." Mentor spoke gruffly, hoping to spirit the old vampire out of his house and be done with him. He would not speak of whatever guilt he took upon himself. Not with Dolan. Not with anyone.

"All right," Dolan said, moving swiftly past Mentor and out onto the walkway. High above, the moon shone clearly, and there was not a cloud in the night sky. "I'm going back to my other prison now."

"God speed," Mentor said, waving a little and beginning to shut the door. He already had turned his attention to the small life evident in the wall just behind him where he heard the scurrying of the tiniest feet. He must concentrate on the sounds so that they would blot out the world. He did not want to think about losing Dolan to despair, did not wish to remember the Craven house he'd taken him from where creatures almost too weak to maintain life lay about like sick dogs. There was only so much Mentor thought he could take, and when he reached that limit, he turned inward to survive another night, another day.

An impediment caused the closing door to jam so that Mentor had to shift his attention to it again. Dolan stood there, his hand holding the door. He looked into Mentor's tired eyes.

"I wouldn't have your job for the world. I would rather be a Craven hoping to die than to be you."

And then he was gone, disappearing on the night wind, a transparent shadow rippling past the leafy limbs of a tall mulberry tree planted close to Mentor's house.

Mentor closed the door with a sigh and walked slowly down the hall, an old man returning to his solitude. He felt no physical fatigue, no pain or ache, and was often completely out of touch with the process that ran the old shell that he inhabited. He was simply tired from living the life Dolan correctly recognized as a royal and total pain. How many times had he embraced a despair deeper than any Dolan had ever experienced and yet gone on? Sometimes he wanted to say to those like Dolan who would take matters into their own hands, "You spineless coward." He wanted to say, "You thought being a vampire would release you from all earthly care. You believed eternal life would be like a picnic, a holiday spree. Who gave you the idea that life, *in any form,* human or vampire, would be without pain and strange, unimaginable horror?"

Oh, he could not teach them anything. He thought about the uselessness of his mission some nights when he was alone, barring the transmission of the calls for help that came through the air like demented radio signals. He could not really teach them how to live. He provided stopgaps in their plans. He talked them out of mistakes. He took young ones, like Dell, and he hoped to see her prosper in her new incarnation, at least for a few years. Eventually, all of them knew despair like an old friend draped over their shoulders, a shroud to warm them. Eventually, they realized their lives were but magnified human lifetimes, lived over and over and over again, with so little changing along the way.

It was less a humanitarian urge than it was for his own sake that Mentor did what he could to guide and to save his kind from total destruction. Once they had lived as long as he, if they ever did, then they would know the ultimate truth. Hope was something you manufactured out of thin air. Not just when you were down and out, when you were depressed and hopeless, but every day, every single minute of every spin of the Earth around the sun.

Dolan was right to realize he was better off as he was than to have to walk down Mentor's path. Dolan was one of the intuitive ones. Dolan was no fool.

And that lifted Mentor's mood the smallest fraction. He had at least not wasted his time with the other vampire. He had been dealing with someone more enlightened than he'd imagined.

Mentor left the lights off and sat on the sofa next to the darkened fireplace. He would shut out the calls for help for just a little while. Ross, the leader of the Predators was coming to him tonight. It would be late, after midnight, when the city slumbered.

Mentor needed his strength for the meeting. He never dealt with a Predator without being at the top of his mark. After all, he had been one. He knew the latent danger inherent in the species. He must reach down and bring up his own power. Any weakness he might show could spell disaster. A Predator would prey, even on his own kind, if he sensed weakness.

He closed his eyes, laid back his head, and listened to the tiny creatures rustling all through, beneath, and just outside of his house. How he loved them.

* * *

Ross, he called himself, having taken a new name for each new body he migrated into. He was the leader of a Predator band that owned and ran the Strand-Catel Blood Bank in downtown Dallas. Because he and his kind did not, for the most part, care to walk free in the sunlight, they had hired enough underlings to keep the bank open and going in the day, while at night the real work was done by Ross' sect.

Strand-Catel supplied blood to Naturals and Cravens throughout the state of Texas and into New Mexico. They had done so for almost a century, calling their operation by different names over the years. It was made clear early in the eighteenth century, when the Americas were being settled, that their kind could not wantonly murder and prey on humans. Some of them still did, many of them, in fact, though they belonged to other Predator sects. But the majority of the vampire population knew that secrecy was paramount for their survival, and taking too many lives left a trail that would one day lead straight back to them.

Ross had run the blood bank for decades without too many hitches. The bank was his baby, his idea, and was granted autonomous operation from the many sects that occupied the Southwest. Everyone knew Ross. Everyone admired his business sense and how he kept up with the country as it moved and changed.

Ross was also feared. Mentor alone could not control the many thousands of vampires in the entire Southwest section of the country. Although the mutated porphyria cells that created them was a rare disease, it seemed to spawn more and more down through the generations, until their kind had gained in numbers. No one vampire could control them all, no matter how powerful. Ross not only watched over the bank's operation, the shipments that went out to the Naturals and Cravens who paid for the blood, and to Predators who needed the extra supplies to help control their hunger, Ross also acted as the chief enforcer over renegades. He was, in essence, Mentor's right-hand man, though neither of them spoke about the arrangement or admitted to it.

Of the two kinds of vampires below Ross, he despised the Cravens most. They lived on welfare, handouts, and begging. In order to pay for their blood, the strongest ones sometimes resorted to petty theft and drug trafficking. They lurked in dark alleyways with little bags of poison to sell, too weak to kill for their living, but not too weak to prey in another way on society.

Ross disliked the Cravens for their poverty and had been determined to make himself wealthy. Though wealth mattered little to most Predators, who were driven by their hunger to the point where ambition died away, Ross saw wealth as a tool that could protect him if things ever got out of hand. Wealth gave him choices, had bought him safe places in the world where he might hide, and it would insure his safety if his operation was ever found out.

It was common knowledge that Ross hated the Cravens. In the early 1900s he'd tried to eradicate the Cravens from the region. It was a famous bloodbath in vampire history. He had been stopped from completing his vendetta by Mentor and a few other ancient Predators who tracked Ross down and demanded he desist. Didn't he know that if they made the choice in death to be a Craven, it had something to do with the soul? If the choice was theirs to make, didn't he know he had no right to take that choice away?

Mentor knew he and Ross suffered an uneasy alliance. Ross thought him soft, a philosophical creature wasting his time with newly made vampires and old, helpless vampires and suicidal vampires. These were creatures Ross would have dispatched without a thought. *Get them out of the way*, would have been his wish. *If they can't make it on their own, we take risks keeping them alive. What do you do when you see a slug on the pavement? You step on it*, he was often quoted as saying. *You step on it and walk away*. That was his philosophy.

"You think because some of us choose to be weak and sick and pitiful that it's ordained?" Ross had asked, furious that he was being held back from the slaughter of the Cravens by Mentor.

"What else could it mean?" Mentor had responded.

"This means all of you believe there is some higher power instructing our existence. Well, you're wrong! We're alone! There is no God, don't you know that?"

It finally came down to a decree. Ross, called Brenton at that time, would leave the Cravens alone or they would all take measures against him. He could not hope to defeat so many as powerful as he. He relented, grumbling and cursing, but never forgave Mentor for his part. "I could have rid the world of them," he'd said. And Mentor had replied, "Never.

There will always be those who choose the Craven way. That is just the way it is, and it's not up to you to change it."

Now he stood in Mentor's living room, towering above him, his body youthful, strong, and beautiful.

Mentor noted how Ross always chose the most beautiful male body he could find. He was as conceited as he was arrogant and dangerous. He was, it occurred to Mentor, the very embodiment of the modern day fictional vampire, with his rarified ways, haughty manners, and impeccable dress. Mentor thought he might have adopted the fiction, seeing himself as romantic, erotic, and dreaded. A ruse, Mentor decided. Or an illusion he favored, but that was all. He was simply a wicked, greedy, ambitious fool who happened to be a vampire leader because he was the smartest, the most ruthless.

Mentor, rested now and ready for him, rose from the sofa, and stood face-to-face with the other Predator. "You called for this meeting. Let's get on with it."

"I don't give a damn about you either," Ross said, twisting his beautiful mouth to show his fangs.

Mentor blinked, catching his own reflection in the wet white glisten of the other vampire's teeth. He knew this was one of Ross' newest tricks to entrance a prey. That he thought it would work on someone twice his age just went to show how pride could go before a fall. If he wanted, Mentor could have wrung forth from his being a fury that would have blasted Ross clear across the room and left him defenseless.

Instead of rising to the bait, Mentor walked to the dead fireplace and placed his hand on the mantel. He loved to show this Predator how unafraid he was of him. "Now that we have the polite greetings out of the way, what do you want?"

Ross turned his back for Mentor to contemplate as he spoke. "There have been quiet inquiries about the bank. Hank called me from Houston. Didn't he call you? He said he was going to."

"Not yet. What did he say the inquiries concerning your bank were about?"

Ross picked up a book from the table near the sofa. He dusted it off, though it was not dusty, read the title, and dropped it. "Our shipments."

"So?" Mentor was losing patience. Didn't the Predator know he was wasting valuable time? There was a new vampire being born right this minute without Mentor there to guide him through death. Mentor resented Ross' appearance and the talk about the blood bank. It was *his* problem. What possible motive did he have for coming to Mentor?

Ross turned so fast that a mortal would not have seen it happen, though Mentor did. "You accuse me of pride, but it's you who think yourself indispensable! I come here to ask for a minute, and you whine in your head about waste. I should rip you apart for that."

"If you think that you can, jump, Froggy."

Ross glared at him before he saw Mentor's small smile, and then he began to laugh. "Froggy!" He laughed some more, his anger all but gone.

"All right, it was rude of me to get impatient," Mentor said. "It must be serious if you've come to tell me personally. Now, what does it mean? I really do have to leave soon."

"It's a woman who runs an HIV testing lab. She has access to all the records of all the blood banks. Federal law requires the blood be tested, I'm sure you know that. She's discovered we ship out blood to other cities before it gets tested. She's called some of my people. She even knows it's been going on for years. She searched back records. She knows something isn't right."

Mentor realized this was indeed serious news. "Do you know if she's told anyone her suspicions?"

"We know she called a doctor in hematology at Hank's hospital. It's how he found out. I haven't sent anyone to investigate her yet. For all we know, she's already called in some federal agency or something. It could undermine our whole operation."

"Yes, it could." The thought of the loss of their blood bank threw Mentor into a sudden anxiety. Even he was nourished by the blood Ross supplied. The strongest-willed vampire, deprived of fresh blood, would turn on the closest victim to satiate his hunger. Naturals could only defeat their craving by having local supplies sold to them. If left to their own devices, many of them would be driven to hunt humans.

Ross was silent a moment. Then he said, "I wanted you to do it."

Taken aback, Mentor flinched inside. "You want me to investigate this woman?"

"Yes. I haven't really dealt with mortals in years except for servant types. I've lost the touch. While you . . ."

Mentor knew he had to do it. He was able to walk among mankind and pass easily as one of them. He made it his number one rule not to separate himself from the world, except for the youth, who changed their fads so often he could never keep up with them. Without staying close to adult society, he could never hope to gain the trust of their souls when the time came to choose the eternal path.

"All right, tell me what you know."

For the next few minutes Ross gave him details, addresses, and other data. Mentor knew what he had to do. He would approach the woman who was about to uncover their secret and he would mesmerize her into forgetting. That way she'd come to no harm. If he failed, Ross would simply kill her and cover up any trail she'd uncovered.

Mesmerizing was an ancient gift that was as real as a cloud, a leaf, or a stream. Magicians, bound by earthly magic, considered mesmerizing another word for hypnotism, but it was far beyond that. Other words for mesmerize were to spellbind, stupefy, and to find entry. To mesmerize people, Mentor had to enter their minds, meld with their souls, and change their memories as one would wipe a slate clean. It had to be done by a master, or it was considerably dangerous. In the beginning when he was first learning how, Mentor had accidentally wiped a few minds that were never the same again.

More guilt. And guilt he had no choice but to live with.

When Ross had gone, Mentor left his home and stood outside, feeling the early morning wind on his face. Earlier, when Dolan had left, the sky had been clearing, but now a few white clouds with dark underbellies coasted near the moon. In another city they might portend rain, but in Dallas they would no doubt scatter and disappear before even a drop of moisture could condense.

He would see the woman, Bette Kinyo, on the morrow. Tonight he had urgent business. It was not in the city, but out in the South Texas countryside near the border with Mexico. A family of Naturals lived there, and tonight one of the women was undergoing the change. The disease had begun earlier in the day when they'd first called for Mentor's help. Now he must hurry, or his charge would be lost. She might become a Predator. That was the fear of her family.

She might anyway, despite his guidance, but at least he would have tried to dissuade her. There were too many of them already, especially along the border where he knew more murders were going unsolved than in all the rest of the state. The authorities thought it was the work of a serial killer who left his victims horribly mutilated, but Mentor and his kind knew what it really was. Too many Predators in the area and too few sources of blood.

What they did not need was one more running loose.

He must be on his way.

With a flick of his will and a mental explosion that changed the very atomic makeup of his being, Mentor dissipated into the Dallas night wind an insubstantial shadow among the clouds sailing south. Just before he'd left the earthly plain, he'd heard the telephone in his house ringing and knew it must be Hank.

He'd speak with him later. He had all the information he needed for the time being.

12

It was not Dell's birthday, that day was in June, after graduation, but it felt like it. On Saturday morning when she woke, Eddie stood at the end of her bed. She'd slept so deeply that she felt now as if she were coming up from a black well of unconsciousness where nothing had ever lived.

She'd heard someone call her name and opened her eyes. "What are you doing?" she asked, coming up onto her elbows. Eddie was bending over the foot of her bed and tugging at her covers.

"Mom and Dad have a surprise for you."

"What kind of surprise?" She threw back the covers and stood to stretch.

"It wouldn't be a surprise if I told you. They're waiting in the living room. C'mon."

Her parents were dressed, standing in the center of the room together, and in her father's hand dangled his car keys. "If you'll hurry and get your clothes on, we'll take you to see something special," he said.

"What?" she asked. "What's going on?"

"Tell her," her mother said to her father.

Her father shook his head, grinning slyly. "We wanted you to see for yourself. So hurry up, we're waiting. And no reading our minds, young lady."

She rushed back to her bedroom and stripped off her pajamas. She put on shorts and a sleeveless shirt.

She almost ran into Eddie when she hurried into the hall. She grabbed him by the back of his shirt. "Tell me what it is!"

"No way. Let's go, they're already in the car."

They drove from the neighborhood, through the suburbs of Dallas, and south, out of the city. When the terrain changed to wheat and cotton farms, Dell could not control her curiosity any longer. "Where are we going? Is it a long way?" She remembered being a little child again, asking her parents every few minutes how far it was to their destination. Vacations must have been tedious for her parents, she realized, having children whine at them for hours on end.

"It's not far now," her father said.

"You're gonna like it," Eddie said, punching her in the arm lightly.

It was a horse! She knew it was a horse. It had to be! She had begged for a horse since she was eight years old. They had never had a pet, not even a dog, and she'd yearned for an animal for years. Her parents told her that most pets sensed they were different and were never happy around them. They would cry and scratch at themselves, they would turn in circles going nuts, and once let outside, they would probably disappear.

Dell had seen it happen before her change when Eddie played over at a friend's house. If his friend had a pet, even if it was a hamster, the animal went bonkers trying to get away from Eddie and the scent the animal picked up that he was not quite human anymore. Eddie always made a joke out of it, saying animals just didn't like him and that was all right, because he didn't like them either.

Gosh, even Carolyn had a pet. It was a big, fat, fluffy cat she named VeryPretty. "That's a dumb name," Dell had said, rubbing the cat's fur and feeling it purr beneath her hands.

"VeryPretty doesn't think so," Carolyn said. "She likes it."

Now, when Dell went to visit her cousin, she knew VeryPretty would shy from her and hide beneath Carolyn's bed. It made her sad to think about it.

But she had not wanted a house pet like a cat or dog. She had always wanted her very own horse. It might be spooked by her, sensing she wasn't human, but she knew she could reach it with her mind, make it comfortable with her.

One of Cheyenne's cousins had kept a horse where she lived on a ranch outside of Dallas. Dell had been visiting the cousin with Cheyenne one day and fell instantly in love. The horse at first shied from her, but after snuffling through its massive nose and prancing away from her twice when she neared it, she spoke to it softly until it steadied. He finally let her rub his nose. She had asked to ride it and Cheyenne's cousin said sure, why not? She hadn't taken the horse faster than a trot, afraid she'd fall off, but once out of the range of her friends' hearing, she had whispered to the horse how majestic he was and how wonderful it was to ride him.

She had been ten years old. The horse was just an old gelding that kids had been riding for years. At home, she had pestered her parents about it. "Why can't I have one?" she'd asked. She'd been told how expensive it was to buy a horse, not to mention its upkeep. They would have to board it at a stable, pay for its food and vet bills, and at that time they simply could not afford it. Everything they could earn went toward living expenses and the cost of the blood the Predators sold.

Crushed, Dell had stopped begging. Her parents really did work very hard. But she'd never stopped hoping to one day own a horse of her own. Now they were driving out of the city and all around them were ranches and farms fenced off from the road with barbed wire and hollow steel rails.

"It's a horse!" she cried, unable to keep quiet. She just had to know. "You've bought me a horse, haven't you?"

Her mother turned from the front seat, smiling. "We thought it would be good for you."

"Oh, Mama, thank you, thank you! Thank you, Daddy!"

"Now don't get too excited," her father said. "It's not much of a horse. We knew it would cost a great deal to keep it boarded, so we had to buy an older one than we would have liked."

She didn't care. She didn't care if it was old as Methuselah, at least she could ride it. She could love it. She could have something of her own.

At the stables where her father turned in, Dell eyed all the horses wandering in the paddocks and standing by the stalls. When the car stopped, she was the first one out of the door. She hurried to a man leading a horse by a halter. "Is that my horse?" she asked, breathless.

"And who might you be?" the stable attendant asked in a friendly way.

"Dell! Della Cambian. You have my horse here?"

"Well, shoot, little girl, I think we just might have it back there in one of those stalls." The man grinned, and a gold crown shone from an upper incisor.

Dell turned to the stalls and saw several horses still closed in there. "Which one?"

Her father was at her side then and said, pointing. "That one."

It was at the far end in the last stall. He had his head hanging over the gate and Dell saw that he was a roan with a white spot right between the center of his eyes.

"Oh!" That's all she could say. To her it was the most beautiful animal in the world. Her father had said the horse was old, and that made him cheaper, but to her the horse was ageless and grand. She ran all the way to the stall, coming to an abrupt standstill just before the horse so as not to spook it.

"Hey," she called softly. "It's me, Dell. Want to go for a ride?" She telepathically talked to the horse in a soothing monotone that she knew he could hear inside his mind. She was so afraid he would fear her. If he feared her, she would never be able to keep him.

Good horse, nice horse, she thought. *I love you, do you know that? I do love you already.*

She felt ten years old again once the horse was saddled for her and she had climbed aboard. His name, the stable hand said, was Lightning. "Not like he's fast anymore," the man added. "He's a little long in the tooth for racing."

Dell waved to her beaming parents and to her brother, who looked like he would split open with joy. She turned the horse with the reins and locked her legs around him. He started walking slowly, and that was all right with her. She was communicating with him silently, knowing he could read her thoughts. *Good horse,* she thought again. *What a fine horse you are. We will be friends, we will be pals forever.*

He took her across a field and to a riding path. He didn't move fast, never went into a trot, but Dell felt she was kissing the wind on the back of a giant, valiant steed. She was free! They were one, she and the horse, moving under the dappled shade of the path, all alone.

She forgot that she was unnatural trying to live a natural life. She was not a vampire who depended on blood to live, but just a girl riding gently through a forest on the back of her very own horse, Lightning.

Time stopped and she had no idea how long she'd been riding when finally the horse, knowing where he was to go, returned to the stalls. Her parents sat at a concrete picnic table in the shade of the stalls, while her brother stood trying to pet a goat tied to a stake. The goat was bucking to free himself, whinnying at Eddies's strange scent.

Dell rode up, pulling at the reins and calling, "Whoa," to Lightning. She dismounted, her legs shaky, the reins in her hand. "This is the best surprise I've ever had," she said.

Her father came over and when Lightning shied

from him, jerking his head back, waited for the horse to calm down. "He's twenty years old," he said. "He was owned by a family whose children all rode him, but now they're all grown and didn't want him anymore. I thought since you always wanted a pet, he'd be just right for you."

Dell kissed her father's cheek. "I love him," she said. "He's wonderful."

"Well, you're going to have to come out here and take care of him. He needs grooming and needs riding to get his exercise."

"Don't worry! I'll come see him all the time. I can get a job this summer and help with the costs."

Her father waved that off. "It's not so expensive. I think I can afford it."

On the way home Dell couldn't stop chattering. She was going to braid his mane. She was going to brush him and get to know him and together they'd wander all over the riding paths at the stables. One day, she'd get her own place where she'd have a stable built, and put him where she could see him every day. How long did horses live anyway? Wouldn't Lightning live for a long time yet?

Despite hearing most horses didn't live as long as thirty years, she thought she'd never been so happy before. She knew her parents had done this to help her adjust into her new life. They knew she needed something of her own to love and cherish, something she could talk to that would never betray her secrets. They were the best parents in the world, she thought, the best there ever were.

That night in her bed she relived her joy in how the horse had been comfortable with her despite what she was. She remembered the excitement of riding Lightning and recalled how time had stopped, dropping her into a timeless world where there were no worries or problems. As the horse walked, she had grown accustomed to his pace and let her body go loose so that finally she hardly bounced in the saddle, but rode Lightning's back as if she were a part of him.

She thought she could probably sneak out of the house and go to Lightning without using a car at all. But she didn't know how to do that yet, how some of them could transform into something else that vanished and reappeared elsewhere. But when she did know how, when she did learn how to vanish and reach her horse without the benefit of human transportation, she could visit him at night when no one was around. She'd make him her best friend of all, her confidant, her closest ally in a world where she was an aberration, an abomination, a . . . dead girl.

He already knew in some way that she was not like others who rode him. Yet he'd accepted her strangeness once she'd spoken to him telepathically, and he had taken her willingly down the riding path just as if she were still human, still just a young woman out for a trail ride.

She fell into a deep sleep while happiness flooded her and burned away all her questions and fears. She would never forget this kindness of her parents and never take for granted whatever sacrifices they were making in order to give her what she'd always wanted.

She might be vampire, she might not be permitted to live as a mortal being, but as long as she had Lightning, she thought she could find a way to cope. Only once did the thought occur to her that because the horse was already twenty, he might live only another ten years or even less and then she would lose him. She banished the thought immediately, not wishing to let reality intrude on her bliss. Deep down, she knew there were going to be a great many losses over the years to come. Not just beloved horses, but friends and relatives who had never contracted the disease. One day she'd lose Aunt Celia. And Carolyn. Like all humankind, she would have to bear those losses and go on, somehow. That there would be more of them than any human ever faced wasn't something she could think about right now.

All that mattered was that she had been given a wonderful gift and Lightning was his name.

13

Bette Kinyo lived alone in a small house she'd purchased in an ethnically-mixed neighborhood. It
was inexpensive and at the time, ten years before,
she had not been making as much as she did these
days. Nevertheless, she hadn't moved, even though
she could have afforded a nicer place. She'd never
felt an urge to abandon either the neighborhood or
the home she'd made in the little house. In the pri-
vacy-fenced backyard, she had a Japanese garden
that had taken her two years to construct. It was
ringed with small conifers and miniature viburnums
and holly. In the center of the greenery was her mas-
terpiece, a raked bed of white pea gravel that she
tended once a week, changing the rake marks and
praying small prayers for a continued peaceful existence as she worked.

Inside the house she had stripped and refinished
the stair rails and spindles that led to a loft bedroom
she'd decorated in Victorian style with bouquets of
roses from her gardens and flowered chintz easy
chairs facing a slanted rooftop window overlooking
the Japanese garden. She took tea there in the late
evening just before sunset, after a spare dinner. In
her living room light glowed like gold, reflected from
Tiffany-style lamps, and bookcases overflowed with
well-worn volumes of history and poetry.

Her kitchen was left as she found it, not even a

dishwasher installed to modernize it. There were open cabinets displaying a collection of Japanese Nippon dishware and on the wall she'd hung hand-woven baskets she bought from local Mexican artisans.

She knew the house and every crevice and corner in it. It was her sanctuary and the most beloved possession she owned. So when the intruder appeared, she knew it even before he spoke.

She had her back to the room, her hands deep in sudsy water washing the dinner dishes. She stiffened and turned her head to look behind her. "Who are you?" she asked in a strong voice. She did not ask how he had got into her home through the locked doors. She knew immediately that he was not human and was in fact something obscene and unnatural. She had felt it the moment she knew he was there, standing behind her on the oval hooked rug in the center of her kitchen.

Unlike Westerners, she had no prejudice against the idea of the supernatural. Though she had attended American universities and was a scientist, she saw no reason to discard the centuries of wisdom that had come down through her family from their ancestors in Japan. The man who had appeared out of thin air in her kitchen might be a spirit of the house only now making itself known to her. Her little home had been built in the late 1800s, and she had wondered if any of the people who had lived in it before would want to communicate with her. But for ten years they had remained silent. Until now.

She was not afraid. She wiped her hands dry on a dish towel, planted her feet apart, and faced the being.

He had not yet spoken. Again she asked, "Who are you? What do you want?"

"You're not afraid," he stated, a little surprised.

"Why should I be? Or . . . should I be?"

"You know I'm not someone from the neighborhood who has broken into your house?"

She nodded. "Yes, of course I know." She gave him a scornful look as she put the dish towel aside on the counter. She took two steps closer to him, wondering about him. "You're not quite real," she said. "I know that much."

He smiled, and she stiffened again, but this time with mounting fear. There was something wrong with the smile, something wrong with the shape of his teeth . . . his eyeteeth. She sucked in air slowly and now she knew a greater fear that crept up her spine and insinuated itself into the lizard part of her brain.

"But you don't know who or what I really am, do you, Bette?"

She sagged a little and reached for the counter to steady herself. "I thought you might be . . ."

"A ghost. Someone from the past who occupied this old house before you."

"Yes," she whispered.

"I'm sorry to disappoint you. I am not a ghost. I am as solid as you. As real as you. Would you like to touch me and see for yourself?"

She shook her head quickly. She waited for him to go on. What could this thing want with her? If it had not come from the many memories imprinted on the floors and walls and ceilings of her house, then where had it originated?

It was after sunset, and the bright overhead light in her kitchen made him appear to be as solid as any man, just as he'd claimed. If it had not been for the glimpse of his teeth when he'd smiled at her, she knew she would not feel this uncommon fear rising as a tide inside her mind. She fought back the edge of panic and glanced about for something she might use against him to protect herself. The small iron skillet on the stove burner? The heavy glass teapot on the counter? She doubted she would ever get the drawer open so she could reach for a sharp knife.

"There's no point in doing any of that," he said, as if reading her mind.

She snapped her gaze back to him. "What are you and why do you want to talk to me?"

"We must have a meeting of minds," he said, coming closer to her. "A *mingling* of minds, Bette."

She stepped back until the base of her spine hit the sink's edge. She brought up both her hands as if to ward him off. He was old, probably eighty or more, but she knew his age was deceptive. She could feel his power as if it were an electrical current springing out and touching her like a force field. It was causing small electrical shocks all along her arms and chest and face. If anyone else would have touched her at that moment, she thought he would have been electrocuted.

"Don't," she pleaded, tearing her gaze from his depthless eyes and staring at the floor. "Please, don't."

"I have no choice, Bette. You'll be in great danger if I don't do this."

What he said made no sense to her and yet in some way her intuition knew what he was about to do was irrevocable. He was primed to do something horrible, she knew that, but did not know exactly what. It wasn't a physical threat; she did not fear for her flesh or her life. He thought whatever he was going to do would keep her from further danger. But what he meant to do to her was far worse; something he was about to unleash would invade and change her. She would fight with every ounce of her energy and strength against it.

"You can't," she whispered in terror, cringing away from him so that she was leaning backward over the sink, gripping the edges with her hands until her knuckles turned white. She turned her head as far away from him as possible.

She had been born with some psychic skills she had never questioned because they were always there, always present. She could sometimes divine the future. She often had dreams about colleagues and friends and the dreams would come true later.

She could sense life beneath the surface of the world, as if there was an alternate reality just beyond the five senses, and although she had never penetrated that world, she had a feeling it couldn't possibly be as dangerous and alien as was the event unfolding in her spare kitchen.

Just as the old man stepped closer to do whatever it was he was determined to do, she heard a knock at the front of the house. Her head snapped back, and she held the being's gaze with her own. "Someone's here," she whispered in newfound joy. She knew he must be alone with her to "mingle with her mind," as he'd put it.

"Yes," said the man, stepping back again. His hands hung at his sides, and she thought she detected disappointment and then sadness creeping over his old wrinkled face. "I'll come back," he said, stepping back once more so that he was at the same spot where he'd been standing when she'd first seen him.

The knock at her door was insistent. She could not move. The being before her was winking out of existence, rippling the way a sheet waves in a wind. "Go!" she whispered breathlessly. "Go away!"

And as suddenly as he'd appeared, he was gone. She was alone in her kitchen, clutching hard at the sink's edge, trembling uncontrollably. She felt tears rise in her eyes and blinked hard to clear them.

The knocking at her door had not let up. It was as if whoever was outside knew she was in imminent danger and was about to break the door down if she did not answer it.

She stumbled across the kitchen, down the narrow hall, and to the front door. She held onto the dead bolt lock for long seconds trying to find a reserve of strength to turn it. Finally she had it unlocked and the knob turned and the door standing open to the night. Her entrance light was on and in the flood of light outlining the front steps stood Alan Star, his face twisted with anxiety.

"I saw your car here and the lights on. I was worried something was wrong when you didn't answer."

"Oh, Alan!" She fell into his arms, so weak she nearly buckled at the knees. He caught her and stepped inside, half carrying her. He reached back and shut the door behind him.

"What happened?"

"I . . . I . . . there was . . ." She couldn't get it out. She didn't know what to tell him. He would think her crazy.

"Someone was here?" He had guessed it. He led her into the living room and lowered her to the sofa. He turned immediately and hurried down the hall to the dining room, then out of it and into the kitchen. He came back, puzzled, and looked up the stairs to the loft that lay in darkness beyond the landing. "Up there?" he asked, about to take the stairs. "Is he up there?"

"No, he's gone."

Alan acted as if he didn't believe her, and then she saw his shoulders slump with the relief of his own tension. He came and sat at her side, taking her hands into his own. "What did he do?"

"Noth . . . nothing. He didn't do anything."

"But if I hadn't come, he might have hurt you! Did he have a gun or something? Was he going to . . . rob you?"

Bette put a hand over her eyes. Rape her, he had almost said. She could not stop trembling. Alan had really thought she'd had a rapist in her house, although he hadn't been capable of saying it. He was not far from wrong, except the power the being had held over her had not been for rape of the body, only of the mind.

She felt Alan's arm come around her shoulders and hug her over into his chest. "It's all right," he said. "I'm here now. I told you long ago you ought to move out of this neighborhood."

How could she tell him it wasn't that? It hadn't been a drugged-out Hispanic or a Black man intent on killing or raping or robbing her. Her neighbors were her friends and watched out for her. She had been accepted as one of them, a minority, one of society's outcasts, no matter what the white population of the country thought of the forward steps that had been made in the name of equality. Deep in their hearts, they all knew they were not truly accepted.

It was normal for Alan, a white man, to think she had been menaced by someone of color, someone who could not find work and so turned to dealing drugs and guns in order to live. In his world that was what people were trained to think. He had no notion of how really protected she was in the racially-mixed neighborhood, how loyal all of them were to one another. If there were robberies, they would be committed far from the confines of her home. At least, that was the way it was in this neighborhood, she thought. She was safer here in her little home than anywhere in the city. Safe until the stranger with the frightening smile and the apparent ability to read her mind showed up in her kitchen, that is.

She removed a shaky hand from her eyes and looked at Alan. When he was perplexed, he squinched up his eyes so that there was a furrow between his brows. He was almost comical to her with his large blue eyes and thin lips, but she could not smile.

"Someone appeared in my kitchen just before you came."

The furrow deepened. "Appeared?"

She nodded her head. "I know you won't believe this, Alan, but it was some kind of man who wasn't human. He wasn't a ghost either. I don't know what he was, but he came to do something to me, something . . . really bad."

"Wasn't human? You mean, like, he as an . . . alien? Is that what you mean?"

With each word his voice had risen because his understanding could not encompass beings that were not human. Even asking her if the apparition was an alien was another way of dismissing what she had experienced. Friends with her since medical school, Alan knew she was born in Japan and had come to the states as a child. He also knew she kept a statue of Buddha on a small altar in her bedroom and that she held beliefs that any Western scientist would scoff at. But trying to explain to him what manner of beast had come to her in the kitchen was not going to be simple.

"It wasn't an alien, Alan. I don't believe in aliens."

He sighed a little, letting out a relieved breath. She mentally cringed at what she would have to tell him. The reality would put the idea of aliens to shame.

"It was some other kind of being. Something supernatural and very powerful. He just appeared in my kitchen while I was doing dishes, and then when he heard you at the door, he left again, twinkling out like smoke. He had a mission that has to do with me, but I don't know what it is. I didn't feel that he was going to kill me. But he was going to do something to my mind. I don't know how, but if you hadn't come, I wouldn't be the same person you have always known. He would have changed me some way. He . . . he promised he'd be back."

Alan didn't say anything. He sat back on the sofa and let go of her hands. The furrow was still between his eyes. That meant he was trying to digest what she'd told him. How could she expect him to understand? Who would? She hardly understood herself, having never come across such a being as this. She hadn't even heard stories of them or of what would cause one of them to be a threat to her.

Then she remembered his teeth and shuddered. She felt Alan's hand touch her arm, and she stilled. She did not think she would tell him about the being's sharp incisors. It was enough that she was asking him to believe she'd seen anything at all. He'd totally discredit whatever she said if she mentioned fangs. Could the old man have been a vampire? From American movies and American culture she had been as immersed in vampire myths as everyone else. Could she have made a mistake and only imagined the fangs?

She began to pray silently as she waited for Alan to come around. She looked down the hall from beneath her eyelashes, worried that she would see a shadow that shouldn't be there. She knew there was no protection from the man and that he would return at his convenience. Except for her prayers, she had no defense. Even if Alan were to stay, or if she moved someone else into her house, the man would come back eventually. He hadn't got what he'd come for, and in the end nothing would deter him.

In other words, she was doomed and there was no help for it. The tears welled in her eyes again, and this time she let them flow unimpeded down her cheeks.

14

Mentor lay on the rooftop of Bette Kinyo's house, listening to how she tried to explain his appearance. He was surprised at her intuitiveness and intelligence. She must have already studied and accepted the supernatural in the world, or she never could have concluded the facts about him she was now relating to the visitor. From where he lay on the roof shingles, he could see her tiny backyard where he could contemplate the Japanese garden there. It was meticulous, right down to the placement of two stones in the raked gravel to indicate rising islands, just as the rake marks indicated swirls of the sea surrounding the land masses. She had built an inlaid stone pathway from her back door to a teak bench beneath a slim weeping willow. From there, she could study the garden in peace. Even the usual noise from cars passing on the street in front of the house was muffled by the trees.

When the man left, Mentor would have to reenter the house and deal with Bette. Ross would not allow her to interfere in the operation of his blood bank. If Mentor did not do something, Ross would dispatch a killer to her door. That would be a shame. This little woman was a shining example of what a human could attain in one lifetime. Serenity. Security in her inner being. The peace of knowing her place in the scheme of the world.

Now he understood why she did not have a husband and children in the house. She had already moved beyond the natural urges of her gender and stepped into another dimension of living. She needed no one in order to be whole. She was sufficient unto herself.

Though he admired her, he would not hesitate to meddle with her mind. Or "mingle" with it, as he had warned her in advance. He would do his best not to jostle or tamper with the part of her mind that had created the wonderful garden and the pleasant home. But he must search out the memories she possessed and eradicate the ones that had to do with Strand-Catel. It would be a tricky procedure. Despite her fears, he was not a demon god, and therefore he was imperfect and sometimes made mistakes.

He paused to listen to the two humans inside the house. The man was full of disbelief, and even a little derision, though he was not voicing it to the woman. Oh, and now he was thinking how delicious she was in bed and had plans to get her there, ostensibly to allay her fears, but in truth it was a selfish motive of a sexual nature.

Mentor sighed to himself and turned his attention back to the empty garden glowing in the moonlight. Sex always made him feel his age, his real and true age. He had not mated in centuries. He had let that portion of his humanity grow lax until, finally, it had died. He missed it—the physical coupling, the overwhelming desire, the heat of congress, and then ultimate relief. He could not remember now why he had been so foolish as to let desire leak from him and vanish altogether.

He had loved a woman once. Her memory was emblazoned on his soul as much as the fact of his vampirism. It had been so long in the dusty past that human women then were an altogether different kind of creature. He had loved her more than his own life and when she'd died, for she had not been of his kind and he could not talk himself into making her one, he had let die his need for any other woman. He did not take a vow of celibacy. His ardor for sex had simply cooled until it was ice, never, he believed, to be rekindled again.

He mentally checked on the couple inside and found them in the loft bedroom, undressing. He might as well not wait, then. The man would probably stay the night.

Lifting straight up from where he lay on the roof, Mentor raised his arms and sailed easily skyward toward the clouds. He would lose himself in them on his way across Dallas to his own home. He would dally in the thin air, clearing his mind of the past and the one woman he'd ever loved. And then, when the morning came, he would return to 2234 Barbary Lane and speak again with the intriguing Bette Kinyo.

*   *   *

Alan made up his mind to watch her house the next day for the being she insisted had come to her. Right now they lay side by side, sweat drying on their bodies. In a moment Bette would rise to shower and afterward, he would bathe, too. Then they would snuggle in the sheets, lying with their arms around one another until morning. Again he wondered why he had not asked her to marry him. It was silly how he fell in love every time he met with her and then left again, the two of them going separate ways.

Perhaps he could broach the subject. "We could use a good hematologist in Houston. They have labs there, too, you know."

All right, it wasn't exactly a proposal, but he would have to work up to it. After all, he'd had no practice.

She laughed a little, her breath warm against his chest, where she lay curled like a soft kitten. "I have my house here, Alan."

"I'll get you another house." There. Couldn't she

see what he was driving at? He would even buy her a home, for Pete's sake. "What I'm saying is . . ." Hell, why didn't he just say what he meant instead of talking all around the bush like a school kid? "I just think we're good together. I'd like you to be where I am. I'd like you to . . ." He was screwing up. He couldn't propose worth a damn.

Bette rose up on an elbow and looked into his face. He knew he was conflicted and that it showed on his features. He was frowning when he meant to smile, but damnit, couldn't she see what he was getting at?

"I don't want to get married," she said simply. To soften the blow, she added, "I love you, Alan. I don't sleep with anyone else but you."

"That's just it. Neither do I. Then why don't we . . . ?"

"It's too perfect the way it is," she said, tracing a finger over his lips to keep him quiet. "I'm happy here. I've made this my home. It's where my parents are and my work. And you . . . Houston is where you belong. It's *your* home. It's where you find the most satisfaction in your work. Besides, we don't need to be married to be in love."

She swooped over him and kissed his lips.

He sighed into her mouth and pulled her on top of him, running his hands down the small of her back to the graceful swell of her hips. "All right," he murmured, "if that's what you want."

One day, he told himself, he would talk her into it. He would give up his place in Houston, which meant nothing to him, the way her home did to her. He would build his research clinic here, maybe, instead of in Houston. He'd speak to Charles Upton right away, telling him his change of plans. It was ridiculous that they only met like this once in while when they could be together every single night for the rest of their lives. But he'd keep it a secret and when he made the move, then he'd see what she had to say. He loved her little house, which to him was as charming as a doll house, and she would have him move in. It would all work out beautifully, she'd see.

Once they had made love again, she pulled him from the bed by the hand and together they showered, washing one another's bodies playfully. As they were drying off, he said, "I didn't tell you why I came to see you."

"It's because of my call?" She wrapped an oversized towel around her petite body and slipped on dainty pink satin slippers.

"How do you do that? Read my mind that way? Yes, it's about your call. I'm doing some . . . uh . . . research for a man. He's . . . uh . . . interested in blood supplies. I thought I'd check out what you said about one of the banks in town sending out large shipments across the state when there's no reason for it."

"What kind of research are you doing? It's not exactly your field. What about your patients?"

He shrugged, wondering how much to tell her. Believing in spirits that showed up in your kitchen was slightly different from hunting down vampires for a disillusioned old man who was dying. Or maybe it wasn't?

"I have someone filling in for me at the hospital. This other thing is important."

"It must be for you to leave the hospital."

"Oh, I haven't, not for good or anything. I'm just taking some leave time now and then. So tell me about the blood bank. Maybe you can show me the records."

She eyed him. "Well, maybe with your help we can figure it out. Like I said when I called, I'm completely dumbfounded. I called the Strand-Catel people and they gave me some nonsense about how my records must be wrong, they don't send out shipments that way. And I know that's a lie. I have to track every pint of blood in this state, and my records aren't wrong. They're hiding something, Alan. I just don't know why."

"I'll go with you to the lab today. Maybe I can visit the bank afterward and get some answers."

She hugged him in all his nakedness and smiled when she stepped back. "I'm so glad you were at my door," she said. "For more reasons than one, that's for sure."

* * *

Alan had spent the morning going over Bette's records and being convinced something was foul in Dallas. He could see how she had gone without noticing the discrepancy for so long. Her office was inundated with reams of printouts and faxes, stacks of government forms and file cabinets of computer documents.

Once sure she was right, that the Strand-Catel blood bank was shipping masses of blood all across the Southwest, he left her office and drove to the squat white brick building that housed the Strand-Catel complex. Inside, he asked to speak to the manager, and was taken down a long bare hall to a door that might have opened on a broom closet, for there was no sign to indicate it was an office. On the other side was a small waiting room with out-of-date and rumpled magazines, a cranberry tweed sofa nubby from use, and a desk for a bored secretary. "He's not in," she announced as Alan and the receptionist entered.

"I'll wait," Alan said, making for the sofa and wishing he'd brought a novel along to read.

"He may be a while," the secretary said.

"That's all right, I'll wait." He was not to be outdone. Someone needed to account for the blood bank's strange actions, and the manager was the one to do it.

It took more than two hours, but finally a man hurried through the unmarked door, a briefcase in his hand. The secretary flicked her eyes from the man to Alan. Alan stood, sore from sitting for so long.

"Hello," he said. "I'm from the Bartok Laboratories. I'd like to speak to you if I may?"

"Of course." The manager, Harold Kreeg, ushered him through another unmarked door into an office nearly as messy as Bette's.

Alan found a chair across from the desk piled with papers, and sat down. He would rather have stood, to get the kinks out of his legs, but it would have been impolite.

"What can I do for you?" Kreeg asked. He placed the briefcase on top of a pile of paper and sank into his chair. He seemed to be a harried man, overcome with schedules and paperwork.

"We have records showing that your blood bank has been shipping untested blood all over the state for many years. It was only discovered by accident, but Bartok Laboratories has a mandate to test blood supplies before shipping and they're wondering what's going on here." He paused and then added, "It would be unfortunate if the federal authorities had to be called in to straighten this out."

Kreeg blanched all the way from his receding hairline to his chin. He leaned forward and placed his arms on his desk, knotting his hands together. "I'm sorry, who did you say you were?"

Alan lied, "I'm a representative of Bartok. Bette Kinyo sent me. She called, but someone here told her that her records were incorrect."

The man sank back again, his hands coming unglued to grip the arms of his chair. "Ms. Kinyo was told the truth. I don't know how she has come up with this information about Strand-Catel. We never ship blood before testing. It's a monumental mistake, Mr. . . ."

"Star. Alan Star."

"Mr. Star. I can show you our own records, if you'd like. Not all of the place is run as . . . messily as my office." He smiled. "In fact, we can show you records going back as many years as you like. They all show quite different information than what Ms. Kinyo has been going on about."

Alan didn't like that. "Going on about" indeed. "It seems, then," he said, "that there is a difference of opinion. I have to tell you, Mr. Kreeg, that Bartok does not make mistakes either. And this being a serious allegation, it will have to be investigated thoroughly."

Kreeg spread out his hands in the air. "I don't know what to tell you. I am stating the facts as I know them as the manager of this institution. You're perfectly free to go over our own records. I can have my secretary take you . . ."

When Kreeg leaned forward to push a button on his intercom, Alan stood and shook his head. "I have no choice but to believe you. I don't have time to check today. However, be assured someone from Bartok will be coming to see you again soon."

Alan left the office, shutting the door behind him without saying a formal good-bye. He was being hoodwinked and he knew it. But it was obvious Kreeg had all the records on hand that would show the opposite of what Bette's records indicated and to get deeper into their true files, if they even existed, would take more than a cursory investigation. Bette would have to send someone from her department to put the heat on these people. They were not going to admit they'd been shipping out their blood supplies without any other organization double-checking their operations.

But what did all this have to do with hunting down vampires? Alan asked himself as he left the building. The idea had been a shot in the dark; he'd known that even when Bette had called with her discovery. Kreeg certainly didn't fit Alan's idea of a vampire. He was florid and heavyset, a middle management type of guy who bought his white shirts wholesale and wore brown wing-tip shoes to work. Besides, would vampires have need of a blood bank? Didn't they just grab people and suck out their blood?

Alan wanted to slap his own face. This was the nuttiest thing he'd ever done—signing on with Upton and agreeing to find him a living vampire. Here he was harassing blood bank managers, for heaven sakes, and imagining they shipped blood surreptitiously around the state for vampires to drink! If he wasn't insane, he was teetering. He had taken on Upton's insanity, that's what must have happened. What was he doing here in Dallas when he was needed in the hospital in Houston? How had he thought he would even pretend to do what Upton wanted?

He chastised himself all the way to Landry's Restaurant, where he ordered shrimp salad and sat alone drinking a draft beer while his food was being prepared. Bette wouldn't be home from the lab until after six. He had told her he would come back and report on his meeting with Kreeg, but he had something else in mind before he did that. One more bit of insane detective work and then he'd stop this charade and go back to his normal life as a doctor and a healer.

He meant to stake out Bette's house. From the time she returned home from work, until around nine at night, he decided he would park at a distance and watch her place to see if the mysterious stranger came back to do her harm. He didn't buy that stuff Bette said about he wasn't *human*. How he'd just appeared and then disappeared. Why was it everyone around him had taken a slow train around the bend suddenly? First Upton, now Bette. Vampires. Apparitions.

He stabbed his fork into the shrimp salad, speared a mayonnaise-drenched shrimp, and popped it into his mouth. He had an hour to kill before he called Bette and told her he'd be late. And then he would drive over to the scary, tumbling-down neighborhood Bette loved so much and sit in his locked car to wait.

15

Dell had slept fitfully the night before, waking in sweats from dreams of pursuit. She would fall asleep again only for the dream to resume.

She had trouble concentrating in class all day. When Ryan Major stopped her in the hall outside their shared history class, she felt sluggish and inattentive. She was not tired, she realized, as much as she was just dim. She might as well be a tarnished mirror sitting in a dark attic, reflecting dust motes. "What?" she asked, unsure of what he'd said to her.

"I asked if you had a boyfriend."

She almost laughed in his face. Boyfriend! She had trouble keeping her best friends from childhood now. She hadn't talked to Cheyenne in days. How could she hope to interest the opposite sex?

Then she snapped to attention, and her eyes widened. Ryan had asked the question because he wanted to know if the field was open.

She looked into his dark eyes and wanted the same relationship he did, in fact, wanted it more. But Mentor had warned her. She should not let down her guard. She changed more and more each day, becoming a separate being, and what boy would understand her? If he did, how could he want to be with her?

"No," she said, carefully, "I don't have a boyfriend. I . . . I . . ."

"I know it was a dumb question, but I didn't know anyone else to ask about you. Listen, do you think we could go out this weekend? A movie? Dancing?"

The word *yes* was on the tip of her tongue, but she couldn't say it. Instead, she pushed past him, mumbling, "No, I couldn't." She knew how rudely she was behaving, and hoped it would discourage him. Yet, she felt him on her heels, his hand reaching out to touch her.

"Well, we could do something else . . ."

She whirled on him so fast kids in the hall turned and looked. "I said no!"

Hurt surprise covered his face as he turned away from her. She wanted to rush after him and take it back. She hadn't had to be so awful to him. It wasn't his fault. He thought she hated him. He didn't know the reason she was treating him so shabbily.

"Ryan," she called.

He turned warily. "Yes?"

"Look, I'm sorry. It's not you. It's me. I'm not . . . not myself lately." She adjusted the sunglasses on her nose as if to emphasize her words.

He shrugged, and she could still see the hurt lingering on his face. "It's okay." He turned and left her standing there, students milling around her as if she were a stone in a swiftly flowing stream.

She hung her head and moved into the crowd, heading for her next class. She imagined her misery was like a billboard hung around her neck. Despair came over her, bringing such a heaviness she thought she would have to run out of the school and all the way home.

He'd just asked her to a movie. She might have gone with him. It wasn't a crime to go to a movie with a friend, was it?

She turned back to see if she could find him in the crowd. She pushed against people, moving through them until she saw him ahead. She didn't know how she could take back the decision not to go out with him, but she was going to try. Looking stupid was preferable to being alone.

Then she saw him stop in the hall and speak to a girl dressed in black jeans. She wore a tattered black top that reached only to her waist, exposing a lily white belly. Dell recognized her as one of the group who called themselves "vampyres." A Loden girl, part of Loden's group. The girl wore black lipstick that caused her lips to pout. Heavy black mascara made her lashes long enough to sweep her cheeks.

Well. Ryan might have picked her for his first choice for a date, but this girl was next on his list. Or had she been the first one he had asked? How many others had he asked before her and how many did he have lined up to ask after the little vamp girl?

Feeling a wave of anger unlike any she'd felt in ages, she turned on her heel and stalked in the opposite direction down the hall. To hell with him. She was right to brush him off. She never should have apologized and she certainly never should have gone after him to let him know she'd changed her mind. She hoped he hadn't noticed.

He was just like the other boys, out looking for a good time with any female handy. He didn't like her specifically or anything; he just wanted someone to go out with and maybe someone to have sex with. He wasn't anything like she'd thought he was. He wasn't *special*. She didn't care who he went out with. Let him get involved with the crazy cult girls for all she cared. They deserved him.

For the rest of the day not only was she oblivious to the instructors in her classes, but she burned with indignation unlike any she'd ever experienced before. Mentor had warned her about escalating emotions. Well, she was in the eye of an emotional storm. All she could think about was Ryan. His very dark blue eyes. His sweet manners and the way he was kind of innocent and gentle. The look of his shoulders and hips as he walked.

The way he bent over the girl in dark clothes, so

interested in what she was saying. The way he hadn't protested when she'd said no, but had turned away at once as if marking her off the list.

At home after school, Dell threw herself on the sofa and turned on the television. Eddie came from his room and, seeing her sprawled on the couch, said, "What's wrong?"

"What do you mean, 'what's wrong'? Nothing's wrong." She stabbed the remote control, switching channels, looking for the Comedy Channel.

"Yeah, something's wrong. You can't fool me. So what is it?"

"Eddie?"

"Yeah?"

"Shut up, will you? And leave me alone."

"Fine." He left the room and headed for the kitchen. "Hey," he called, "you hungry?"

"No!" She wished she'd never gotten sick, never changed, never had to taste blood again. If she were alive, she could date Ryan, the way she'd wanted to. She could go out with anyone. She could have lived a normal life, gone to college on a scholarship, had a career, married and maybe even started a family. Now all she had to look forward to was misery and a sense of bereavement. She would make loneliness her friend and separate herself from the real world.

She leaped from the sofa, dropping the remote control on the coffee table. Her parents weren't home from work yet, so she'd let Eddie know her plans. "I'm going to ride my horse," she yelled toward the kitchen.

"I thought you did that on weekends?"

"Oh, go to hell, Eddie. Leave me alone. I'll be back before dark, just tell Mom for me."

She hurried out the door and to the car. She remembered what Mentor had told her about controlling her emotions, riding rein on them and staying master of her actions, but she couldn't seem to follow the advice.

Well, to hell with Mentor, too. He didn't have to

go to high school and pretend he was one of the others. He didn't have to push away relationships and spend every weekend alone, dateless, like some ugly duckling no one could ever love.

Before she reached the car she saw Carolyn coming down the sidewalk. "Hey," she called, smiling, waving.

Dell stood waiting for her, unable to wipe the frown from her face.

"What's up? Were you going somewhere?"

"Yeah. To ride my horse."

"Oh." Carolyn looked disappointed.

"I'm sorry, I need to get away for a while."

"Oh."

Behind Dell came Cheyenne's voice. "Hey, you two, can I join in the fun?"

Jesus, Dell thought. *It's turning into a block party.*

"Hi, Carolyn. Dell, were you going somewhere?" Cheyenne was looking at the car keys in Dell's hand.

"To ride my horse."

"Horse! You got a horse? Oh, my God. I know I haven't been over lately, but when did this happen? Why didn't you tell me?"

Dell didn't know what to say. She looked to Carolyn for support.

Carolyn caught the pleading look and said to Cheyenne, "She got it for her birthday."

"That's not till June. An early birthday present! Anyway, that's seriously cool, Dell. I know you always wanted a horse."

Dell melted, remembering how Cheyenne cared for her and had been her friend for so long. They'd shared everything until now. "I can go another time," she said, holding up the keys.

"Not on your life. Go on, I'll see you at school. Nice to see you, Carolyn. Call me, Dell, okay?" Cheyenne waved and turned back the way she'd come.

Dell looked at her cousin. "Thanks. I got tongue-tied."

"No problem. I guess I'll go back home, too. Cheyenne's right, you should ride the horse before it gets too late in the evening."

Dell hugged her and opened the car door. She saw Carolyn leaving and called out, "Tell Aunt Celia I'll come over to visit this week."

"Okay. See you."

Dell sat in the car a moment, noting that her earlier anger and frustration had leaked away. She started the car and backed onto the street. She had thought she would never be able to live as a Natural, interacting with humans and behaving the way they did. Not when she felt so much anger. So much envy. But as long as she had friends and family who loved her, she might make it.

It was all so new. Before the change, she'd never felt so much anger and never been envious of anyone. Her whole personality was evolving and not for the best, she thought. She was letting the fury overcome and take away the hurt. It was all she knew to do.

The tires squealed and as she punched the accelerator. Riding could help. She would take Lightning on the riding path and be alone. She only wanted to forget all the things in the world she was going to miss now. Most of all she wanted to forget Ryan was going out with Lori on Saturday night.

* * *

Rebuffed by Dell, Ryan stopped a girl named Lori and asked her out for Saturday night. He picked her at random, liking the way she looked. Although she was not as pretty as Dell, she was no dog. She accepted, but suggested he might like to accompany her tonight to a party with her friends. "Loden's friends," she amended.

"Who's Loden?"

"You'll see." She smiled. "You'll like our friends." There was an intriguing twinkle in her eye.

The rest of the day Ryan wondered if he would.

Like Loden's friends, that is. Lori's friends. He knew who they were. The kids who were into heavy metal, gothic literature, body piercing, and thumbing their noses at society. But Lori herself was pretty cute. She was as perky as a cheerleader in Halloween drag. She was no Dell, that was true. But Dell had made it obvious she wasn't interested. It had cut him deeper than he thought it might. Damnit.

Well, Lori was going to show him a good time, introduce him to some people. She'd help occupy his time, help him fit into the new school, at least with the cult. He wasn't a jock, he had no aspirations as an academic, where else was he to fit anyway? He was really sort of a country boy, a ranch hand, used to hauling hay and cleaning horse stalls on his grandfather's land. The ranch boys didn't have a group, though, so that left him on his own.

It worried him that he might not fit in with Lori's group either. What did he know about Dracula and body-piercing and tattoos and drinking blood? Nothing, nada. Maybe Lori would instruct him. He really was looking for something besides a girlfriend, and why not what a cult had to offer? At least he'd check it out; no harm in that. No harm at all.

That night at the party he had a chance to reassess his own idea of "harm." First, he wasn't exactly accepted on sight. The other people in the house, which was apparently given over for the night to the younger generation with no parent present, rigorously ignored him. Lori said, noticing his discomfort, "Don't worry about it. They'll come around."

"Which one's Loden?"

"Oh, he's not here yet. He doesn't own a watch, doesn't go by time. No telling when he might show up. If he does." She shrugged.

Maybe the others would come around. Maybe he should have made a concerted effort to dress in black clothes and move his body as if it were mired in molasses. It seemed the people in the house were drugged on something that slowed them to a crawl.

Quaaludes, pot, something. Their eyes were dull and their gestures small. They seemed unsteady, but mannered in the way people were when having to be careful where they put their feet in case they might stumble. At one point he was offered a hit off a monster joint and declined. Another faux pas, evidently, because after that no one made the slightest attempt to engage him in conversation.

Lori sat beside him on the sofa. He tried to ask her about the scene they were stuck in, but she evaded him. Instead, she talked about school, her plans to go to Europe and stay in hostels after graduation, and how cool it was not to have to "perform" at a party like this, how it was just enough to "be."

He had to admit he just didn't get it. He really didn't get it when the first bloodletting began. Lori touched him on the arm to direct his attention. He'd been daydreaming, idly munching potato chips from a bowl in his lap, wondering if there was anything good on TV. He'd seen one in the family room. When he turned at Lori's touch, he saw a skinny young man slip his black turtleneck over his head. He brought a pocketknife from his pocket and opened the blade. Ryan saw lamplight shine off the blade and it made him shiver deep inside. Oh, man. Oh, man.

A girl, his girl, Ryan guessed, was kneeling at the boy's feet. Without preamble, and before the crowd gathered so that Ryan could not see what was happening, the knife was making five quick slits in the boy's upper arm. They weren't deep, but blood welled immediately. As soon as he'd cut himself, he wiped the blade on his jeans, folded it shut, and slipped it into his pocket. Then he bent over the girl on the floor, thrusting out his arm to her. She bowed her head and began to lick at the blood, a look of ecstasy on her face.

"Oh, Christ," Ryan said, grimacing.

"He's been tested," Lori said, thinking his disgust might be at the thought of the girl getting AIDS.

"You do that sort of thing, too?"

"Sure." She glanced meaningfully at his arm. "When I feel like it," she added.

Ryan watched the couple giving and receiving blood and felt a catch at the back of his throat. He had seen a lot of things; it wasn't as if he was so straight he was a Republican or something. But licking and sucking at bloody wounds was way beyond anything he'd witnessed before. No wonder they were all so lethargic, he thought. Maybe they weren't drugged out of their skulls, after all. Maybe they were depressed and weak from giving blood. Never mind AIDS—not that testing protected them, since the tests didn't always detect HIV in the early stages. But hadn't they ever heard of anemia? And whatever godawful thing might be in someone else's blood?

He laughed to himself, and Lori looked at him with dark eyes outlined in black eyeliner pencil.

"Most people who see this for the first time have a squeamish reaction," she said, as if to forgive him.

"But what's the philosophy behind the ritual? I mean, I know they're not doing it because they're . . . well, hungry."

She smiled and shook her head. "No, they're not hungry in the way you mean. There's no, uh, philosophy. It's like a way of life. A lifestyle. We're intimate when we share blood. We're brothers and sisters. It's a way to distinguish us from the rest, the normals. And, believe it or not, it's an incredible turn-on."

"Oh, it is, is it?"

Lori and Ryan turned at the interruption and saw Dell standing nearby, hands on her hips. She was scowling.

"Hey, Dell. What's up?" Lori said.

Ryan noticed Lori hadn't missed a beat.

"I know I shouldn't be here," Dell said to Ryan, ignoring Lori's greeting. "I wasn't invited." This she directed at Lori. "But I heard there was a party, Loden was throwing a party." She looked around and saw couples beginning to get into the bloodletting business. Ryan saw her look quickly away again.

He started to stand up to offer his seat to Dell. "Want to sit down?"

"Not on your life," she said, anger in her voice spiraling close to the surface. She faced Lori. "What made you bring him here?"

"Hey, he wanted to come." She tugged on Ryan's hand and made him sit down again.

"What's the point of all this crap?" Dell asked, angrier now.

"Call it crap if you want, but maybe you ought to wait until you're invited somewhere before you begin calling names." Lori was blowing her cool. Ryan didn't know what to say. He was really surprised to see Dell and more surprised to see her so angry. He saw some couples close to them move away and some people were beginning to leave. Others, couples involved too deeply in their blood rituals, hadn't yet noticed Dell on the scene.

"You think this makes you a vampire?" Dell asked. "Why do any of you think you know what the hell you're doing?"

"You don't know what we know," Lori said.

"I know this. I know this kind of thing is crazy as hell. This no more makes you a vampire than wearing a jeweled crown makes Miss America the Queen of England." Dell turned to Ryan, her cheeks flushed. He saw the pupils of her eyes were dilated so that her eyes were extremely dark and intense. "Is this really what you want?"

Ryan realized suddenly why she was so angry. She liked him. Liked him enough to show up at Loden's party and make a scene on his behalf. He said, "I'm not sure what I want, Dell."

She threw her head back in exasperation. "Well, you'd better make up your mind."

"Who says it's up to you?" Lori asked.

Again Dell ignored her. She said to Ryan, "About Saturday night . . ."

He nodded, almost afraid to breathe until she finished.

"We'll go somewhere together, like you said. Somewhere there's no blood dripping all over the place." With that she turned and left the room.

"Whoa, boy," Lori said, shaking her head. "A little overwhelming, isn't she?"

Although Lori was right in a way, Ryan didn't like to hear criticism of Dell. "She's just worried, I guess."

"None of her business. As far as I can tell, you're a big boy."

Maybe so, Ryan thought, but he was glad Dell had let him know how much she cared. If she hadn't cared, she wouldn't have walked into the middle of a cult party and said the things she'd said. He thought her brave, and the logic she'd employed was impeccable.

As the night wore on, the thought of cutting himself and watching Lori drink from him was more distasteful in his mind than some little kid playing in his own excrement. Not only was it unsanitary, but it was such a taboo, almost as bad as cannibalism. It certainly wouldn't turn him on. He had to be missing something integral to the notion.

He kept silent and didn't share his doubts. He continued watching the couple and then other couples as they followed suit with blades and bloodletting. Soon, half the people at the party were down on their knees taking blood and the other half stood, giving blood.

"I think I'm going to have to leave," he whispered to Lori. She hadn't moved in long minutes, frozen in place by what was going on.

"Okay," she said, reacting slowly as if waking from a trance. "You'll get used to this later. Forget what Dell said. Most of the time we don't bring first dates to this kind of party, but I knew you'd be cool."

He was cool, all right. He was cold as a corpse. All he wanted to do was get the scent of blood out of his nostrils. He thought he was going to gag and

176 Billie Sue Mosiman

that wouldn't make his date happy. He stood and Lori with him. She said good-bye to a few people and they left the house. Outside, in the fresh air, Ryan took a deep cleansing breath. "Maybe we should have worked our way up to this," he said.

"It's what Dell said, isn't it?"

"Not really."

She linked her arm in his as they walked to the car. "I hope I didn't scare you away. Not everyone does this. It's not like you *have* to or anything. It's more like you want to once you realize how close it can bring two people. Or a group of people. We're like family. We'd do anything for one another."

Ryan thought they already did anything for one another. He'd be damned if he'd take a knife to his arm, or any other part of his anatomy, and watch someone drink from him. As for being the drinkee, well, that was totally out of the question. Ugh.

He drove Lori home through the night, but all he could think about was Dell showing up at the party. He thought of her long red hair spilling around her shoulders in spirals. He thought of how her eyes had looked, deep and dark and amazingly impenetrable.

He tried to listen to Lori while she made her case for what he'd seen. He wanted to understand. He wanted to make sense of it. Finally he gave up trying and decided it was just the shock that he was working through. She'd said they all got over the initial disgust eventually. She suggested he read Bram Stoker's *Dracula*, and he said he would. He would, really. Read it slow, she said. Read it like you've never seen a book before and this is the first one you've ever read. I'll try, he told her, honest, I will.

"And after that," she said, "I have a whole list of new books for you to read. People are publishing books every day just for us."

"For you?"

"For the real believers."

"You don't really think you can be a vampire, do

you? Dell asked that, I know. But you don't, do you?"

"Oh, of course not! But we can get close to it if we really try. We become one of the underground the books are really written for. It's a society, Ryan. If people really knew what we thought, they'd have to get a little scared. Not because we're going to turn into bats and bite their necks, but because we don't think at all about things the way they do."

He didn't think it made much sense to want to be so different you created a whole myth around yourself and you made rituals up out of the whole cloth. He didn't say it to Lori, but as far as he could determine, the kids at the party weren't a danger except maybe to themselves. He wasn't afraid of them. He wasn't lured.

He would, however, read *Dracula*. He'd always meant to anyway. He'd just read Mary Shelley's *Frankenstein* last year and that had been an eye opener. The monster was nothing like he was portrayed in the movies. He expected Stoker's monster would be more interesting, too. But nothing was going to make him want to partake of blood. He was about as far from that as he was from the moon in the sky. Dell really hadn't had much faith in him if she'd thought otherwise.

When he went to kiss Lori good night before she left the car, meaning to give her a friendly little peck on the lips, she grabbed him around the neck and kissed him back so hard he found himself trying to pull away. Breathless once loose, his mouth still filled with the taste of her, he said, "That was . . . intense."

She grinned at him and said, "Yeah, wasn't it?"

He watched her enter the house before driving away. He was too stunned to leave earlier. He had really liked what she'd done. He thought he could go for an aggressive woman.

Then he thought of Dell and knew the truth. He would go out with her exclusively, if she'd let him. He had no interest in blood drinkers and cults and warped philosophies. Lori was a sweet thing and a terrific kisser, but Dell was someone he couldn't stop thinking about. He was happy she'd changed her mind about going out with him. All he needed was a chance.

*   *   *

Mentor took a direct route to Bette's house when he returned. She knew he was coming back. This time he would make her let him inside. He walked down the long street fronting her house, noting the small children playing in the street after dark. If only they knew what kind of creature he was, the mothers would never let their children be alone outdoors again.

Teen boys, all wearing black baseball caps with some kind of red insignia, congregated on a corner across the street. They watched him quietly, but did not move to intercept him. He projected an aura of danger their way. They might be tough little hooligans, but in each of their brains an alarm sounded that caused them to hesitate. Dallas had its share of minority gangs, and this one dominated the neighborhood.

A white man in his forties sat on a house stoop near the sidewalk. Mentor touched his thoughts and found his mind scrambled by heroin. His personality was near disintegration, and it made him angry and dangerous. As he lifted his head when Mentor neared, Mentor sent a message telepathically. *Don't come near me,* he told the man. *You'll be sorry if you do.*

Finally, Mentor was in front of Bette's walkway. He looked up to the front door and the windows. Lights glowed lemon yellow through lace-covered windows. Her car was in the drive. He telepathically searched the house and found no one there but the woman. Now he would make her invite him in, and he would finish the job he'd begun the day before.

When she answered his knock, he hit her with his

strongest suggestion. *Ask me in,* he said to her mind. *You know me as an old friend.* He watched her expression change from horror to recognition and, finally, to happiness. She reached out for his hand and tugged him into the house. "I haven't seen you in so long," she said.

"And I bet you missed me, didn't you?" Mentor stepped through the doorway and closed the door behind him. He should have done it this way the first time instead of letting her see him as he really was, allowing her to understand his real intentions. He didn't like to trick them so easily, though, and unless he had to, he usually let a human face him on his own terms. But he hadn't any more time to waste on the woman.

Once they were in her small living room, he entered her mind fully. This caused her to stiffen and become as still as a statue. His own frail body also froze, waiting for his mind to return to it.

Inside Bette's skull he rifled through the area that held her lifetime of memories, shunting aside those that were too personal, those that concerned her childhood or her parents or her friends and relatives. He searched diligently for the memories that had to do with her work. She was a bright woman; he admired her and would not touch anything in her mind that would change her too much if he could help it. Of course there was always the chance of an accident when doing such delicate operations, but Mentor took special care because of the goodness he found in the woman.

It took several long minutes before he located her work memories, and then he went through them gently, stirring them this way and that until he found the exact ones he needed. She had memories from textbooks and classes taken at a university. These memories were tangled up with flashes of meetings with the man who had been in her house the night before, when he was much younger. When they both were much younger.

She had volumes of information stored about hematology and her lab work involving blood. If he ruined too many of these memories, she would never be useful as a scientist again. He meant to be careful, realizing he was trampling among stored data that she needed in order to fulfill her life's training.

And then he found what he needed to expunge. He moved through a memory of lifting a long computer printout close to her face and noticing the shipments from Strand-Catel. There was confusion surrounding these memories, like clouds shrouding a summer moon. She was not sure what the data meant and it left her befuddled. He took these memories and folded them the way one folds a newspaper, then he stuffed them behind a set of memories that dealt with other blood banks. For her to recall them again, she would have to have a traumatic brain injury that might possibly jiggle them loose, but even then it was an improbability. In other words, short of near fatal injury to her brain, she would never remember them again.

He lifted every memory he could discover that had to do with Strand-Catel and folded and stuffed until the whole inquiry she had started had been swept clean and put away in very deep storage within her brain.

On his way out of her mind, he almost tiptoed over to the area of memory that held personal data. He was tempted to look in on the love she had devoted to the man who had spent the night with her. But he knew that was snooping. It was an urge he should not indulge. What he might find there would no doubt throw him into a conflict about his own lack of a love life. It would depress him. Better to stay out of this woman's love affairs and leave before he caused some kind of accidental and irreparable damage.

He stepped out, hovered in midair just for a moment, and then reentered the skull of his old body. Just as he did, the woman collapsed forward into his arms. Her eyes were closed and he checked to see if she was breathing well. She was. She was sleeping like a newborn.

He lifted Bette and carried her to the sofa. Then he made her comfortable with a pillow under her head and smiled down at her slight body.

"You see? That wasn't so bad, was it?"

He left the house, happy that it had been so easy. He was reasonably sure he had not harmed her, except for taking away the memories that would get her into trouble with Ross. He walked down the sidewalk through the neighborhood the way he had come. The gang was gone, and the drug-addicted homeless man was missing from his stoop. Even the children had fled the street. The neighborhood seemed to have emptied, and he expected it was because they had unconsciously felt the danger he represented. They had gone inside their homes and bolted the doors. He smiled, showing his teeth. He thought how wonderful it was to be able to command this much power over not only the sweet, unassuming Bette, but a whole neighborhood of people who might not have even seen him. Without catching sight of him, their instincts knew something was walking close by that they did not want to encounter in the darkness of the night.

Mentor had seen a bus stop near the edge of the neighborhood. He decided he would take public transportation over to Ross' house to tell him the news. Mentor had not been on a bus in years, though in the past he had loved bus rides very much. *Leave the driving to us,* he sang in his mind. Yes, he would do that. Sit back and watch mankind moving from this place to that unaware that in their midst rode someone who, with very little effort, could mesmerize every one of them into a catatonic sleep.

He must never separate himself too far from man, he knew. He must renew his study of man and their modern ways, or he could not hope to be of service to his youthful charges like Della Cambian.

As he rode, he watched an old Asian man fiddle with a leather pocketbook attached to his belt loop by a chain. He listened in on a conversation between two young women who seemed more interested in their dates this weekend than in anything else in the world. He moved his attention among the passengers, letting it pick up this and that observation until he wearied of their daily cares and frustrations, their minor joys and triumphs. Finally, he settled back in the seat and rested, leaving the driving to them.

* * *

Alan woke just as Mentor left Bette's house. He whispered a curse and sat straight up in the seat of his car. He gripped the wheel and gritted his teeth as he watched the old man come down the walkway and turn up the sidewalk. How could he have fallen asleep! It was as if something came over him, blowing out the candle of his awareness. It might have been because he ate too much dinner. Used to canned goods, a real meal often caused him to grow drowsy. But he would not have fallen asleep tonight, not when he had to watch Bette's house and keep her safe.

He cursed himself as a fool again and turned in his seat to watch the old man saunter down the walk beneath streetlights and crape myrtle trees that grew along the sidewalks. The street was eerily quiet, with no one else around. Had that been the stranger who'd frightened Bette the night before? Or was he just an old friend who had stopped by for a visit?

Alan was torn between rushing into the house to see about Bette or following the man who had come from her house. He decided to see about her as fast as he could. She was his primary concern. He rushed across the street and into her house. When he found her sleeping, he touched her face, felt the pulse in her wrists, and, satisfied she was all right, he hurried out the door again.

He had to follow. He was as drawn to the old man as if there were an invisible rope attached to him that was pulling him along.

He started the car and put it into gear. He turned his car around in the empty street and cruised slowly toward the old man. He had not closed in on him before he saw the man sit down on a bus stop bench. In the distance a bus lumbered toward him. Alan pulled into a parking spot at the curb and waited. He'd make another U-turn in a minute and follow the bus. Something told him he must know where the old man was going. Whether he was Bette's friend or foe, there was something magnetic about him that made Alan want to get closer to him. He was very curious about the old man's destination.

16

Ross lived in a modern ranch-style home at the edge of Dallas. He had bought twenty acres so that he would have no close neighbors. He had hired the best of the city's architects and given him enough money to build a castle, but what he created was an oddly shaped monstrosity sitting out on the edge of nowhere, it seemed to Mentor.

The bus lines did not extend to Ross' property, so Mentor left the bus and walked two miles in the night to reach the place. Sometimes he walked like this, rather than travel supernaturally. The night was tropical and balmy, the sky overhead so clear that once he was out of the city's interior he could see the stars. He was happy he'd decided on the walk where he could spend a little time tuning himself to nature's rhythm.

Just as he had enjoyed the hour-long bus ride across the city, now he reveled in the cooling night air. The houses and lights dwindled until darkness settled over the long vista. Mentor took solace from the sounds of night birds, the slither of snakes through the green grass that grew along the highway, and the sparkling clarity of the air he breathed.

He knew Ross was at home, could sense him there, even at this distance. Once he reached the house, he marveled, shaking his head at the overwrought construction. A peaked roof soared two stories tall, and from the entrance portico two wings spread out on each side. With a little squint of the eyes, the house looked like a giant predatory bird squatting in the low grass, its wings extended. In the rear was an Olympic-sized swimming pool, a full tennis court, and a long sleek building that Mentor knew was Ross' own indoor handball court. Ross was nothing if not extravagant. But it was all for show. Ross did not need to exercise. He swam in the pool sometimes, Mentor knew, but he rarely used the other facilities.

Mentor shook his head in consternation. He always felt that way when he visited Ross' home. While the Naturals worked like slaves in the human world in order to buy blood from the Predators, Ross lived like a king off the profits. He had no compunction about the inequity involved. He had chosen to be a Predator and excess was in his nature. Still, it saddened Mentor to see one of his kind so obsessed by possessions that he would take so much without giving back any more than the bare sustenance the Naturals and Cravens required to stay alive.

Cravens lived on welfare and their wits, handing over what money they could scrounge to Ross' people. And here Ross was, living like a king.

He would only stay a few minutes. He did not feel comfortable beneath the two-story ceilings that ended in an overhead vault of glass. The collected artwork on the walls was disturbing to Mentor, since it probably belonged in a museum instead of a private collection. He'd never inquired, but he suspected some of the paintings were original masters, procured illegally. The imported rugs and the modern, garishly colored, stilted furniture that Ross preferred only deepened Mentor's feeling that everything was on display to make visitors feel insignificant.

Also, he had checked on Dell during his bus ride and found that her parents and little brother were frantic with anxiety. Dell had sneaked out of the house after dark, and they did not know where she had gone. They had tried to contact her telepathically, but she apparently had blocked out her family. They had been sending messages to Mentor for more than an hour, asking if he would find her. They knew Mentor, with his greater powers, could get the job done.

Mentor, hearing Dell's family calling for him, went on a mental search and, after little difficulty, found her outside of the city. She was with the horse her parents had bought as a gift. He must go to her and explain things. Though he understood her need for solitude and the companionship of the new pet, she should not worry her family. He was also concerned about how wild and free she was acting as she rode alone through dark woods. She was giving in to the dangerous part of her vampiric nature.

Once a Natural took to the wild, it was only a matter of time before giving in to the blood call. Even a Natural might take to random kills if she did not stay close to the human community and continue living as she always had. If Dell ever gave in and listened to the call her soul made for abandoning the real world, she would be a renegade and lost to her family forever.

Ross met him at the entrance, swinging wide the twelve-foot-tall, ornately carved door to let him inside. "Did you take care of the woman asking questions about Strand-Catel?" he asked without preamble.

"Yes," Mentor said. "She won't be a bother to you again."

"Good! I was about to take a swim. Care to join me? I have extra trunks."

Mentor was inside before he saw two women sitting side by side on Ross' sofa. He knew from their scent they weren't vampire. Had he not had his mind on Dell, he would have known they were there before Ross admitted him.

The women wore bikini swimsuits and seemed to

be in a stupor, their eyes glassy and out of focus, barely registering his presence.

"What are they doing here?"

"Oh, them," Ross said, flicking long delicate fingers in the women's direction. "My dinner companions, that's all." He grinned and Mentor shuddered.

Ross would play with them as if they were puppets and when he tired of their company, he would take them one by one, having his way with their bodies before draining them dry.

"I don't know how you live with yourself," Mentor said, moving again for the door. "I'm leaving now."

"Well, hell, if you weren't going to stay, why didn't you just call?"

"I wanted to walk. I didn't know you wouldn't be alone."

Ross stepped to the door and held it as Mentor exited. "Your sensibilities bore me, Mentor."

"And the lack of yours bores me." Mentor did not turn back as he left the house.

A low growl came from Ross suddenly and Mentor turned back to him. "What is it?"

"Did you bring someone with you?"

"I certainly did not."

Ross swung his head from one side to the other, peering out from beneath a frown. He looked like a buzzard, checking for prey. "Are you sure no one came with you?"

Mentor now looked about too, scanning the property. He sensed a human, but he did not want Ross to know it. He did not want more bloodshed. The two women inside were already doomed. Why give Ross another?

The human was male, a lurker, near the windows. Let Ross take care of that, if it came to it. If he saw something he shouldn't, Ross would know that as well. For right now, Mentor would not divulge the human's whereabouts. "There's no one," he said, lying easily, waving away the idea with a gesture of his hand. "Go back inside."

"Are you sure you won't have a taste of my love-lies before you go? When was the last time you had a warm meal?"

Mentor heard his laugh, and it followed him down the driveway to the highway. If he had his way, all Predators would be wiped from the face of the Earth. They not only preyed on mankind, but they were truly heartless creatures. They were too fully engaged in the world, taking from it all earthly delights and then discarding their dead as if they were refuse for a landfill. They controlled the Naturals by being their only supply of blood, and if given the chance, they would murder every Craven who came near them.

Mentor wondered why God in heaven had ever allowed them to exist, but he wondered, too, why *any* of them existed and why God had no answer for him. Just as there were criminals and humans without souls walking among the normal population, there were the unholy and despised living alongside the Naturals. There was no good reason for it; it simply was how things were arranged. Mentor felt he would never really understand it all until the day he no longer lived on the planet. Whenever that would be. . . .

Sometimes he worried. He tried to be religious. He tried to believe in a Supreme Being. He hoped God was there, looking down, taking notes on his conduct. He had done evil things, but he'd shown regret and tried to mend his ways. He worried, still. For if there was a God, there might be a Devil, there might be hell.

Waiting for him.

He shrugged off the thoughts, relentless as they were, and turned his attention to the human hiding near Ross' house. He tried to send him a warning, but seemed to be blocked from telepathically reaching the man. The stranger's fear crowded his mind, keeping it locked solidly against outside interference.

So be it. The curious always got what they deserved. The man never should have gone near a vampire's house.

Now he must go to Dell, thirty miles away, and speak to her about the rebelliousness that had overcome her since she had been given the horse. It was not the horse, per se, that had triggered it. She probably would have acted this way no matter what. Many of the young ones made mistakes, unsure of themselves and their powers, confused by their new lives and the changes that were taking place.

He spent half his time trying to teach them control. He could not have them turning out like Ross. There were quite enough unruly, unfeeling vampires in Dallas already.

He was not too far from Ross' house when he gathered himself together and changed so quickly it was like a lamp turned off in a room. One moment he was walking along the side of the road and the next he had vanished. What he had really done was take to the skies with such speed his movement would have blown away a supersonic fighter jet.

* * *

Alan thought he might have made a pretty terrific private investigator. He tailed the bus easily enough, watching for the old man to leave when the doors opened, but once his target was on foot, that was another problem altogether. He parked on a deserted street where small businesses were closed for the night, entrances barred by heavy black iron grilles and metal curtains that rolled down to cover wide windows. Here, roving dogs nested behind trash bins, and people scurried home to be safe from the night. Alan turned off the headlights to sit in the darkened car. His heart beat fast. He felt both scared and elated. He was in a frightening part of town, but he was excited by the hunt.

He watched the old man move deeper and deeper

into the lonely darkness that spread out from the edge of the city into fields and pastures and farm-lands. Where could he be headed and why?

Alan had to know. He had come this far, following the bus on its circuitous routes through city streets, and now he had to make another decision. Did he leave his car and walk, too, keeping his distance so the other man did not know he was being followed? Or did he give it up as a bad job and drive back to Bette's house?

He looked at his wrist watch. It was almost eight p.m. He had told her he would be back by nine. He had an hour. He might as well finish what he had begun. Besides, he hadn't walked anywhere like this in ages. Except for health-conscious joggers, did any-one walk anywhere anymore, he wondered? Now he wished he'd been more athletic.

He eased out of the car, shutting the door quietly and locking it. One could not leave a thirty-thousand-dollar car unlocked in a deserted place like this. It was a poor business district and not much business at that. A few storefronts, some of them with painted signs in the windows announcing they had moved elsewhere. The only working streetlights stood just over where he was parked at the broken concrete curb.

He set off into the dark, wondering why he felt so compelled to act in this manner, and yet unable to stop himself. It was the excitement, he realized. It made him feel so alive.

He could barely see the figure of the old man ahead of him, and that was good. If the man turned, he would have a difficult time detecting that he was being followed. Alan was ready to move off the high-way and hide in bushes along the way if he had to.

Only two vehicles had passed them so far, a brown Toyota with a dinged front fender and a pickup truck that spewed black smoke out its tailpipe. Alan gave them a wide berth, afraid he would be seen in their lights as they passed.

After a mile of walking, he was sure the old man was absolutely crazy. There were no houses, no lights, nothing but a few cattle barns and rows of barbed wire fences. Hadn't there been something in the news about some cattle mutilations going on for a while out here? he wondered. Was this the highway where they'd found the cattle lying dead, no footprints or tire tracks around them, and they had been cut, their genitals taken, half their jaws, parts of their stomachs? What was *that* all about?

Despite the fact he was a medical doctor, he was not a surgeon. He couldn't fathom how anyone without knowledge of animal anatomy could perform such delicate surgery in the middle of an open field. Or why they'd want to. People who perpetuated hoaxes had never made sense to him.

Alan shivered, though the night was warm. He saw some cows in the distance, like black dots at the horizon in the fields behind the fences. God, he was glad he was not a cow. Eating grass and waiting for something to descend upon them to surgically and cleanly remove most of their blood and vitals. Or if not that, the slaughterhouse.

He walked another mile, keeping far back from the old man, always alert and ready to fall down into the high grass of the ditch if he thought the old guy might look behind him. Not far ahead he saw lights illuminating a house. A very large house, tall in the middle and long on both sides. There were small domed pathway lights along a gravel path leading up to the massive doors.

That's where the old man was headed. He was not crazy, he was just being careful. Alan watched him near the house, and then enter it after a moment or two at the door.

Going up the gravel driveway was out of the question. It would be like turning on a foghorn to announce his presence. Instead, Alan walked on the thick lush lawn, now wet with dew, skirting the front and approaching the windows from an oblique angle.

When he got to the wide, leaded-glass picture window on one side of the door, he crept close and peered inside. He saw two women in bathing suits, sitting on a sofa together. They weren't talking. They weren't doing anything, but sitting, looking kind of spaced out. Drugged? He couldn't really tell, but it sure looked that way to him.

To the right of them, he saw the old man talking to a younger man dressed in bathing trunks. There was something about this man that gave Alan the willies. He was handsome and fit, very tall and broad in the shoulders, but there was an unmovable cruel expression on his face that could make you go jelly-kneed. Alan couldn't make out what the two of them were saying.

He looked around and found a thick stand of cypress near the corner of the house, close to the window, and stepped behind them. He was just in time. The door opened again and the old man stepped out. He heard the younger man call to his back, "Are you sure you won't have a taste of my lovelies before you go? When was the last time you had a warm meal?"

Taste of his lovelies? The girls inside? Taste them, as one would a . . . a . . . meal?

Alan cringed, knowing without doubt that the man meant exactly what he said. He wasn't talking about tasting them sexually or he wouldn't have added the stuff about a meal. Jesus, were they cannibals? This was too bizarre for words.

The old man made some reply, then stalked off into the night, back down the road toward Dallas. Alan watched him go and heard the younger man close the door. He stood up, watching and waiting. As he tried to decide when he could leave his cover and follow, he saw the old man disappear into the night. Alan stepped out from behind the cypress trees and took a step forward. He stopped, staring hard at where the old man had been walking, sure he had made a mistake. It was a trick of the night, the lack of light along the highway, the utter isolation of this place. It was because he was tired and felt dumb for playing at detective work. Surely a person could not just vanish.

He began to walk toward the highway, searching everywhere, hoping for a glimpse of the old man. Maybe he had suffered a spell or seizure and fallen down so quickly Alan hadn't seen it happen.

When he neared the spot where he had last seen the man, he looked around on the pavement, in the ditch, even over the fence and into the pastures. The old man had simply vanished, all right. He was nowhere. There were no hills, no obstructions, no place where he could have hidden himself. He was just gone.

Just then Alan heard screams from the house and he turned, hunching his shoulders. He hurried back to the cypress trees near the window. The man inside had drawn the curtains, but Alan could see through a slit into the lighted interior.

The screams were from the women he'd seen on the sofa, and they were unending. The screams rose from the house and into the night like sirens at full blast. Peering through the slit, Alan saw what was occurring, but his mind could not comprehend the scene. He fell back, putting both hands over his eyes, his lips tight and teeth gritted. He lowered his hands to look again.

The man had straddled one of the women, bending her back over an ottoman. He held her arms down with one hand and her head down with the other. She was screaming piteously. The man had torn flesh from her throat with his teeth. A gout of blood gushed from the wound, covering the ottoman and the tiled floor. The man chewed the flesh as one would a mouthful of steak.

The other woman seemed to have come out of the trance she had been in and was standing, screaming, beating at the man's back with her fists to try to stop him.

As Alan watched, sickened and stupefied, the man

whipped around, dropping the wounded woman onto the ottoman where she slipped limply and unconsciously to the floor. He grabbed the other woman who had been fighting against him, bent her over his knees, held one arm against her forehead so as to bare her throat, and then he leaned down and bit at her savagely.

She screamed until the scream changed to a strangled gurgling.

Alan turned from the window, stumbled back, and vomited into the grass. His dinner at Landry's Seafood Restaurant came up, all of it, and the beer mixed with it. He retched dryly, stumbling farther and farther from the house and into the darkness. He hurried to the road that would lead him away from the bloody massacre, afraid to look behind him.

17

Dell rode Lightning as fast as she dared, crossing a ravine in the darkness, past low hanging limbs that whipped past her face, around and through stands of cottonwoods and pine and soaring oaks. Something had entered her, and she was trying to get it out again. It was the memory of the dark wood where the moon shone blood red and the giant Predator, king of them all, swooped down toward her from out of the crimson sky like a monstrous prehistoric dinosaur with wings.

It felt as if The Maker was here again, coming for her in the night as she rode the horse. She raced from him, flying as fast as she could, as fast as the horse could be made to run. "Go, Lightning!" she yelled, swatting at his flanks with her reins, leaning forward so that she was as close to him as possible. Branches pummeled her back and whipped across her lowered head.

"Hurry, Lightning, hurry!"

The remembered dream that was now so real had come on her in a flash. She'd just been trotting along in the darkness, thinking about Ryan and Lori at the Loden party. She thought she had done the right thing showing up and confronting them, but she couldn't seem to get rid of the anger. She knew where it originated. Ryan was with someone else. He should be with her. He had to be with her.

Maybe she should have stayed home and talked it out with Carolyn. Or maybe she could have visited Cheyenne and asked for advice. Instead, she'd come here on her own, and now the memories raged through her unsettled mind.

When she had first saddled Lightning and taken him out along the riding path, it was delicious to know she had slipped away from everyone, taken the car to Loden's party and then to the stables. After leaving the party, spending time alone was what she needed most.

She had never disobeyed her parents before or done anything remotely rebellious. Her conscience gave her a twinge when she thought they might be wondering where she'd gone.

But now that she'd done what she pleased, she realized how much fun it was to feel like a runaway, a brat, an unbridled spirit who had no master. She could say anything to anyone; she could ride in the night like a blithe spirit.

She glanced up once at the moon risen partway into the sky, and saw that it was a full milky orb surrounded with a halo of silver. Without warning the dream came on her, returned to reality. The tremendous fear it had instilled in her very soul when she lay dying returned full force. Suddenly it burned in her mind with clarity and emotion. All thoughts of Ryan and Lori left her. Fear was at her back, lifting a clawed hand to capture her brain.

She had kicked Lightning to send him off on a marathon race, plunging through the thickets and woods as if the very hounds of hell were on their heels.

Now that they were spinning out of control, she didn't want to stop it, wanted, in fact, to run the horse until he could run no more, lose her way without any thought as to how she might get back.

The monster was at her back, and she would outrun him. Together, with the help of her marvelous steed, they would show him that he could not have her, never. Never would he have her!

When they reached a shallow creek running silver in the moonlight, Lightning dashed across it, sending sprays of water to each side. Laughter erupted from Dell and fell around her like diamond droplets, filling her with so much pleasure at her escape that she thought she might burst. Beyond the creek lay an open field where she could push Lightning flat out and no one could catch her. She would ride across it and into another world, ride over the horizon and into oblivion.

Then she saw him appear. Mentor. He stood ahead of her, straight in the path. She hauled back on Lightning's reins, trying to halt him before he ran down her only friend. Lightning was responsive, but not quick enough to avoid a collision. The two of them, girl and horse, ran through Mentor as if he were a ghost.

Dell turned the horse, got him under control, and trotted back to where Mentor waited patiently, none the worse for being run through.

"What's gotten into you?" His voice was stern.

"I'm . . . I'm sorry, Mentor. I didn't see you in time." She was wet with bloody sweat, her hair hanging in dark damp strands around her face. The horse was breathing heavily, foam dropping in huge globs from his mouth. He lifted his head, hoping to take off again on a run, prancing yet, unable to still himself.

Mentor walked closer and put his hand on the horse's nostrils. Immediately Lightning settled and hung his head as if full of patience now, eager to please the old man.

It was as if Mentor had touched her, too. She could not remember why she had been racing the poor horse and why it was so important to treat him that way. She remembered being upset over Ryan, but she didn't know when that had turned into a nightmare about the giant Predator. She slid off the saddle, holding onto the reins, and stood shakily. It was as if all the bones below her waist had liquefied. She held onto the stirrup to keep from falling on her face.

"I don't know what happened," she said. "I was riding, just riding along slowly, and then . . . I thought . . . Oh, Mentor, what's wrong with me?"

He came to her aid and helped her sit on the ground. He took the reins and patted the horse's neck, calming him further. "You can't do this," he said.

"I know! I didn't mean to. Something came over me and I . . . I . . . got scared."

"You shouldn't have left your house. Your family is worried sick about you. They asked me to find you and bring you home."

She looked up at him guiltily. "I didn't think it would matter. I wanted to be alone with Lightning. He's my . . . my friend."

"I'm your friend, too, Dell. And I'm telling you that you can't go off on a whim. You can't give in to whatever urge strikes you. It's dangerous. It's what Predators do. Dell, do you hear me? You're treading down the wrong path. It could lead to your destruction."

"I'm sorry, Mentor." She wiped sweat from her face and then dried the bloody dampness on her jeans. She was as tired as she'd ever been and wondered if she could even stand up. She was hungry, too, her veins screaming for blood.

What might have happened if Mentor hadn't found her? How far might she have gone; to what lengths might she have driven her animal in order to escape a phantom?

"You could have killed the horse," he answered her thought. "You might have run him until he died."

"No!" She struggled to her feet and reached out for Lightning. She fell against him, her head against his side, and put an arm over his back. "I'd never hurt him."

"Yes, Dell, you would. You were out of your mind. You were vampire only and there was no human left in you. Don't you feel it? Don't you even now want to lash out at me for stopping you? For keeping you away from the thrill of the ride and the slap of the wind against your face?"

She admitted to herself that he was right. There was a tiny part of her that wanted to mount the horse again and whip him into a run so they could cross the pasture as fast as possible. She looked behind her, searching for shadows, feeling a touch of panic again and a fear that someone was watching.

"The dream came to you again," he said. "You had The Maker on your back."

"Yes." She hugged the horse closer and shivered. "What happened, Mentor? What's wrong with me?"

"Get on your horse and let me lead you back to his stall." He helped her into the stirrup and then into the saddle. The horse raised his head, eyeing Mentor as if for direction.

As they walked slowly back into the woods and across the creek, Mentor explained to her the way desires would take hold and, unless she squelched them, would override every human caution and lead her into violent action. It might be riding a horse too hard or it might be finding a weak human and being filled with a craving she could not control. She was a Natural only as long as she disciplined herself and held herself accountable for everything she did. She must not let fleeting thoughts of pleasure lead her toward excess. It ended with blood and death.

He told her of his meeting with Ross, the Predator leader who supplied their blood every week. He told her how Predators engaged in wanton gratification, how they were smart enough not to get themselves in a bind and be caught, but that they took whatever they wanted when they wanted it. It was this tendency to live larger than life that filled them with violence and caused them to attack, even though they might have refrigerators full of blood, chilled and cleaned and neat.

Did she want to be like Ross? Did she want to leave her family behind in their struggle to live decently and without doing harm upon the Earth? Was being a vampire so thrilling that it superseded morality and good judgment?

Properly chastised, Dell told him no, she did not want to live that way. She did not want the life of the real vampire, the deadly intruder in the night, the monster who lived in madness and depravity. She did not want to hurt Lightning or worry her parents. She would never do this again. She promised.

Yet, in the depths of her being, she felt the pinch and the tug of need that prompted her to add, "Mentor, will you help me? What if I'm not strong enough to resist?"

"I'll help you as much as I can," he said, walking ahead and to one side so the horse could follow. "That's why I came here at your family's urging. But in the silence of the night, in the privacy of your room in your home, the real choice is left up to you. I may not always be available to stop you. Now that you know there's a danger, you'll have to be on the lookout for it yourself. In the end, Dell, we are all on our own."

"Even you?"

"Even after all these years and despite whatever wisdom I've been able to glean . . . yes, even me."

18

Alan sat alone in his locked car, nausea still rising in his throat and making him sick. What he had witnessed at the isolated ranch house was nothing short of astonishing. It wasn't simply murder. It was brutal and evil, the most contemptible thing he'd ever seen happen to another human being. No one bit out another's throat! Jeffrey Dahmer, maybe, but no one else he had ever heard of. And Dahmer had been some kind of aberrant monster himself.

Upton, with his volumes of lore, was right. There were creatures walking the Earth who should not exist. They killed wantonly, taking life without a thought. And Upton wanted to be like that. He wanted to live forever even if he had to kill over and over again to remain living. What did that say about him, except that he was as corrupt and insane as the monster Alan had seen murdering the two women?

Turning the ignition, Alan looked around at the bare streets under the pools of lamplight and wondered where he could find a phone. He must call the police and report what he'd seen. He wouldn't be able to get involved, so he would have to make the call anonymously.

Ten blocks back into the city he saw a pay phone outside a closed convenience store, pulled in, and, after twice dropping quarters from his shaking hands, managed to dial 911. He told them where the house was located, what was going on inside it, and described the killer, who obviously owned the house.

He hung up abruptly, got into his car, and drove as fast as he could without getting a ticket to Bette's house.

He knocked on the door. When she didn't answer right away, he tried the doorknob. It was unlocked. He let himself in, calling to her. "Bette?"

He found her still sleeping on the sofa in the living room. She had not moved since he'd checked on her earlier. She had not changed her work clothes. She still wore a white lab jacket over her prim white blouse and dark brown, calf-length skirt. He shook her awake. "Are you all right?"

She blinked at him and sat up groggily. She brushed hair back from her face. "How long have I been sleeping?"

"All evening, I think."

She pulled at the sleeve of her lab coat. "I didn't even take this off. I must not have had dinner . . ."

"Are you sick?"

"No. I'm hungry." She hesitated, bringing a hand to her bosom and laying it flat between her breasts. "I don't think I'm sick. I must have been more tired than I thought."

He sat with her at the little kitchen table while she made herself a cold-cut sandwich and poured a glass of milk. "You're sure you don't want something?" she asked.

He raised his hand, tasting the remains of a dinner that had come up again. "No, no, thank you. Bette, who was that old man who came here tonight? Was he a friend of yours?"

"What old man?"

Alan felt an alarm go off. "The old man. The one who came here tonight." She still looked confused. "I didn't tell you, but I was outside watching the house. I saw the old man walk down the street here to your house. You let him in. After a little while he came out again. I rushed in here to see if you were all right, and found you sleeping soundly. I left again, following him. I had to know where he was going, who he was."

Bette shook her head as she sat at the table, turning the glass of milk around and around, watching the wet circle it made as water condensed on the outside of the glass. "I . . . I must be sick or something. I remember coming home and putting down my purse and car keys. I think I was very tired. I must have let in someone. I think I remember going to the door when there was a knock, but . . . I'm just . . . having trouble remembering what it was about."

"Never mind. At least he didn't hurt you. Is he someone you know? You have to think, Bette. It's important."

She raised her gaze to meet him. "I guess I know some old men. Friends of my father's from the neighborhood. There's Mr. Chang, who runs the Chinese store. And Mr. Graber, who operates a barber shop."

"Well, this old man has a secret. You need to think about who he was.'"

"What do you mean?"

"I followed him from your house, all the way outside of town, to another man's house. I had to walk about two miles, following him when he got out of a bus and started off. He would have seen me in my car. He went to a house way the hell out in the middle of nowhere, outside of Dallas. He met with a younger man in a huge, isolated ranch house. Anyway, when he left the house, I started to follow him again. Then I heard screams."

"Screams? Alan, I don't know what you're talking about."

"Screams, Bette, people screaming. There were two women in the house with the younger man, the owner of the place. I heard them screaming, so I hurried back and looked through the front windows. They were being . . . he was . . ."

"What? What did you see?" She was leaning forward, gripping his hand on the table.

"He bit them," Alan said, knowing how absurd it sounded, how it wasn't believable. He wouldn't have believed it either, had he not seen it with his own eyes.

"Bit them?"

"On the neck. He . . . tore at their necks with his teeth."

"My God. Did you call the police?"

"As soon as I could find a phone. But, Bette, what about the old man? He left you here, he went to a killer's house, and then he vanished, and I mean he *vanished*, as far as I can tell, into thin air. I was behind him and he was on the side of the road and then suddenly he wasn't."

Bette sat back. This reminded her of the stranger who had appeared and then disappeared in her kitchen the night before. Remembering that incident made her shiver where she sat. "What did he look like?"

"You saw him! He was here."

"Alan. What did he look like? Was he Chinese?"

Though puzzled, Alan complied and told her. "No, he was an old white man. He was about my height, wide in the shoulders, white hair that was kind of frazzled, like it was always windblown, deep creases on his face. He looks like he's eighty."

"That's him," Bette whispered, bringing a hand to her lips to hide her horror.

"Who? Graber?"

"No. Graber's a little Black man, bow-legged, you'd know him right off. I'm talking about the man who was here last night. In my kitchen. When you knocked and scared him off. That's who you're talking about."

Alan didn't understand. "But he was here last night, too. He knocked on the front door, and you let him in. I saw you. Why would you do that?"

"I never would have let him in."

"But . . ."

"Alan, I wouldn't have let him in. He isn't real.

He's some kind of . . . some kind of . . . I don't
know! A spirit. A golem. A devil."

"Do you think that's why you don't remember he
was here and why you slept so long?"

He saw she was trying to think back to discover
any trace of the meeting. She shook her head finally.
"I just can't remember. What did he do to me? Why
can't I remember?"

She began to cry, and Alan scooted his chair
around the corner of the table and held her in his
arms as she sagged against him. He didn't want to
say what he thought, but he knew he had to, no
matter how crazy it sounded. There was no one else
he could confide in.

"I think he's a vampire," he said, getting the worst
of it out. "The other man, the killer of the two
women—he was one, I know he was by the way
he . . . by how he killed. And I think the old man is
one, too."

He expected Bette to refute him, to tell him he had
seen too many movies, that he was imagining things
and letting his judgment get twisted. He was surprised when she stopped crying, shuddered in his
arms, and said, her face buried in his shirtfront, "I
think you're right. That's what he must be. He's a . . .
vampire. It's how he can be there one minute and
then wink out. That's why he could come to my
house tonight and make me forget he'd ever been
here."

"Of course, on the other hand," Alan said, hoping
to dismiss his own theory, "there's no such thing as
vampires. We're taking what little evidence we have
and leaping to one hell of a conclusion. We have no
rational explanation, so we're making one up."

"Are we?" She drew away from him and stared
into his eyes. "And the man who devours women is
nothing more than a demented killer, is that it? The
man who emerged from nowhere into my kitchen,
then just as swiftly left it, the man who came for a
visit that I can't even recall—that man's just a magi-

cian, a hypnotist. Does that make any sense either? Is it more logical? Why is one explanation more reliable than another? Because it's respectable and rational? Because that's how we've been taught to look at reality? Or could the myths that last for hundreds or thousands of years have some kind of basis in truth?"

Alan couldn't answer her. He had been reading about vampires. Was on a mission to find one, and that could cause him to deduce he had seen them, just because he was predisposed to seeing them. His was the kind of investigation that only produced bad science and tainted evidence. But what about Bette, who understood more than he that the world wasn't always as it seemed? If she agreed with him and the evidence, no matter how it was gathered, pointed toward it, then perhaps it really was vampires.

Except that the idea, the conclusion, was too crazy. If he accepted it, he would have to rearrange his whole notion of what life was, what being alive meant, and how the world was constructed. If the world admitted creatures who lived on blood and never died, then there might be miracles, a spirit world, a true God and a calculating Satan. There might be leprechauns, for all he knew, and water sprites, and fairies, and ogres.

If the world admitted vampires into reality, there could be *anything* . . . and . . . everything, some of which no one had ever imagined yet. That was why science fought so hard against superstition. If a thing could not be proven by repeated experiment, then it was not a verifiable truth, but merely an odd aberration. If an apple falls from a tree once, it must always fall from any height, for gravity is dependable, it doesn't go away. There is no other explanation for gravity the way there might be other explanations for what he and Bette had seen and experienced.

He spoke his thoughts aloud, "If it happens again and again, so that we can cross out other possibilities, we might be onto something. I'm not sure we should be saying what something is, beyond all doubt, just yet. I need to investigate more."

"I don't think that would be a good idea, Alan."

"Why? Because I might be hypnotized and have my own throat torn out? You've got a pretty good point. But I have other reasons to pursue this."

"What other reasons?"

"Didn't you wonder why I came up here to find out about the strange blood shipments you discovered?"

"I thought you missed me." She gave him a weak smile.

He kissed her then and said, "I did miss you. Terribly. But there's something else I haven't told you."

"Tell me."

He moved his chair back. "Go ahead and eat your sandwich. This will take a while. And when I'm done, you may not like me very much anymore."

"That could never happen." She took a napkin from beside her plate and neatly layered it over her lap. "Nothing," she said, "could make me like you any less."

He thought about that for a moment before he began to laugh and she joined him. Nothing could make her like him *less*! That could be taken in two ways, one not so flattering. "I'm going to marry you one day," he blurted. "I really am."

She smiled enigmatically and lifted half her sandwich to her lips. "I don't do Houston," she said, before biting into the bread.

"Then maybe I'll learn to do Dallas."

"I was afraid you'd say that."

He drank from her milk, set the glass back into its wet ring on the tabletop, and prepared to tell her about Charles Upton and the strange covenant they'd made.

Outside, in the dark rectangle of window over the stove, neither Alan nor Bette noticed a figure pressing its face against the pane of glass. The face stared at them unblinkingly. No telling breath fogged the window, for no aspiration was taking place in the being's lungs. There was no heartbeat ticking in the chest of the beast that watched and listened just beyond the thin barrier, glaring at the couple.

* * *

Ross sensed the advance of strangers coming to interrupt him long before he heard the sirens and the crunch of tires over his gravel drive. They were miles away, but they were coming, he knew that for certain.

Immediately he was reminded of the presence he'd felt near his house. It was when Mentor was leaving. Mentor had told him no one was there. And he had been too dazzled by the thought of taking the two women waiting on the sofa to sharpen his senses and discover the intruder.

Now, he was furious, both at Mentor and whoever had been outside his home. A stranger, a *human* must have seen something. He must have called the police.

Ross moved swiftly to the two dead women, lifting both bodies onto his shoulders, and he strode through the house to the back, pushing open the door with his mind. He rushed into the night with his burdens. He took them acres behind the house, dropping them like the garbage they were. They rolled over scaly dry ground into a natural gully. Coyotes and other wild predators would take care of the rest.

He was back into the living room of his home in seconds, cleaning blood from the Spanish tile floors. He finished the job quickly, licking at the pools and splatters the way a cat laps at a dish of milk. He took the stained ottoman and stuffed it into a closet in a bedroom at the rear of the house. He could dispose of it later. Back in the living room, he surveyed his work and found it good. Without using every available forensic tool, the police would never suspect there had been a slaughter.

He met the solitary policeman at the door, let him in, offered him coffee, asked what he was doing this far from the city. While Ross was talking, he tapped the deputy's mind and plucked from it every shred of suspicion.

Once the county sheriff's car had left, Ross, still furious at the intrusion and the accusation he'd found in the policeman's mind, went out the front door and walked all around his home. He found a man's scent near the windows. It was very distinct, filled with fear and loathing. It was strongest behind the stand of cypress at the corner of the house. Checking further, following the scent, he found evidence of human effluence.

Ross howled, opening his mouth wide and baying as a wolf does at the moon.

He would trace this scent if it took him the rest of the night. He would follow it to its home and find the man who had dared come onto his property, leer through the windows, and then call in the authorities after he'd evidently seen the two women die.

And now here he was, pressed against the little foreign woman's window, watching them. She was Bette Kinyo, the woman interfering in his blood bank operations. The man was her lover, a doctor named Alan.

His lips pulled back from his teeth in an automatic gesture of threat, but he swallowed the growl threatening to erupt. He had come merely to find the unwise human who had invaded his private space and dared to report his activities. He would decide when and how to take him later. First, he wanted to know what the man knew. He wanted to see how much he would tell the woman.

He really wanted to play with both of them. Watch and intrude the way he had been intruded upon. Learn their secrets and in the end display his intimate knowledge of their lives before he dispatched them to the Devil. Nothing, at the moment, could give him greater pleasure.

He sank back from the glass, vaporizing into the molecules of a thin fog, and insinuated himself beneath the tiny crevice at the bottom of the kitchen door.

Once inside, he wafted into a corner near the humming refrigerator, curling around its side until he was behind it. From there he listened, and what he heard increased his fury until his molecules danced like starbursts of electrical energy giving off cold heat and light.

How he hated humans. He could not remember what it had been like to be one. Sometimes he convinced himself that he had never been one, but was always Predator, always since the beginning of time.

He settled down again, resting at the base of the wall behind the black coils of the refrigerator's condensing unit.

He heard the man talking about a billionaire in Houston who was dying of a disease and wanted to find a way to beat it and beat death at the same time. That kind did not deserve eternal life. The diseased. The old and weak. The greedy and impure. They should die and do the world a favor.

The humming of the machine so close to him lulled him a little and the edge of his anger subsided to mere disgruntlement. He listened to the couple's idle talk about searching for vampires and the making of a research center and the possibility of life after death. Part of Ross' attention wandered to the window over the store. He sensed something approaching there and began to concentrate so that he might discover what or who it was.

His fury returned when he realized it was another vampire. It was another Predator, in fact. He could sense the being's frightful power. He was out there, infringing on territory already inhabited by Ross.

The creature was a Predator, but had not supped in days. He was hungry, but he was not coming to kill and feed. He wasn't looking for would-be victims in the foreign woman's house.

It was a hungry Predator who had stopped preying. Only one of them was fool enough to do that. *Mentor.* Always where he wasn't supposed to be. Always judgmental and grating on the nerves. And now he was calling to Ross, requesting he leave his hiding place and come outside.

So you want to pow-wow, thought Ross. *You track me down and get in my way all the time, you ass.*

Ross did not want to leave his cozy little spot behind the machine where the humming vibrations soothed him, where the darkness and privacy were so appealing. He had more to learn about the humans' plans. He had wanted just a taste of the woman with the short, shiny hair and moist, slanted, beautiful eyes.

Trust Mentor to throw his designs into chaos.

He would have to come out, leave the house, find out why he was being summoned. He would relish telling Mentor that even though he might have cleared the woman's mind about Strand-Catel's blood shipments, the man who called himself Alan was right there to remind her and to give back her memories. He should have wiped both their minds to insure they'd leave the blood bank alone. How would Mentor like failing for a change? How would he like knowing he was not infallible and that he could not control humans nearly as well as he thought?

The couple rose from the table and exited the kitchen. Ross spread out along the floor, sliding from beneath the refrigerator, and out again on the side nearest the back door where he flowed at the couple's heels. His fog-self curled and edged over the threshold into a hall where they had disappeared. He rose up in the shape of a head with eyes that sought after them. Then the fog folded onto itself and slid underneath the door like a regretful lover. In a second he was himself again, housed in flesh, and scowling fiercely at Mentor.

"Who asked you to come here? I thought I was through with you for the night."

"They're harmless," Mentor said, ignoring Ross's rude sarcasm.

"The man saw me take the two women. He was the presence I asked you about at my house. You lied to me, and I took your word for it. Not very trustworthy, are you?"

Mentor looked surprised at the news. He hesitated a moment before saying, "I can make him forget he was there and that he saw anything."

"The way you made the woman forget? She brought up the memories again when the man reminded her."

"I'll do a better job this time."

"And why shouldn't I just cut off their heads and throw them into an alley instead?"

"You are the beast you are because you're able to ask that question, Ross."

"One day you're going to go too far." Ross stepped closer as if to embrace the old vampire in a kiss.

Mentor smiled and his incisors emerged, large and deadly in the reflected light from the window. "I already have. Hundreds of years before you were born. I have gone entirely too far to ever turn back now, and too far to be intimidated by the likes of you."

Ross reconsidered a confrontation. He hated to admit that Mentor could frighten him. As boastful as he sounded, he knew any fight with Mentor could not have a predicted outcome. Mentor might very well bind him long enough to set him afire.

"All right," he said, "I'll let you handle this one more time, and if it doesn't work, you have to step out of the picture and let me get rid of them. They're just . . . just . . ."

"Pests? That's what you feel about all humans, isn't it? Inferior and useless unless they're doing what you want or providing you with blood."

Ross began to shimmer and disappear. He sent one last thought to Mentor. *I warn you. This is the last chance they'll have.*

* * *

Mentor sighed and turned to the woman's Japanese garden. He walked to the bench and sat beneath the willow limbs. They rustled sweetly in a breeze, brushing gently and softly against his sagging shoulders. He sat looking at the raked swirls of white gravel glowing in the moonlight like a pale river snaking through the darkness. He studied the shadows cast by the large boulders. They were alien mountains rising in a white sea.

He would not intrude into the house and the lives of the couple just for the moment. He was tired of dealing with people. It had been a long night and there were hours yet until dawn.

When he thought of the woman, Bette, he felt a quickening in his chest. She was nothing like the human woman he'd loved and lost in the past, but something about her made his passion rise. When he'd entered her mind earlier and searched for the memories to erase, he had felt comforted. The soul which had created the garden he now sat in was unusually humane. He had discovered none of the bitter ugliness that often swamped the minds of most adult humans. Her mind was as clean and straight-forward as any he'd ever been inside. It was *good*. A rare mind, unlittered by the folly of self-aggrandizing or bits of evil stimuli that led to evil deeds.

He shook his head slowly and put his hands on his knees. His shoulders fell further until he was hunched. He had deadened his emotions for so many years it was a miracle anyone could have stirred him. He didn't know if he should be grateful or angry. To love was too human. It was too fraught with the possibility of rejection, danger, and loss. He had never honestly wanted to love a woman again.

He sighed heavily once more and closed his eyes. Ross would certainly destroy her, and the man, too, given the chance. There had been others who ferreted out the existence of vampires, and it was Ross and his minions who had dispatched them without a qualm. He might even have done it tonight if Mentor hadn't halted in his walk to the stables with Dell and felt the alarm Ross projected once he'd entered the woman's house.

Mentor must do something with the couple. And he must do something about his burgeoning feelings for the woman. She was human. She already loved someone. He had no right to interfere with that part of her life.

He turned his head, straightened his shoulders, and looked toward the house. The lights were out. They had retired for the night. He wouldn't go to them now. He feared he'd find them in a bliss that could blind him with the truth of his deprivation.

Better to return to his own home where thoughts of the woman might dissipate. He could come back just before the sun rose over the city. If only he could sleep. Sleep and forget.

He stood, pushing aside the willow branches, and stepped into the moonlight. It was times like these when he wished he could fly away and never come back in touch with either man or vampire.

He had not slept in a century, his attention always alert and active, on the job to rescue others from their dementia and bad choices. He had never run away.

He glanced up into the clear sky to the stars. God had forsaken them. Perhaps vampires were not his creatures and he had nothing to do with their creation or their future. None of them might be worthy of redemption. They might have to roam the Earth until all humans had died, and all animals, and then, finally, their kind would die, too. It would be a mercy.

He thought at times, when he tried to communicate with the source of all power and all life, that one day the Creator would respond to him. He didn't just hope for communication, but believed with all his heart that one day he'd be answered. As yet, the Creator remained silent.

19

The morning after her wild ride, Dell apologized to her parents for disappearing. She admitted she didn't know what had gotten into her. Tears came to her eyes and she began to stutter until her mother put her arms around her and said, "Dell, you're going to be all right now. We don't want to hold you down. We just don't want you to get into trouble, so that's why we called Mentor to help."

"I know, Mom. It's a good thing he came. I'm glad you sent for him."

Her mother gathered the papers she needed to take back to the office and took up her purse. "I'll try to get off early," she said.

Dell knew she didn't want her left alone. "Don't worry, Mom. I'll stay home."

Her father entered from the hallway, tucking his shirt into his slacks. He smiled at her. "Another day, another dollar," he said cheerfully. She realized, not for the first time, how the years passed, but her father never aged. He seemed not that many years older than she was now.

"Maybe I should get a part-time job," Dell said, feeling her parents' weariness of going to work every day, always struggling to make ends meet.

"You stick to the books, young lady. We'll bring home the sausage."

Dell laughed. "Bacon, you mean."

He wrinkled his nose. "Ugh. I don't remember what bacon tastes like. Kind of thick and greasy, I think. But sausage, now . . ."

The thought of cooked animal meat made Dell want to gag. She hurried out the door to catch the bus, waving at her parents as they made for the cars.

At school all Dell could think about was the Loden party and Ryan sitting next to Lori on the sofa, watching the kids begin their blood rituals. When she'd decided to show up and blast off at Lori, she thought her aims were pure. She would save Ryan from getting involved in something stupid and dangerous. But the truth was more complicated. She had been jealous, the jealousy fueling her flight with Lightning across the night landscape later in the evening.

She knew she really had to get herself under control. It was as if she were in a maze, zigzagging down pathways that led her to dead ends where she had to turn around and find her way back again to another route.

Cheyenne stopped her in the hall at school and said, "What have you been doing, Dell? I know you go horseback riding and like that, but you could call me. My mom said maybe you're depressed and need some St. John's Wort tea."

Panic rose in Dell. She had forgotten her friends. She needed excuses all the time now. It was harder to straighten out her affairs and keep the humans happy.

"Tell your mom I'll think about that." She smiled, trying to make light of her absence from Cheyenne's life.

"So what's up? I heard you made a little racket at one of Loden's parties last night."

"You heard about it?"

Cheyenne nodded, clutching her books to her chest as they walked down the hall to classes. "Lori's telling everyone."

"Lori needs to keep her mouth shut." Anger

bloomed in Dell, threatening to get out of hand. She tried to soften her voice. "I mean, Lori's kind of silly, isn't she?"

"Crazy, if you ask me," said Cheyenne. "So, what was the deal?"

"You know the new guy, Ryan? I think he might be in your trig class."

"I know him. Real cute, tall, from North Dallas?"

"That's him. He asked me out."

"No way!"

"I turned him down, I don't know why, don't ask me why. So he went out with Lori last night, and I found out where she'd taken him. I got hot about it, I guess. You know what goes on at Loden's parties."

Cheyenne made a face. "Boy, do I. You know Shirley Lott? They pulled her into their group. She went from straight As to failing in one semester. She looks like a hag now, all black long skirts and raggedy old tops. Talk about someone who needs St. John's Wort."

The bell rang and Dell hurried into her classroom, waving at Cheyenne as the other girl sprinted down the hall.

I know what I'll do, Dell thought. *Before we go out for real, I'll ask Ryan to go riding.* She had to make sure he wasn't going to get mixed up with the Loden bunch. *And maybe on Sunday I'll go swimming at the pool with Cheyenne.*

In the hallway after their class together, she saw him watching her. She smiled and walked close to him. He had seen her passionate side at the party. Now he'd get a chance to see the real Dell, the one who was beginning to fall for him. "You ever ride a horse?"

"A horse? Sure, since I was a kid."

"Would you like to meet me after school and ride? I've got a horse at the Dove Stables, south of Dallas. It's between here and Ennis. Five o'clock?"

"I don't have a horse," he said.

"They'll rent you one. We'll go riding so we can talk. Okay?"

She hurried to her next class feeling triumphant. She knew she could get him away from Lori. She could save him from the "vampyre" scene.

There were so many things she could tell the kids in Loden's group, secrets that would stand their hair on end and give them nightmares. She ought to bring a Predator to one of their rave music, bloodletting parties and let them see for themselves what being a vampire was really all about. They'd wet their pants. She sort of understood the lure, sure she did. She knew they wanted more, something supernatural, something different. But what they were headed into wasn't the way. She'd be damned if she'd stand by and watch Ryan fall into their hands.

She knew what Mentor would say. He'd warn she was interfering in the lives of humans out of selfish motives. Maybe she was. She liked Ryan a lot. But she felt she had to do this. She wouldn't tell him the truth—heavens no. Not about vampires. Not about herself. But she needed to make him understand. She didn't know exactly what she'd tell him, but she had to do something.

* * *

It was ten after five when Dell saw Ryan pull up in the parking lot at Dove Stables. For a few minutes she feared he would stand her up. He almost had a girlfriend now. What did he need with someone who had rejected him outright the first time he tried asking her out, someone who tried to bust up his date?

She was relieved and let out a happy sigh when she saw him park. He got out of the car slowly, a tall, lanky boy with hair that was long on top and unruly where it fell across his brow. He squinted toward the stables where she stood waiting for him. He smiled and came through the gate and down the well-worn path to where she waited. She even liked the way he walked. She'd seen old ranchers walk that way, bronco riders, horse trainers. It wasn't so much a bowlegged gait as it was a leisurely rolling motion from hip to hip, with long legs moving at a graceful, slow pace. It was definitely a cowboy walk, but regal for all that.

All he lacked to fit the part of cowboy was a Stetson hat. He already had on the washed-out blue jeans and softly worn tan leather boots.

"Hi," he said, reaching her side. "Sorry I'm late. Traffic. People getting out of work."

She smiled up at him. "That's okay. I haven't been here long." She was lying. She'd come to the stables straight from school. If she'd still been human she'd have had enough time to have drunk two Pepsis and go to the bathroom three times.

"Well, which one is your horse?"

Dell turned to the stables and led him to Lightning. She told him the horse's name, then laughed. "I should rename him. He's too old to be a racehorse or have a name like that. But when he wants to, he really can take off for me." She almost winced, recalling how she'd run him nearly to death.

"Lightning's a fine name," Ryan said, rubbing the horse's neck just back of the ears. "How you doing, boy?"

"Here's one I picked out for you," she said, pointing at a bay two stalls down. They walked to the bay, and Ryan began to rub it down along the neck, too.

"It seems friendly," he said. "I've been riding since I was little. My grandfather owns a ranch. Cattle, a few horses, you know," he said by way of explanation. "But still, I like a quiet, friendly horse. Riding's no fun when the horse wants to act like a fiend out of hell's gate."

"Have you ever gone on the trail ride across Texas they have in March?" She also reached out to pet the bay, on the opposite side of the neck. It shied a bit until she reached out with her mind to soothe it.

"No, but I bet it would be fun." He gave her an

interested glance. "What about you? Ever gone on the ride?"

Dell shook her head. "I never had a horse until now. I got Lightning as a birthday present."

"Happy birthday!"

She smiled. "Oh, it was days ago, but thanks."

"So you're fifty-two now, huh?"

"Eighteen!"

"Sorry. Eighteen. I knew that."

Once on the trail, riding their horses, Ryan broke the silence first. "So, what did you want to talk to me about?"

"You might think I'm out of place, doing what I did last night when you were with Lori, but . . ."

"No, go ahead."

"It's just that those kids are into some weird stuff. It wasn't any of my business, but you're new here and I was worried about you."

"You mean not everyone drinks blood?"

She looked over at him, surprised. She saw he was about to burst out in laughter. "It's not funny," she said.

He sobered. "No, it's not funny, I guess."

"It's . . . I think the blood stuff is dangerous. People could get, well, they could get really sick doing that."

"I know. I didn't partake after you left. Not that I was going to anyway."

But will you? she wanted to ask. "Ryan, that's what they do," she persisted. "It's part of who they are."

"Look, if you're worried I'll turn into a vampire, rest your mind. I've started reading Stoker's *Dracula*. The nightlife doesn't appeal."

She smiled to herself. He'd not get much from Stoker. "They might not want you hanging with them if they find that out."

He shrugged. "Maybe."

They had reached the little creek. Dell pulled up Lightning and got out of the saddle. "Let's let them drink," she said.

Ryan dismounted and led his horse to the sparkling water. Sunbeams glanced off its surface and threw glitters of light into the nearby stand of shadowy weeping willows. A noisy bluejay flitted from branch to branch high up, making a racket. A mama bird, no doubt, protecting her nest of eggs.

The horses snuffled and bent to the water, wetting their front hooves in the stream's edge. In the distance, the sun was beginning to set, a flaming burnt-scarlet ball radiating purple and pink against low clouds. Dell thought there couldn't be prettier sunsets anywhere else in all the world.

"Why do you really care if I get into the vampire stuff," he asked suddenly.

Taken aback, Dell stared into the running water of the creek. She didn't wish to look at him and betray herself. "It's just that I know them," she said, "and it's the danger in it, that's all."

"You wouldn't want me to get sick," he said, more softly.

She felt as if he were peeling her open the way someone shreds the skin of an orange to expose the soft center. "I wouldn't want anyone to get sick. Lori. You. Those others. I think it's just a dumb thing to be doing, that's all. It's not very responsible."

"So it's not me."

She turned to him and saw he'd moved from one side of his horse next to where she stood. "Not you, what?" Ignorance was always a good screen.

"Not me you wanted to save. I'm incidental. This ride was meant to be just a plain old warning that you'd want to give to anyone new in school, right?"

She was looking in his face, into his eyes, and she couldn't lie to him. She found she'd stopped breathing. She didn't need to breathe and in times of distress or during lapses where she daydreamed, she forgot she was supposed to be human. She took in a showy breath and let it out. She looked away from him, turned, began to rub down Lightning's coat.

"I guess so," she said, answering him finally. "I guess new kids need some warning."

"Dell, Dell, Dell."

She turned back to him.

"You can't lie, so you blow smoke instead. Why didn't you say you'd go out with me when I first asked you? Why did it take Lori and the cult thing to get you to notice me? Lori was a second choice. I don't have any interest in her world. It's you I wanted to be with, until you made it plain you didn't want it."

Tears sprang to Dell's eyes and she had to look down. She couldn't cry in front of him. He'd see her tears were made of other than salty water. "I . . . can't . . ."

"Like me? You can't like me? Am I that terrible? Do I have four eyes or six fingers on each hand? Is there a booger hanging from my nose?"

Now she laughed, and the threat of tears vanished. "I like you," she said, laughing at the face he was making and the gesture of a finger at his nose. "Stop that."

He stepped close and put his hands on her waist, suddenly serious. "We'll try one date. How bad could it be, after the Loden party? We'll see a movie, eat pizza, go to the mall, whatever you want to do this weekend."

"I like movies," she said.

"I won't even kiss you." He let her go and stepped back, his hands raised. "I promise. No funny business. I'm not one of those guys always out to score."

He made her laugh. She loved how he made her laugh. He was telling her serious things in a way that didn't scare them both.

"I don't know if you have to go that far," she said.

"Okay, I take the promise back. Maybe I'll kiss you, maybe I won't." He turned and leaped onto the bay, hauling back on the reins so it wouldn't get skittish. "It was the booger thing, wasn't it? Something about boogers gets girls every time."

They laughed and talked during the rest of their ride together. When they stabled the horses and were at Ryan's car, Dell felt good about everything. Damn what Mentor said. She wasn't going to be lonely and an outcast. She wasn't going to deny herself good times with Ryan. She didn't have to, damnit. She could handle herself. It was her life.

"Friday night, eight p.m.?" He was inside his car, the window rolled down. The way he was looking up at her, the curve of his lips, the sweep of his hair over his forehead, made her want to lean down and kiss him. But she didn't.

"Friday," she said. "Yeah."

She watched him drive away. She wanted to give Lightning a brushing, so she meant to stay a while. And the whole time she'd be thinking about Ryan. How cute he was, how funny and sweet. She wanted to think about how good she felt, better than she'd ever felt before, and how that could not be a bad thing. It was only a date. She wasn't marrying the guy.

What could Mentor say?

* * *

Mentor said nothing. He knew of Dell's interest in her young man, and he kept silent about it. At least a fourth of all vampires fell in love with humans at least once. Some of them kept the relationships until their humans died. A very few turned their lovers into immortals, in order to keep them. But most watched their humans die and grieved so deeply they rarely ever allowed themselves to fall in love that way again.

Mentor had been one of the latter. He'd loved Patrice with all of his soul. He had wrestled for months over whether he should or could make her vampire in order to save her from death. In the end he knew he had to let her go. When she closed her eyes for the last time, she whispered a thank you to him. She had lived with him for fifty years and knew the terror of his life. She did not want to be like him. She wanted instead to die peacefully in her own bed and go to her Creator, whom she believed in totally. She also believed that one day, when he was allowed to end his existence as a vampire, he would be with her again.

Mentor prayed she was right. He hadn't much faith in that future meeting, but he continued to love and miss his wife, and he resisted loving another mortal.

He had warned Dell, and that was all he could do. He could not dictate to her or force her to do something she didn't want. He feared for her, but then he feared for dozens of others like her who had decided to plunge into a love affair with a human. There was nothing he could do.

He had to shake off his regrets because he was close to Bette Kinyo's house, and he had work to do this morning. He had been too careful the last time when he'd entered her mind and tucked her memories away. This time, unfortunately, he would have to do a better job of it or else Ross would murder her. Mentor also had to erase the man's memories as well. Both of them were getting too close to the truth.

As he walked up to Bette's front door, Mentor paused and let his power probe the rooms of her home. He wanted to know where she and the man were, what they were doing. He really did not want to interrupt an intimacy. Truth be told, he didn't want to be here at all. Every time he saw Bette, he was reminded of Patrice, and he seemed to fall in love all over again. He really didn't want to have to contemplate such an event.

As he searched the rooms, he easily found Bette, showering in the bath off her upstairs bedroom. She smelled of soap and lavender shampoo. She diligently washed her trim, healthy body, humming as she did so. But he could not find Alan. He searched again, thinking he had been too interested in finding

Bette and had overlooked the man's scent and presence.

No, he was right. Except for Bette, the house was empty.

Mentor frowned. Where was the man? Now what would he have to do in order to get to him? Ross would surely kill him if he spoke to anyone about what he'd seen at Ross' home. Mentor cared nothing about the man. In fact, he was secretly jealous of both his humanity and the love Bette had for him, but he did not want to see him taken from Bette. He liked her enough to be selfless.

He searched the house supernaturally for a third time, unbelieving that he could not find the man. He had to find out where he'd gone.

He was inside and waiting for her when she came down the stairs dressed for work. Her hair was still damp, falling appealingly across dark eyes that looked on him with dread. She halted on the stairs upon seeing him. "Go away," she said. "I didn't invite you in this time."

"No, you didn't. But something has to be done, Bette. You're in more danger now than ever before. Your life hangs in the balance."

She began to back up the stairs, never taking her gaze off him. "I don't know what you are, but you must leave here," she said.

"Bette, come down the stairs to me."

She paused with a foot poised above a riser behind her. She began to move mechanically down the stairs again until she reached the ground floor. Mentor found it incredibly easy to manipulate the actions of humans. They were no more than puppets under his power.

"Please," she pleaded. "Don't."

"If I'm to save your life I have to, my dear. You're a beautiful woman in the prime of your life. You're engaged in important work. You're too young to die at the hands of my colleague. I'm afraid it's the fault of your young man. He told you information he should never have found out. Neither of you will be allowed to share it."

"We're right, aren't we? You're a vampire." Her eyes were wide and terror-stricken. She began to shake with tremors so that her hands danced on the ends of her arms.

He stared into her eyes, hypnotizing her now, coming close to reach out and touch her pale arms. "I am vampire," he said. "And you must forget I told you so."

It took only seconds, but to Mentor it seemed to be a long voyage beyond time. He found himself lost in her mind's fears. He stumbled through torrents of emotions that shook him and made him fall back before moving forward again, as if against a hard gale. He found all the information that pertained to the blood bank discrepancies, the memories of what she thought of him and of Ross. He found everything that pertained to vampires and every word Alan had said to her. He made sure this time she would not be able to recall them, even if someone were to try to trigger the memories. He was like an electroshock machine, scrambling the electronic impulses of her brain in a specific area holding these memories. They vanished under his assault, the way memories go dark and die away from electroshock waves.

When he finished, Bette again collapsed from the trauma to her mind. He lifted her gently and set her down on the sofa, straightening her legs, slipping off her shoes. She had such small, delicate feet, such shapely legs. He drew back from her. She would wake in minutes and remember nothing about his visit. And nothing about what Alan had told her.

While in her mind, Mentor found the information he needed to track her lover. It seemed that the man had left her early, going before daylight, driving south to Houston. He ferreted out the man's last name, his profession, where he worked, the name and address of the old man who had sent him on a search for an immortal, and Alan's apartment location in the city.

Before leaving, Mentor stood looking down on the woman. Her face was a little more square and her eyes a little more Oriental, but she did remind him of his beloved Patrice. It was as if Patrice had come back and incarnated into this small Japanese woman—if only he could believe in reincarnation—which he couldn't. Over the years he'd walked the Earth, he'd never had any proof such a thing existed. Still . . . Bette Kinyo bore such a strong resemblance in so many ways. She awakened in him all the old memories, his old feeling of love and tenderness for a woman.

He reached down and brushed the damp hair from her high forehead. He bent from the waist and pressed his lips there, feeling her warmth, tasting the slightly tangy fresh soap scent that lingered on her skin. He whispered, "I hope never to see you again. I don't want to love you."

And then he was gone, vanishing from the room, going in search of Alan Star, the man who would take his fantastic story about vampires back to Houston to a desperate employer eager to believe him.

Ross communicated at a distance, just as Mentor was leaving Bette's house and entering the atmosphere beyond her roof as no more than a wisp of shadow.

"Did you do it?" Ross inquired on a mental wavelength.

"Yes, yes, it's done," Mentor lied, hoping Ross would not discover the man had got away. No one could ever lie to a vampire except another of his kind, one with the power to make it stick. Mentor always tried to be truthful, but he found himself breaking all the rules with Ross.

Mentor left Bette's house and sailed south, flying high above the city like a passing breeze, relishing the feeling of freedom he always experienced when transformed from human flesh into nothing more than molecules of energy.

20

Alan gnawed at worry all the way to Houston. He had begged Bette to come with him. He didn't want to leave her alone. She resisted. "I'm not a child, Alan. I can take care of myself now I know what I'm dealing with," she'd said.

Alan left before she woke, debating whether he should wake her and try again to convince her to accompany him. But he knew Bette well. Once her mind was made up, there was no moving her.

He drove directly from Dallas through the dark morning light to Charles Upton's building in downtown Houston. It was late morning when he arrived, and his stomach growled hungrily. The Styrofoam cup of coffee he'd purchased at a gas station sat in his midsection like a roiling sea of acid. He found a bottle of Tums in the car pocket and shook three into the palm of his hand. He chewed them on the elevator ride up to Upton's penthouse.

It wasn't the empty stomach that caused his real discomfort. He didn't really want to make this report to Upton. He had left the penthouse weeks before believing he was on a wild goose chase for a demented billionaire. And now he was returning with news that the old man was right. There were vampires walking the land—at least that was how it looked. He couldn't be sure. He had to make Upton understand that.

Lately it had seemed to Alan that reality was rapidly shifting. It wasn't just the fact he'd stumbled upon the lair of what appeared to him to be a murderous vampire or that a spiritlike, shape-shifting being had come to Bette and made her forget she was interested in Strand-Catel's blood shipments. No, there were other things going on in the world and being reported by top news agencies that completely baffled Alan.

On the car radio he'd been listening to on the way to Houston he'd heard a report of a UFO in the sky above a farmhouse in Alabama. The farmer had run outside with a video camera. What he taped was being reported as straight fact. The video apparently showed a huge circle of bright light illuminating the farm as it passed over, and once it passed there was deep darkness in the sky, like a black hole, blotting out the stars behind it.

That was odd enough. UFOs reported as if real. Were they? Could they be? If so, what did it say about reality and life on Earth?

On the same news broadcast was a report from China that a "Bigfoot" type creature had been sighted. Left behind were sixteen-inch footprints and tufts of tangled hair.

Either the world was changing, allowing these phenomena that seemed downright bizarre, or else humankind was going insane, maybe suffering from some sort of mass hysteria.

Is that what affected me? he wondered, as the elevator door opened onto Upton's suite. *Am I hysterical and about to report as truth some kind of momentary psychosis that happened while I was outside the big ranch windows?*

Upton's very proper, very British butler was waiting for him. Alan had called before he left Bette's house, saying he was on his way.

"Mr. Upton is waiting to see you, sir," he said, leading Alan through the rooms to the massive bedroom. Upton was propped on pillows in the bed, as he usually was, but his color was high and there was excitement evident in his pale, watery eyes.

Upton threw back the sheet and swung his legs to the side of the bed. He sat straight and looked stronger than Alan had ever seen him.

"Alan! Come in, come in. Are you hungry? You look famished. Please bring Dr. Star some breakfast," Upton commanded his butler.

"Yes, sir."

Alan watched the butler bow formally before leaving the room, presumably to tell the cook to make a meal for him. His mouth watered at the thought of bacon and eggs, and his stomach churned. He burped behind his hand. "Sorry," he said. His mouth tasted of chalk from the indigestion tablets. He frowned.

"Well, sit down. Tell me the news. You found them, didn't you? You wouldn't come here right from Dallas if you didn't have something for me."

"I do have something for you," Alan said, taking one of the ornate French chairs near the bedside. God, how he dreaded telling the old man anything. He sensed something bad would happen once he did. Something he couldn't even predict and most certainly would not like.

Upton clapped his hands together in a prayerful attitude. "I knew it. I knew they were out there. I've dreamed about them, you know. It's as if I'm walking with them in my sleep. I see a big one, just monstrously huge, bearing down on victims in a very dark wooded area where there is a red moon. Can you imagine? It's so real I wake weeping and shaking, scared to death. Because in the dream, or nightmare, if you will, the monster turns on me, finds me hiding, and comes my way. But you don't want to hear about my silly dreams. Tell me, what did you find?"

Alan shivered from the cold air-conditioning vent that blew frigid air down the back of his collar. "I first interviewed the manager of a blood bank in Dallas where there have been some odd shipments out of the city across the state. I was deliberately lied to and misdirected."

"Yes, yes . . ."

"Then I followed a man. It's a long story, but he was suspicious and he seemed to have something to do with the blood bank situation. He went outside of the city. Walking. I had to leave my car and walk, too, to follow. It was night and pretty spooky. He went for miles and then there was a big ranch. He went up to the house."

Upton still had his hands pressed together tightly before his lips. His eyes glittered and behind his hands Alan could see the rictus of his frozen smile. He continued, "When the man I followed left, I stayed behind a few minutes, looking through the ranch house windows. I saw . . ."

"Yes, yes!"

"Murder."

Upton's hands lowered from his face. He gripped the covers around him. His eyes blazed now. "What kind of murder?"

"That's what I've come to tell you. The man inside the house didn't use a weapon."

"No?"

"He tore out the throats of two women with his . . . teeth."

Upton sucked in a big breath and held it.

Alan continued, "Then he . . . he seemed to . . ."

"He drained them of their blood."

"Yes," Alan said, glad he hadn't had to say it.

"You're sure?"

"I was standing right outside the window. I had to stumble away and throw up, it made me so sick."

"He didn't see you?"

"No."

"So what did you do then?"

"I hurried back to where I had my car parked. The man I'd followed had disappeared. In fact, even as I watched him on the road he seemed to . . . disappear.

When I got back into town and found a phone, I called the police."

"You did *what*?" Upton fairly leaped from the bed. His back straightened, his hands flew up, his immovable face showed great shock through wide open eyes. "How could you do a thing like that?"

"But it was murder. I saw . . ."

"If you believe you saw a vampire who killed two people, didn't you stop to consider that by reporting him you were letting him know he'd been observed? Are you out of your mind?"

Alan didn't like the direction the conversation had taken. Upton, so elated, now appeared to be about to have heart attack. He was frantic, clawing his way from the bed, scooting his skinny old legs around until he could slip his feet into black velveteen house slippers. He staggered as he stood. "You have done a terrible thing by calling the authorities. You've let the vampire know someone was there. He'll find you."

"Oh, I don't think . . ."

"He'll find you!" Upton screamed. "And if he finds you, he finds me! What have you done?"

Alan stood, overwhelmed by Upton's fury. When Upton advanced on him, he began to retreat to the bedroom door. "I don't see why you're so upset. He didn't see me, didn't even know I was there so he wouldn't know who I was, who called the cops."

"Oh, God, you are so naive and ignorant. Didn't you read the material I sent with you? Don't you know what you're dealing with? I never thought you'd do something so stupid."

"Look here, calling me names is uncalled for. I did what you wanted."

"Yes! You found vampires. Yes! But you ruined it by reporting them. Now either the authorities will find out something, or the vampire you discovered will hunt you down."

"That's ridiculous. How would he know . . . ?"

"He's a vampire, Alan. Think about it. He'll know.

And he'll come for you and anyone you told. He'll come for me."

Alan thought of Bette. He had told her first. Was there anything to what the raving Upton was saying to him? Could he be correct? Oh, Jesus, oh, hell, he had to get back to Dallas; he had to warn Bette.

Then it occurred to Alan he was behaving just as crazily as Upton. Hell, he might have been mistaken in what he'd glimpsed through the ranch-house windows. He might have had some kind of medical condition that made him fall into a trance or dreamlike state where he imagined the things he saw. Was he now firmly in control of his faculties and, if so, how could he possibly believe he'd witnessed the acts of a vampire? All his education and training told him there couldn't possibly be such a creature.

Upton's butler entered carrying a tray of fragrant food. Bacon, ham, eggs, grits, toast, orange juice, coffee. Upton said, "Put that down and help me dress."

Alan stood by, unsure what to do. Had he been dismissed?

"Are you . . . are you leaving?" Alan asked.

"Of course I'm leaving. If you're being hunted, I'll be found, too. I can't imagine it would take the creature long to get to us. I don't want to die at the hands of the vampire. I want to find one to help me. I have to go away now, where you won't know where I am, so he can't trace me through you."

Alan began to make for the door. Upton was just as insane as he'd ever been. It had evidently rubbed off.

"I'll call you," Upton shouted. "I want you to go back and find me another one, one less powerful, a young one. Do you hear me? If you want this grant, you'll do as I tell you."

Alan felt for one instant like turning and telling the old man to take his grant money and stuff it where the sun didn't shine. But the impulse passed. He said instead, without turning to face the old man, "I'll do what I can."

"You'll do it, just as I said," Upton shouted again, "and then you're out of this. But right now I advise you to go underground. Get away from everyone you know and tell no one where you are. Do you hear me? No one."

The smell of the breakfast followed Alan as he crossed the living room and entered the elevator for the lobby. He hadn't even had breakfast yet, and he was already dealing with a maniac. A man shouldn't have to do that.

But on the way down in the padded silence of the elevator, he reconsidered Upton's response and his advice. He reconsidered what he'd been telling Upton about there being real vampires in the world and how he'd seen one.

It made a little sense. Not a lot, but a little. He might have stumbled on vampires or he'd run into one of the worst killers in the state of Texas. Upton's response sounded like paranoid ranting. But what if the vampire could find him? If there was a vampire. Or what if it could find Bette? He must return immediately to Dallas and take Bette with him. She wouldn't want to go anywhere or leave her house, but he'd make her. Even if there was a shred of danger, he had to do that.

Paranoid or not, they might be dealing with the supernatural. Who knew how the supernatural worked? Who knew what the UFO was that sent a circle of bright light streaming down over a farm? Who knew what left behind sixteen-inch footprints?

But, more importantly, what did any of them know about the existence and motives of vampires?

* * *

Mentor hovered high over an area just outside the city limits of Houston, Texas. He was near the presence he knew to be Alan Star, and was just zeroing in on his location when he heard an urgent mental call. It was as if a siren went off in his subconscious, wailing . . . screaming for his attention. "Mentor! I know your name. Come to me now."

He paused in his shadowy flight, filtering the voice from all the others that clamored in a cacophony of calls for aid. He found it belonged to a woman. A human woman. *Now what is this about?* he wondered. Not once in a century had he had communications from humans, psychics who had somehow tuned into the channel of his subconscious. It always surprised and unsettled him.

He turned toward the direction where the voice emanated. North of his location. He searched farther and found it came from Dallas. Who . . . ?

She called him again, as if speaking directly into his mind, clearly enunciating every syllable. "Mentor. Come back. Leave Alan alone. We have many things to discuss first."

Bette Kinyo. She reached him over a distance of hundreds of miles. She was indeed an enigma. A gifted enigma.

He gave Alan Star one last moment of his attention, waffled between going directly to him to wipe his mind of all memories involving Ross, but then he sighed inside and turned back North. Bette called for him. This meant she remembered him. Not only that, but she had learned his name.

It took him mere minutes to respond and move his intelligence and the energy of his being to Bette Kinyo's home. He went through the wall into the kitchen where he sensed she would be found. As before, when he'd first ever appeared to her, she had her back to him and her hands deep into a sink of bubbles.

"You called for me?"

She turned purposefully, taking a dish towel to dry her hands. Her eyes were dark and heavy with meaning as she rested her gaze on him. He stood before her in his old man body, the cold old body that sometimes he could cause to contort enough to frighten the life from a mortal. He did that now, scowling fiercely, showing the row of upper teeth and sharp incisors.

* * *

Bette had come awake on the sofa after her session with Mentor. Confused, she staggered up the stairs to the small altar in her bedroom. Falling to her knees before the statue of Buddha, she bowed her head and began to weep. She knew she had been violated in some way, but did not know how or to what extent. She prayed to the god she adored to save her sanity and restore her spirit.

For many long minutes confusion reigned. Her mind skipped about like a child on holiday. She continued to pray. She lit incense and breathed deeply, letting the scent of sandalwood help concentrate her mental processes.

I am strong, she told herself. *I am a child of heaven. I will recall myself and who and what I am. I will overcome this violation and set my house in order.*

After a time her mind did settle, and she was sure the master vampire had come to her home and done something with her memory. There were holes and gaps, leaving her with black images, like overdeveloped photographs. The more she tried to plumb the missing part of her mind, the more panicky she felt until she had a breakthrough and finally, finally, she saw in her mind's eye what she was not supposed to ever recall.

Vampire!

The old man. He had told her he must do it to save her life. She cursed him for the lie. For if she died, she would die knowing all, being queen of her own spirit and soul. She would not live with holes in her mind, vast black holes hiding secrets.

She began to pray to know the master vampire's name. If she could find his name, she could call to him and make him hear her. No one knew Bette had these abilities and sometimes she doubted them herself, but in any dire need she knew she could call upon an innate strength and belief that the world was knowable. In all its permutations. In all its vast multitude of dimensions. She had only to open herself and call out for the world to respond with the answers she needed.

When the vampire had first showed himself to her in the kitchen, she had been aware in a psychic way that he was not human and the visitation was supernatural. Now she went in search of the supernatural, embracing the part of her soul that understood the shadow world beneath the real world.

She first found the vampire, moving more rapidly than the wind to the south. Two hundred miles in the distance. She found him and opened her soul and sent out the distress signal that bore his name. *Mentor.* She had to make him understand he was not the only one who could enter and ransack another's private memory banks. She had found his name within his own being. It was how he described himself. How he had been known, she finally understood, for hundreds of years—or longer. Mentor.

While she waited for him to appear, she rose from her knees, giving thanks to Buddha for his grace, and went down the stairs slowly to her kitchen. She had not washed the dishes. They lay in jumbled disarray on the countertop—cups, saucers, plates, silverware. She ran a sinkful of hot water until steam came up to meet her nostrils. She plunged her hands in, scrubbing hard at the dishes while focusing on the real world of hot water, soap suds, the solid feel of glassware.

When she felt the old vampire at her back, she turned to face him, unafraid. If he killed her, then so be it. She'd made up her mind she must try to stop the violation he intended to do to the man she loved.

He said, "You called for me. I would like to know how you accomplished such a feat."

She said, "You are not the only creature with powers. I called because you must not do to Alan what you tried to do to me. It's evil. And I don't sense that you are as evil as you would like to appear."

"Am I not?" He waited and when she did not reply, he said, "How is it you can reach me when you're not like me? Where does your power come from?"

"Not a vampire, you mean? My power comes from the universe. I depend on my god."

"Would you call yourself an angel?"

She almost laughed. The smile played around her lips as she suppressed the laughter. "No, I'm no angel, Mentor. I'm not supernatural. I'm simply a devoted woman with my own small skills. I have found the pockets of memories you tried to eradicate. I remember the story Alan told me of the vampire who murdered two women. And I remember the problem with the blood bank—that surely has something to do with you. It's why you came in the first place."

"I don't know how you reversed my work," he said, "but this puts you into grave danger. I did what I did only to save you from a horrible fate."

"You must not interfere in my life," she said stubbornly.

"Then I'll have to watch your life taken. I wanted to avoid that."

She turned her head to the side, scrutinizing him. "Why do you want to save me? What am I to you?"

His lips lowered over the teeth, and now he did not look so much fierce as defeated. "Never mind my motives. What do you think you can accomplish by overriding my work and by insisting I come to you? Aren't you afraid at all?"

"I'm not afraid," she said honestly. "I believe we have some kind of connection, you and I. Now we must have an understanding. I've called you here to make a promise. I'll stand by that promise, knowing I forfeit my life if I break it."

"Yes?"

"I won't pursue the discrepancy with the Strand-

Catel Blood Bank. I won't speak of the murders Alan witnessed. I won't bother you the rest of my life. But you must promise never to come to me again to tamper with my mind. You must leave me alone, forever."

"That's an admirable trio of promises, Bette, but what about Alan Star? He's not like you, is he? Not as . . . gifted."

"No, he's not. But I'll prevent him from pursuing you and your friends. He loves me."

The old man glanced aside as if unable to meet her eyes. "I know," he said softly.

"Then is it a deal? I know that if you want to, you can take my whole mind, all of it, and turn it in such a way I'll never be myself again. I know you can kill me as easily as snapping the neck of a little wounded bird. I know your power, Mentor. But if you'll go away and stay away, we will—Alan and I—stay out of your business."

He seemed to think it over. His eyes still would not meet hers. He looked everywhere in the little kitchen except into her face. She felt an overpowering urge to step forward and take him into her arms, to hug him close to assure him all would be all right. It was not the proper urge for one she thought of as an abomination, an enemy, but there it was anyway. The feeling confused her so much she shook her head a little and glanced down at her hands as if seeing them for the very first time. The small, delicate fingers, the little square white nails. She wanted to put those hands on the old man's face and stroke his cheeks in a loving way.

She suddenly turned her back on him in order not to act on the strange urges rushing through her body. She knew he was not causing her to feel this way. It did not come from outside herself, but from inside, in the core of her, and it left her baffled, and a bit afraid.

"You must keep your promises," he said.

She nodded her head, not trusting her voice.

"If you break your vows, the next one who comes

to you will not be me, Bette. It will be one who will suck your very soul from your body and leave you separated from your god. Do you understand me?"

Again she nodded, holding fast to the sink edge with both white-knuckled hands.

"Speak it," he commanded.

"Yes! I understand you. Yes!"

In just seconds she sensed he was gone. She turned, sighing in resignation at the pact she'd made. She clamped her trembling hands together. For now she had saved both herself and Alan.

All she had to do was to convince him he must forget what he'd seen. She hoped he had not yet told Charles Upton. If he had, then her promise was already broken and they were all doomed.

21

Dell walked alongside Ryan through the mall, hoping he would take her hand. Wishful thinking, she told herself, but it would be nice if he did.

They stopped at a booth in the center aisle of the mall and looked at gold jewelry. Ryan picked up a gold heart with scrolled edges, but put it down again quickly. "That's pretty," she said, smiling.

He looked at her. "Yeah, it's nice."

They moved on, mingling with crowds, passing other young couples and groups of kids from their school. "You want something to eat before the movie starts?" he asked.

She glanced over to the food shops and shook her head. Lately, just the smell of real food put her off. She did not want to go near those places, but would suffer it if he was hungry. "No, thanks, but you eat something if you want."

"I'm all right."

They browsed in a bookstore, and he bought her a bookmark imprinted with angels. "Here, to mark your place," he said, handing it to her once they were out of the store.

"Thanks!" She slipped it into her purse, secretly happy that she would possess something he'd given her, a talisman.

As they strolled the mall some more, window

shopping, commenting on clothing, she asked if he were going to college.

"A and M," he said.

"Aggie bound!" She grinned at him. She had thought that was where she would go, too. She had applied long before the change. If she were going to live for more than one lifetime, she would need education. A lot of it. Perhaps she would be a perpetual student, come right down to it. It might be the only way she would stay current during all the decades of whatever society she inhabited. "I'm going there, too," she said. "I was admitted just last week."

"What major?" he asked.

"English literature, at least to begin with. I guess I'll just go for a liberal arts program. I really love libraries, you know? Quiet, clean, so peaceful."

"Good choice. I'll be in veterinary medicine."

"Wow. I hear you have to be on a list for years to get into that. The waiting list is supposed to be impossible."

"I think my parents signed me up when I was in diapers."

She laughed. "So you like animals a lot, huh?"

"Better than people, sometimes. They don't talk back, they don't get jealous, and they don't drive sport utility vehicles."

"What's wrong with sport utility vehicles?"

"They can't do what a pickup truck can in an open field. They're really for looks, most of them."

"I guess that means you like trucks. That's kind of typical Texan, isn't it?" she asked, teasing him.

"What's wrong with that?"

"Nothing, I guess, as long as the truck has a sticker on the bumper that says you're an NRA member."

"Aw, c'mon." He smiled. "I'm refinishing an old truck I keep on my grandfather's ranch. It's a 1952 Ford and ugly as sin, but when I get through, it'll take you wherever you want to go."

"What color will you paint it?"

"I don't know yet. Right now it's gray and rust.

Maybe you can help me out with the color when I get ready to paint it."

"Fuchsia's nice."

"Oh, man."

She laughed happily. "Lime, then. Lime's good."

They talked about college and how they were both happy about going off to school, what they wanted to do when they had degrees, where they might want to live one day. The whole time Dell found herself full of excitement to think they'd be on the same campus.

At show time, they entered the mall theater lobby and he stood in line to buy them popcorn and cold drinks. She just couldn't tell him she wanted nothing without arousing his suspicion. She was learning quickly how to fake the eating of food and drinking of liquids. Sometimes she disposed of things when no one was looking by using her burgeoning skill at sleight of hand. Sometimes she just pretended to sip on a straw until she could set aside the drink. No one ever really watched another person consuming food or drink. It wasn't very difficult to trick the limited vision of a mortal.

He was so sweet to her, she thought, watching him as he paid for the goodies. Not anything like some of the other boys in her school. He wasn't full of ego, wasn't acting like a Romeo out to get whatever he could. He was polite to her, and so honest, his face showing every emotion that crossed his mind.

In the darkened theater seats, she placed her drink in a cup holder and let it sweat. Once in a while she took a handful of popcorn, bringing it to her mouth, then carefully dropping it to the floor. She smiled into the darkness when he slipped an arm around her shoulders and pulled her a little closer to him.

She knew it was crazy, but she really wanted to go a little nuts and kiss him full on the mouth when he wasn't expecting it. She stopped herself, knowing it might throw him a little. She would let him make his own moves, in his own time, but she wished that he would hurry. She could hardly concentrate on the movie for thinking of how good his arm felt around her shoulder, how great it was to have his hand brush the edge of her arm.

Her mother had told her just the night before how her emotions would be larger than before, her appetites greater. They had been discussing the night she left the house and rode Lightning too hard. They advanced from horse riding to the discussion of relationships. She was warned about feeling rage she would have to control, anger that might spiral out of hand, and all sorts of overwhelming desires she would have to contend with.

"It's as if you've matured by fifteen or twenty years," her mother said. "You'll want to do things . . . well, things you haven't done yet."

If she could have, Dell would have blushed. Her mother had never openly talked about sexual things before. She knew she was talking about virginity and having sex, and she had assumed, correctly, that her daughter had not yet had intercourse. Assumed, or she'd read her mind.

"I have to ask something, Mom."

"Anything, sweetheart."

"Can I become pregnant? I guess I can, since you did even before you changed, but I need to know these things and how they work. How they'll work for me."

"Yes, you can have a baby. Your body works just as it did before. If you feed, you'll remain healthy. So you can conceive and have children, but . . ."

"But I shouldn't mess around with mortals, I know, Mentor told me."

"It's just that . . ." Her mother seemed at a loss for words. She finally said, "It's just that if you conceive with a human male, the child will be . . . different."

"Will it live?"

"Oh, yes, absolutely it will live. The fetus of a vampire mother is always strong and vigorous. But if the father is a mortal, it won't be vampire. But ... it won't be human either."

"I don't understand. That makes no sense to me."

"We have a word for it. The child of a mixed union is called a *dhampir*."

"What does it mean?"

"Human, with supernatural abilities, but not with the need for blood that we have. Truly alive, truly mortal, but with more strength, better vision, keener hearing, enhanced stamina, quickness, and some other abilities I just don't know about. I don't know any dhampirs. Some of the Predators do away with them."

"They kill them?"

"Oh, yes. They're a little dangerous to keep around."

"But what's wrong with being a . . . a super-advanced human? It's the best of both species, isn't it? Why haven't we all mated that way?"

"Because there's a drawback."

"Oh."

"The mixed-blood child sometimes grows into a . . . a . . . killer."

"A killer?"

"A hunter. A killer of vampires."

"But why?"

"Because it knows both worlds, it's a product of both, it feels and knows everything we know and feel. The mixed child comes to despise the parent who is the immortal, and often tries to destroy him. Or her."

"Jesus. Is that why Mentor warned me about having a mortal boyfriend?"

"I'm sure that's part of it. He left the rest to me. The other part, as you know, is the finite life of humans. The pain of separation when death takes them from us is awful. The aging they undergo, while you stay the same age, at least to the visible eye. It's a terrible thing, Dell, a horrible agony if you love someone. I wouldn't want you to have to go through it. That's why I'm telling you everything I know about it, and I'm asking you to be careful in your choices."

So here she was, sitting in a darkened theater with just the person her mother told her to shy away from, and she wanted to kiss him, and she wanted to hold him, and she wanted . . .

She stopped her train of thought and directed it to the screen. She could control herself. She knew she could. She had to. She simply couldn't ravish Ryan like a succubus, no matter if it produced a child or not. She couldn't live in a wanton manner, taking whatever her desires dictated, taking chances on unforeseen outcomes. She had not lost her virginity before now for these same reasons.

On the other hand, she'd never felt this serious about anyone before either.

I knew it wouldn't be easy, she thought, reaching to her shoulder to take his hand. Feeling his warm flesh beneath her cool fingers, she wondered if it would be impossible to keep her distance. The hormones, or whatever it was that caused her to want to find a mate, seemed to be operating at full throttle. At this point, the urge to love someone and have him love her back was stronger by far than the ever present hunger for blood. Because he was human, she wanted him for her lover. No, she thought, that wasn't right. She wanted him because he was Ryan. And because she was vampire, she knew she should never have him.

* * *

Ryan came away from kissing Dell with something in his brain sparking like moths striking against a hot lightbulb. He thought: *Wow!* He said, "Uh . . ." and then she flung her hands around his neck and kissed him again. He nearly fell right over a precipice of reason into a valley of deep desire.

They sat in his car in front of her house. Outside a night bird called in a tree at the edge of her yard. He was only going to kiss her gently, a good-bye and thank-you kiss, but it had turned into something hot and unworldly. He felt zany and bedazzled, as if he were in a fairy tale and was bowled over with a spell.

When she released him, he sat back panting, feeling startled and aroused.

"I don't think I've ever been kissed like that before," he said.

She remained silent, but she touched his cheek with her fingertips before letting herself out of the car. He watched her run up to her front door.

He put the car into drive and drove slowly away. Sweat had broken out on his brow and he now wiped it away. "Whew," he said, reaching for the air conditioner control to see if it was working.

His mind was made up. Lori was a kisser, all right, but compared to Dell she was a rank amateur. Dell made him forget where he was and what the hell he was doing. He didn't think something like that could happen and was so amazed he nearly ran a stoplight before noticing the light was red and slamming on the brakes. He got home in a shaky state and let himself into a dark house. His parents were already in bed asleep. It was a good thing, he thought, since if they could see his face they'd know something had happened. He knew of no way to explain it. A kiss that knocked him for a loop. A kiss that seemed to sear into him and seal him tight to her.

I think I'm losing my mind, he thought, going for the kitchen and a glass of milk.

He wondered if she'd go out with him the next weekend. And the next. And every weekend of his life.

"You're a crazy person," he muttered, putting the empty milk glass in the sink. "Ryan, you've just flipped out, man."

On the way to his room he realized it was true what he'd told himself. He'd flipped out. He was way over the moon. Dell Cambian was a magician, and, just like the song said, she'd put a spell on him.

22

Alan drove directly to Bette's house, so worried that he drove too fast and was stopped for speeding just inside Dallas city limits. Frustrated with the delay of signing for the ticket, he arrived at Bette's house frazzled as a half-dead mouse who had been toyed with for hours by a particularly energetic cat.

Bette, to his relief, met him at the door looking serene and beautiful. She had donned a hip-hugging, ankle-length, traditional Japanese gown. It was turquoise satin, embroidered all over with tiny black flying birds. He had seen her in traditional dress only once before when he'd arrived to take her to dinner. It always took him aback to remember that though she was thoroughly American, she upheld the past traditions of her forebears.

"You look a fright," she said, smiling and leading him inside. "Would you like some tea?"

It was as if she knew he was coming back. There was a Victorian rose hand-painted tray on the coffee table holding two cups and saucers, sugar, creamer, and a bamboo-handled teapot.

"How did you know I was coming back right away?" He leaned over to touch the teapot and found it still warm. How could she have possibly known?

"Sit down, Alan. I have something to tell you."

'I think you do." He sat on the sofa while she poured tea, dropped two small cubes of sugar into his cup, stirred, and handed it over. "And I have something to tell you, too."

"You first, if you like," she said.

"I went to Upton and told him about the vampire. He went crazy. He said the one I'd seen would track me down, and finally, it would find him. He really just freaked. When I left, he was packing and preparing to go away somewhere to hide. He told me to do the same thing."

Through the recital Alan saw that Bette nodded her head, sipped her tea, and didn't seem at all tense. What did he have to do, spell it out? That's what he'd do then.

"Bette, they might come for us."

"Now I'll tell you my news," she said, putting down the teacup. "They've already come for us. We just didn't understand what was going on."

"What do you mean?"

"You know the old man who showed up here a couple of times? And the last time my memories about the blood bank seemed to elude me when you tried to discuss it?"

"Yes."

"Well, that man, the old man, he's sort of like a leader. He's one of the most powerful ones. He came again not long after you left."

Alan inched forward on the sofa's edge. He wanted to leap up and stomp around, do something physical. He felt wound as tight as a cheap alarm clock.

"What did he do?"

"He invaded my mind again and tried to take away all my memories. Even as he was doing it, I caught the impression that he was going to find you next and do the same thing. I can't tell you how I knew it, but I did. When I woke, he was gone, and I knew something was terribly wrong, although I didn't remember yet that he'd been here. I went up-stairs to pray."

Alan knew about her altar and the faith she put in her religion. He nodded, thinking her response was a normal reaction to her victimization.

"Alan? I haven't told you everything about myself. I thought you'd laugh or ridicule me."

"I'd never do that."

She shook her head. "You might have. You weren't raised my way and you don't know my faith. You also don't know that I have had . . . abilities . . . since I was a child."

"Abilities?"

"Maybe you might call them 'powers.' I can get in touch with other people, a sort of telepathy. I've even done it with you sometimes when you've been down in Houston and hadn't called for a while."

"I never knew that."

"No, of course, you didn't. I just sent a subtle message that you should feel as if you needed to call me, get in touch. I could have just picked up the phone and called you, but then that's not the same, is it?"

He stared at her. He wasn't sure exactly what she was telling him. She could do what? Manipulate people by some kind of mind control?

"Yes," she said, smiling slyly. "I can manipulate people when I want to."

Alan sat back abruptly. "How'd you do that?"

"Read your mind?" She laughed. "Look, our reality isn't as it seems. There's work going on in physics that astounds the physicists. Down at the atomic level, things are going on that we never even imagined. Subatomic particles aren't predictable. They sort of wink out and back into existence. No one knows exactly what that means yet. It does mean things aren't the way we thought. And you know reality isn't as simple as it appears. Not now that you've been witness to murders performed by a vampire. You followed the old man, you said, and then he suddenly disappeared. How difficult is it to believe that I can also perform feats that seem fantastic? All humankind can do these things, if they're trained, and if they believe. It's not as rare as you think."

"Is that what you wanted to tell me?"

"That's not all," she said. She stood and began to walk the length of the room, holding her small hands clasped in front of her. The satin of the dress swished against her legs as she moved. "After I prayed, the memories the old man had taken from me were restored. I knew what he'd done. So I . . . I sent him a message."

"The way you sometimes did for me when I was in Houston?"

She turned and came back toward him. "Yes. And the old man appeared. Alan, he was on his way to do something to your mind. My call stopped him. If I hadn't done that, you wouldn't even remember now what it is we're talking about."

"So he came back? What did you do when he came back?"

"I made a pact with him."

"You what?"

"I told him we would drop all this. We wouldn't interfere with the vampires in this city. We'd never tell anyone. But . . ." She sank into the chair, her chin almost touching her chest. "I was too late. You told Charles Upton, and now he knows, too."

"Bette, how are we supposed to let this go? We discovered there are vampires and we're supposed to keep it to ourselves? That's impossible! And besides, I was hired to find them and report back to Upton. I did what I promised him I'd do."

She raised her head, and in her eyes he saw pity. "You still don't understand, do you? I made a promise. In order for the two of us to stay safe, I promised we'd let it go. I imagine the old vampire will know you told. And he might forgive you, on my behalf, because I made my promise after you revealed the secret."

"And if he doesn't forgive me?"

"He'll kill us. Or let us be killed, same thing."

"You don't really believe that, Bette."

She took up her teacup and sipped slowly before replying. "Oh, yes, I do believe that, Alan. I believe it with all my heart. I know it."

"What can we do?" He was prepared to go along with what she said. He couldn't help but believe she knew more about what was happening than he did.

"We can wait. And we can never speak of them again, Alan. Ever. I've promised."

Alan thought about a world where vampires lived and shipped huge amounts of blood all over the state, vampires who could enter a person's mind, and wipe out memories, vampires who took innocent life without any regret. He shuddered uncontrollably. He was a man of science dropped into an alternate universe where nothing was as it appeared. Where monsters dwelled and telepathy was practiced easily by the woman he loved.

He brought his hand to his forehead as if to make it all go away. He didn't want to know what he knew anymore. He would have been happier if the old vampire had come to him and cleaned his mind of these unholy bits of knowledge.

"You know," Bette said, reading his mind again. "There is no unknowing. But you have to let it all go now, Alan. For my sake, if not your own."

"And we just hope we aren't going to be murdered in our sleep, is that it?"

"There are no alternatives," she said. "Would you like more tea?"

Alan slumped back into the sofa and let his hands rest alongside his thighs. He was so tired. He'd driven to Houston and back all in one day and it had left him drained. Night was coming fast outside the windows where moonlight crept through the panes onto the floor.

'Yes," he said finally, "more tea, please. And turn on the lights, if you don't mind. It's getting dark in here. I hate the dark lately."

* * *

Upton's butler served equally well as his chauffeur. They were in the black limousine waiting in the parking garage when Alan left the building. Upton had hurried, carrying with him little more than credit cards, cash, and an overcoat. He was easily chilled by the air-conditioning in cars.

They followed Alan from the city onto the freeway north to Dallas, always keeping a safe distance so that he wouldn't notice the unusual car tailing him. When he parked in front of Bette Kinyo's home, they drove past and around the block then back again, parking down the block a bit. Upton could just see the front walk to the little home and knew if the couple looked outside, they'd never spot the limo.

George, Upton's butler and chauffeur, killed the engine. He said, "Should I get you anything, sir?"

Upton wanted a Coke. And Fritos. He also wanted a hot dog. His tongue tingled with the thought of the bite of mustard, the crunch of relish and onions. "Is there a store nearby?"

"I'll find one, sir."

Upton explained what he wanted to eat and sat still and peaceful in the comfortable leather seat waiting for George's return.

A dark-skinned child neared the window where Upton sat and tapped gently. Upton lowered the window a few inches. "What do you want?" he asked.

"Are you lost, mister?"

"No, young man, I am not lost. Now go away."

"I was only trying to help."

"Shoo, shoo, fly, shoo," Upton hissed, raising the window again. He knew the limo stood out in the old rundown neighborhood, but what choice did he have? The hood characters would never get to him anyway, even if they used baseball bats. The limo was special order, the sort used for politicians, for presidents. It was nearly impregnable, a fortress on wheels. Unbreakable glass that could stop bullets, reinforced tires, and locks on the doors that could not be jimmied.

When George returned half an hour later with the food, Upton fell upon the hot dog ravenously. He hadn't eaten since breakfast. "I hope you got yourself something," he said. "We're going to be here as long as it takes."

"I ate on the way back, thank you, sir."

"Right." Upton ripped open the Fritos bag and began to shovel them into his mouth. His lips, frozen, and without any feeling at all, impaired his eating, but did not completely deter him. He thought the junk food scrumptious. He hadn't eaten hot dogs in years.

* * *

Mentor arrived at Dell's house late. He'd been quite busy with new Naturals making the change. Of course, had he not been present to help them when they died, they might not have chosen to be Naturals, and he'd have been neglecting his duty. Still, he'd kept tabs on Dell and knew all about her involvement with the mortal, Ryan.

He knocked out of courtesy, but the door opened instantly as if Dell's mother knew he was on his way. They were all able to sense one another, even at some distance.

"You've come to see about Dell?" she asked. There were worry lines on her brow. Not only was her young son coming to an age when he would soon have to leave the family or be suspected of being some kind of abnormal child who never aged, but now her daughter, a vampire, was falling in love with a boy at her school. Life was never easy for a parent.

"Yes," he said. "I'm taking her for a stroll."

Dell appeared in the entrance hall just as he spoke. "You want me?"

"I thought we'd go for a walk, Dell. We have things to discuss and you missed your evening meeting at my house."

Real surprise showed on her face. "Oh! I forgot, didn't I? I'm sorry, Mentor."

"Don't apologize. Just come along with me."

They walked through the quiet neighborhood in the dark. Now and then a car turned down the street, splashing them in their headlights. Parents coming home from late hours at work.

"This is about Ryan, isn't it?"

"You're getting good with that."

"With what?"

"Knowing. It's part of your powers."

She shrugged. "I guess so. That means it is about Ryan. We've already talked about that. And I've talked with my mom, too."

"And neither talk deterred you from the direction you're heading?"

"Hey! Do I have my own life or what? I'm eighteen now. I go to college next year. I'm not a baby all of you have to keep scolding, you know."

"Temper, girl." Mentor's voice had dropped several registers, enough so that it sounded menacing. He saw Dell cringe.

"I'm sorry, Mentor, it's just that I can't help it. I get mad easy, all the time I'm angry, and I just don't know what the big deal is anyway. I like him, that's all. It's not a crime to like someone, is it?"

"I'll try to answer that question. Let's take a trip. Take my hand."

"What?"

"You're going to try your first transformation. Take my hand."

"I'm scared, Mentor."

He had her hand and held it, looking into her face. "I'm going to be with you. Nothing's going to harm you."

"Tell me what happens then. I'm still scared."

"You know that all matter is made of atoms." She nodded her head. Mentor continued, "We're super-natural now, not diseased or dead, but supernatural. Our atoms are under our control. Our minds can cause them to separate, without destroying us. Our minds stay intact, though the atoms scatter and become invisible. The very first of our kind stumbled on transformation by accident. Since then, we have all been able to transform. We can cause the atoms to gather again, through willpower. They can create another form, if we were to want one. Most of us don't do that often because *form* affects *mind*. If I were to become an eagle, I would be me, but eagle as well, do you understand?"

"Kind of."

"Only experience teaches. My words can merely describe. That's why you're going with me on your first trip. I'll keep you safe. After this, you'll be able to do it yourself. Are you ready?"

She hesitated. "I guess so."

"It's natural to be afraid. You've felt some of the emotions and heightened sensory abilities of a vampire, but this is different. I promise you'll be all right. I'll be at your side every minute."

As he stared at her, he turned all his attention inside himself, feeling the molecules that made up his physical body begin to spin and bump one off the other. The world outside dimmed only a moment as he transformed, and then it was bright and real again. Directing his attention to where Dell had been standing beside him he saw that she was coming along nicely, her corporeal body shimmering as if stars danced inside the shell of her skin. She winked out, at least to the human eye, but he could sense the darkness she became, darker than the surrounding night, and he tugged at her, bringing her with him as he ascended toward the sky.

She was crying out for him, terrified, and he sent her soothing thoughts. She would have to learn how to do this on her own eventually. It would not terrify her then. He sped with her clasped tightly to his consciousness across the skies and higher, higher until they were beyond the atmosphere and the world below looked like a blue globe swirling coldly through black space.

He was taking her to the monastery. It was located half a world away from Dallas, Texas, in a remote region of Thailand. Vampire monks had inhabited it for centuries. The monks were the guards, unusual men who devoted their lives to the monastery. Had they been human, they would have been men who joined a religious retreat. Mentor's clan kept it as a safe place, or used it as a prison when needed.

Mentor and Dell descended in a flash, the world having turned enough that Thailand was just below them. Pulling Dell along with him, he drew her earthward again and through the red-tiled roof of one of the monastery's buildings arranged in a semi-circle in the isolated enclave.

Then he let her go.

With his silent guidance she began to shimmer into existence from the darkness. He also waited for his own molecules to group again, creating the being known as Mentor.

They stood on a stone floor in a dim room with thick wooden rafters overhead. It was a gloomy, damp place, smelling of wet stone and rusty iron.

Gasping for breath, the way a mortal might, Dell jerked this way and that, throwing out her arms and twirling. He touched her arm and she was suddenly still, her eyes focused on his. "Dell? You're all right. You're in your body again."

She glanced down at herself with surprise. "What happened? I thought I saw the Earth at my feet. It was making me sick. I thought I'd passed out. Where are we?" She looked finally around at their surroundings.

"We descended so high into the stratosphere that the Earth turned below us. When we descended, we were at another place on the globe. We can do that, with practice. I'm sorry it shocked you so badly, but this was important to your development."

"And this place?"

She wrapped her arms around her body and shivered, looking around the dismal room.

"It's our safe, secure place. We're in Northern Thailand. This is an old monastery and the original order of monks deserted it a long time ago. We took it over. Now it's run by monks who are like us."

"Naturals?"

"Well, not really. They actually border on being Predators. They have, shall we say, 'aggressive' instincts. They stay here. Some have been here for centuries."

"What do they do here?"

"That's why we've come, Dell. I wanted you to see someone who is kept here."

"Kept?"

"She's imprisoned."

"Is she vampire?"

"Oh, yes, she is." He took Dell's hand and whisked her down a corridor. As they passed one of the hooded monks, Mentor nodded and the monk barely acknowledged them with a glance before moving on.

"They're not surprised we're here?" Dell asked, looking back at the monk as his orange robe swept along the stone floor behind him.

"No, I come here quite often. They know me well."

Mentor led her down stone steps into an underground corridor, this one with low, soot-stained ceilings. Electric lights hadn't been installed. Iron sconces flickered with candlelight. Along each side of the corridor were cells with iron gates that served as doors. Mentor paused at one. He brought a key from his pocket and slipped it into the large black iron padlock hanging from a hasp. He unlocked it, and swung open the heavy door. "Go in," Mentor said.

Dell stepped inside and moved toward a figure

who had its back to them at a primitive oak writing table. As Dell approached, she saw it was a woman. Her hair was long, to her waist, and very shiny, sparkling with light from the candle sitting on the table next to her. She was dressed in a plain dark dress that buttoned at her throat. Around one of her ankles Dell saw an iron collar attached to a heavy chain. "Hello?" Dell said.

The woman did not turn. She said, "Mentor, your little new-girl vampires are a bore to me. How many years do I have to bear this intrusion?"

"As long as there are others like you," he said. He touched Dell's arm and said, "Madeline here was like you. She fell in love with a mortal. Didn't you, Madeline?"

"You tell the story, Mentor. I'm busy."

"Madeline is writing her memoirs." Mentor indicated the shuffled papers on the desk. "Madeline is kept here for her own good. When her mortal lover died, she tried to kill herself. But first, she tried to attract attention from the world media. She was going to cause a scene, weren't you, Madeline?"

Madeline refused to answer. She kept her head down over the papers on the desk, writing furiously.

"You're scaring me, Mentor," Dell said, her face looking heavy and sad.

"I wanted you to see what becomes of vampires sometimes when they take a mortal lover."

"As if you didn't!" Madeline turned in the chair, her long hair swinging wide over her shoulder. Her face was deformed with rage. Her incisors showed, her lips were pulled back from all her teeth, and they shone yellow in the light filtering in from the barred corridor.

Dell turned to Mentor. "What does she mean?"

"I'll tell you what I mean, girl. Mentor fell in love and married a mortal, too. He should be here with me, chained for eternity in a cell with nothing of the world but paper and pen."

Mentor spoke softly, "Madeline, I didn't lose my mind when I lost my mortal."

Madeline rose and Dell stepped back, startled. Mentor stood his ground.

"Oh, didn't you?" she shouted. "Didn't you lose your mind, Mentor? Are you saying you're impervious to the pain of separation? That you're heartless? That you didn't beat your breast and weep and gnash your teeth?"

"Calm down, Madeline. You get this way every time I come to visit. It's tedious."

"And why shouldn't I get enraged?" The chain attached to her ankle and connected to the wall clinked like doom as she stepped toward them. "Why shouldn't I let your little secret out? You're as mad as I am. You've been mad for a hundred years!"

Mentor saw her rash movement coming a second before she made it. She always attacked him. She was always furious when he brought a youth to see her, to witness her madness and imprisonment. He reached up and grabbed her raised clawed hand before it could touch him. "We're leaving now, Madeline. You're a terrible hostess. You need to work on your manners."

Now the chained woman went for him tooth and claw. Mentor threw her back against the writing desk and ushered Dell through the open door before Madeline could recover. He swung the door shut with a crash and with his key locked the door.

He looked at Dell. "Do you understand?"

"Was she right? Did you love a mortal, too?"

"Yes, I did. And that's why I want to spare you that kind of pain. Madeline never got over it. You can see she's insane and vengeful. She would tear me apart if she could. She'd do great damage if she were let loose in the world. She wants to bring us all down. Make sure we're hunted and found and killed. It's her mission now, so of course we can't allow her freedom. Ever again."

"Why doesn't she do what we did? Transform and leave?"

"Someone's attention is turned on her all the time, every second. One of the monks is assigned to her. Many of the captives here don't know they can transform, but Madeline knows. She was quite talented in her day. And she knows she wouldn't get far. Her monk would come for her and bring her back within seconds. It would be a useless gesture on her part. Not that she hasn't done it. But she's given all that up now and sits in the cell, finally realizing there is no escape."

Mentor led Dell up the stairs. As they stood in the big open room where they'd first appeared, monks silently came and went, hoods shielding their faces, ignoring the presence of the two outsiders.

"I don't want this for you, Dell." Mentor hoped she could see what might happen to her if she continued falling in love with her young man.

"But you didn't really lose your mind, did you, Mentor?"

"No. At least not to the extent Madeline did. And others like her. They're all here, locked away for their own good. For the sake of us all."

"But it's my choice, isn't it, Mentor?"

Mentor sighed. "Yes," he said. "It's your choice. I've just shown you the usual repercussions of such a choice. I only want to help you, Dell."

"I'll think about it."

Mentor took her arm and said, "Yes, you must. You must think about it."

This time, knowing it was time to go, Dell began to transform before Mentor had to bring her along. Soon they were but heavier clouds of darkness near the rafters and then they were beyond the red-tiled roof and the green treetops, rising rapidly through clouds into cold dark space.

*   *   *

"Where are we?"

Mentor had set them down on the sidewalk in front of Bette Kinyo's house. He turned to Dell, who was just finishing returning to her body. She was yet a bit transparent, but even as he watched, her body filled in and was whole again. She had already learned enough to transform and reappear on her own at will.

Mentor glanced around to be sure there was no one nearby who might have seen them. He had checked before appearing, but he always had to make sure. Seeing the sidewalks empty, the curtains in the houses closed, he was sure they had gone undetected. He answered Dell's query. "We're in Dallas again, in front of a house owned by a woman named Bette. She's a . . . a beautiful Japanese-American female."

"Why are we here?"

"I wanted you to know something."

"Yes?"

"This woman has stumbled onto us. She's psychic and possesses powers of a true wizard, or medium, if you like. If Ross had had his way, she'd be dispatched by now. For she's a scientist, you see. And she knows enough to expose us."

Dell looked at the front of the silent dark house, perplexed. "So why are we here? Are you going to take her to the monastery?"

"Oh, no. That's only for our kind. No, I'm not going to hurt Bette. And I won't let Ross hurt her. Can you figure out why I'd do that? Risk our safety for this mortal?"

Dell stared at him and he opened his mind to her, his heart. She reached out to touch his consciousness, and knowledge dawned in her eyes. "You love her," she whispered. "Oh, Mentor."

Mentor reached up to rub his forehead as if he could make his mind obey his command to release him from this insanity. "Yes," he said, "yes, I've fallen in love with a mortal again. After being so

long alone. After suffering the loneliness of a century.
After knowing what I know. After visiting Madeline
and those like her held prisoner so they won't do
harm to all the rest of us."

"And after warning me so many times," Dell added.

"Do you see all the dangers, Dell? Don't you understand the agony of it? This woman does not love
me. She has a lover and will likely marry him. They
will have children and grow old together and die.
That is as it should be. I'll attend this woman's funeral in the future and I'll grieve. I'll love her from
a distance, stay separate from her, never be a part of
her life, never feel her hand stroke my face or feel
her gaze of love grace me. But I will do that
because . . . why? Why would I not try to make her
love me back, Dell? I probably could if I tried, you
know. But why wouldn't I?"

Dell didn't answer though he was certain she knew
the answer. She simply hung her head in sadness.
Mentor put his arm around her shoulder. "Let's go
home," he said. "You must think this all over. You're
not a child anymore. You understand the complexity
of who and what you are and the consequences of
whatever decision you make in this matter." *And I
have done all I can do,* Mentor thought.

He glanced back at the house as they walked away.
He wished he'd never gone there, never seen Bette
Kinyo. It was a tragedy in the making, the woman
in that house. He might have to protect her from
Ross or other Predators who found out about her.
She might even cause a war among the ranks of vam-
pires in this city. All because he had foolishly let his
heart feel something again.

"I'm so sorry, Mentor," Dell said.

"I know," he said. "So am I."

* * *

"Did you see that?"

Charles Upton had his face pressed against the

dark glass of the limo window, hands on each side of his face.

"George, did you see that?"

"No, sir, see what?"

"That man and the girl. They weren't there a minute ago. They just . . . they just appeared!"

Upton felt excitement rush through him like bared strands of electricity touching and sparking. "Start the car, George. Follow them."

By the time George had the car turned around at the next intersection, the old man and girl were several blocks away. "No, wait," Upton commanded. "Stop the car, pull over there, to the curb."

George did as instructed.

"I've got to go on foot. They're going to see this damn big boat following them. Come on and help me, George. Help me!"

George got him onto the sidewalk and gave him his cane. He walked beside him, ready to catch him if he stumbled or fell on the cracked and heaving chunks of concrete sidewalk. It was difficult for Upton to get around on his own. It was painful. But he was onto something, and he would not let it get out of his sight even if he had to crawl or have George carry him. At least the couple wasn't moving fast. He'd never be able to keep up if they upped their pace.

"I'm all right," he said to George. He had his balance now and was careful where he stepped. "Go back and get the car. Stay way behind me, do you hear? Don't get close enough for them to see you. Just keep me in view in case I need you." *In case I break my damn neck,* he thought ruefully.

George turned and hurried back down the sidewalk to the car.

"I've got you now," Upton whispered to himself. *One of you will do as I want,* he thought. *One or the other of you will give me eternal life. I'll* make *you, by God. I* will.

23

When morning dawned, Dell groaned and rolled from bed feeling as if she were hung over. She dressed slowly and dispiritedly. She thought she'd ask to drive the car today. She couldn't face riding the bus.

In the other rooms she heard her parents rushing to ready themselves for work. It was all they did. They rested, they slept, they paid Ross' lackeys for blood, they went to work. It was the same routine every single day. It was not so different a life than humans lived, but shouldn't it be more, she wondered? Shouldn't such powerful creatures as they were live more comfortable and less stressful lives? If only they could . . . could kill. But then they wouldn't be Naturals, the closest any of them ever got to being human again.

School, too, was the same routine. Every single day. School was a drag. Each day was harder to get through. Dell felt sullen and out of sorts. Once at school, she steered clear of her friends and attended her earlier classes with only half her mind paying attention. She went off by herself at lunchtime, walking out to the front of the school to sit on the steps alone. No one came here at lunch. They grouped together in little cliques, believing they really were Somebodies.

Mentor's little supernatural-assisted trips had sobered her. She'd seen the pain written on his face, felt his loneliness and helplessness. She'd felt the depth of Madeline's unwavering rage and her helplessness, too.

Mentor surely was right. It was not worth it to get involved with humans. Eventually she'd be out of school, go on to college, begin to see the world from the vantage point of a vampire. One day, maybe, she'd meet another of her kind and form a union so she that wouldn't be alone like Mentor. She'd be like her parents.

Oh, God! More routine and discouragement. Nothing new, nothing bright and exciting. It just didn't seem worthwhile.

Nevertheless she really had to stay away from Ryan Major. It was unfair to him. It was a form of death to her to think she'd love him so much one day that she'd be locked in the monastery after his loss.

"Hi, they said I'd find you here. Are you all right?"

Dell pushed her sunglasses tighter against the bridge of her nose. It was Ryan. He was sitting beside her now on the steps, folding his long legs before him. She could smell him. He had a very masculine scent, sort of lemony and sunny. She turned her head away from him and picked at the seam of her jeans.

"Dell? What's wrong?"

"Nothing." If she were rude and ugly and mean to him, he'd go away.

"Nothing? You look like you lost you best friend."

"Would you mind leaving me alone?" There. That should do it.

"I don't want to leave you alone. Something's wrong. Did I say something, do something? Can't you talk to me?"

He had his hand on her hand and she jerked it away. She was cold. Dead. He would know that one day and he'd despise her. He's be horror-stricken. She couldn't take that. She never wanted to see his face change with understanding and horror filling his eyes.

"Go away," she said.

He didn't. He sat quietly, not trying to touch her again. Finally, when she saw he was not going to leave, she turned to him. She felt anger rising. Why wouldn't he let her be? She was trying to save both of them so much trouble.

Spiraling anger caused her to lash out. Words tumbled before she could catch them, before she could monitor herself. "So you like vampires, huh? You like Lori and her little pretend bloodsuckers? You don't even know what a vampire is. You probably think they're like your little friends. They want to be alone and pretend they're different, special. They want to drink one another's blood, they want to try out kinky sex. They're the ones you ought to hang out with. Go find them, Ryan, and leave me alone!"

"I don't understand . . ."

"No, you don't. People die, don't they? They live a little while and then they die and turn to dust. Well, what if some of them didn't exactly die? What if when they did die, they became something else, they changed, they had a special disease that made them live on? What if they turned into something . . . weird? Something no one under heaven could accept? A monstrosity, a freak of nature? What if I told you that's what I am? You wouldn't like me so much then, would you? If I told you I can't eat food or drink anything anymore, what would you say? What if I said I have to drink blood from a vampire blood bank? That it comes in bags and we drink them? And what would you say if I told you I can't die except under very special circumstances? And that I'm cold, Ryan, COLD! My heart doesn't beat. My blood only sits there, renewed by the blood I have to have, but my heart never moves it. And if I wanted to, I could disappear. Right now. In front of you."

She saw the look on his face, the amazement, and she wanted to scare him, scare him so badly he'd never want to come near her again. She began to concentrate and her molecules slowly began to dance, bumping and moving apart, until when she looked down at her hands she saw them shimmering, light flowing right through them, making them transparent.

You see? She sent the thought to his mind. *Watch closely and see a miracle. I am vampire, Ryan. I am a true monster.*

She completely disappeared, except for a darkness in the air that hovered just above the steps she'd been sitting upon. She moved higher and watched Ryan's shocked face as his gaze followed her. She lowered again to the steps, came back to herself, transforming into her corporeal body. She looked fully into his eyes and said, "Get away from me. Get away from me now before I do something you won't like."

Ryan stumbled back up the steps on his hands, pushing with his feet to get away, and finally he leaped to his feet and hurried into the school building. Dell turned back and looked out into the empty yard. A wind blew past ruffling her hair. It smelled of magnolia flowers blooming on a nearby tree. She closed her eyes and felt the tears come, filling her eyes.

"Are you happy, Mentor?" she whispered into the wind. "Are you all happy now?"

* * *

Dell lay on her bed, one arm thrown over her eyes. It was after eight p.m. and she'd sent Eddie away when he'd come to see about her. When her parents came to her door to inquire after her, she sent them away, too. "I just need to be alone," she said. "Please."

She knew they were discussing her in the living room, thinking of calling for Mentor, but she didn't really care what they said or what they did. She only wanted to be still. And to think. She wasn't sure she could even go back to school again. She wasn't afraid that Ryan would say anything to anyone. Who would believe him, after all? But she did not think she could stand the rigorous standards that humans demanded in an institution like high school. She didn't want her friends anymore. They cared about clothes and cars and boys. She had nothing in common with any of them. Her problems were much deeper and more personal.

She couldn't have Ryan. Couldn't date him like a real girl could.

She cared little about her subjects and if she wanted, she could speed-read every book they gave her and retain the information, the way Eddie did.

Maybe she should quit school and forget college and just learn what she had to learn from books and from the world. She could take classes from a university on the Internet. She might even go away from her parents, leave Dallas, hide out somewhere so that she could think and find a way to live this new life she'd been given.

Her family probably thought she was getting suicidal. She could tell them how wrong they were and relieve their worry. She couldn't sustain the thought of fire, of setting herself alight and twirling until she was but cinder and soot. She simply needed to change her life now. Get away. She could transform, since Mentor had shown her how. She could travel above the Earth, so far away there was no air, no heat. She could go to another country or into the wilderness in this one. She could live on the blood of small animals and grow her hair longer and let it tangle. She could live like the wild thing she was. She needed neither shelter from storm nor anything else the world offered. Why more of them just didn't go away into hiding she couldn't understand. Or maybe they did—and no one spoke of it. Maybe there were thousands of them, millions! All of them hiding out, living alone, miserable until the end of all time. The vampires who tried to live with humanity and couldn't. The ones who were so depressed and alone they had to go away forever.

"Oh, God," she said quietly.

After a tentative knock at her bedroom door, Aunt Celia stuck her head into the room. "Dell? Can I come in?"

Dell turned onto her side away from the door, keeping silent. She felt the weight of her aunt when she sat down on the bed's edge. She waited for her touch, and when it didn't come, she turned over. "Why did they call you?"

"They know something's happened. This isn't like you. Can't we talk about it?"

"I don't really want to talk."

"It's that boy, isn't it?"

"They told you about Ryan?"

Celia nodded and now she did place her hand on Dell's shoulder. "Carolyn's nearly your age," she said. "And though you might not believe it, once I was young too."

Dell had to smile. "I know. It's just . . . I can't talk about this."

"All right, I won't press you. I'm having dinner here tonight, and Carolyn will be over later. When you feel better, maybe you can come out and be with your family."

"I'll try," Dell said, sighing deeply.

Celia rose and left her alone. The door snicked closed, and Dell lay on her back, feeling sleepy. She'd try to get up later and let her family know she was going to be all right. She hated to make them worry.

She must have fallen asleep because everything went hazy and she felt the hairs at the back of her neck stand up. She knew herself under scrutiny, and when she lifted her gaze to look around she saw she was not in her bed, but lying on forest debris in a dark wood with a blood-red moon overhead. It was the dream of her death—and she was back again.

* * *

Ryan stood on the steps at Dell's house, hesitating, his fist raised to knock at the door. It frightened him to be here. Yet he'd felt compelled to come. He had seen for himself that Dell had been telling the truth. Not only did she make herself disappear and reappear, but just before and after he had seen her teeth, the sharp incisors, the look of hunger in her eyes. They were no fake dental appliances she'd slipped into place. The disappearance was no magic trick. The strange look that came over her was unearthly. And it was real.

She was a vampire. That was a fact. He knew it for certain, absolutely. Although it was against all logic. It was truly insane. But it didn't detract from the fact that he knew what he knew. He'd seen what he'd seen. He'd experienced a vampire, a real one.

And he was here at her door because . . . because he loved her. That was another verifiable fact of life. There were vampires. And there was love. Neither could be disputed. They were universal truths that nothing he could do would ever change. He guessed he'd loved her the first day he'd entered school and sat behind her in English class. He didn't even know that love at first sight existed, but then there were a lot of things he didn't know.

Suddenly the door opened and Dell's little brother, Eddie, stood there, glaring at him. "What do you want?"

Ryan stepped back a step, but then he straightened his shoulders and looked the boy in the eyes and said, "I've come to see Dell."

"She doesn't want to see anybody."

"I know. But I have to talk to her."

"That's impossible." Eddie began to shut the door.

Ryan stepped forward and put his hand up, holding it open. "Please, Eddie. I know all about you, about your family. She told me."

He never got the chance to say more. Eddie's eyes widened, then he grabbed Ryan by the collar, and though he was smaller than Ryan, he dragged him easily from the front step into the house. "Wait here," he said, "God *damn* it."

Shaken but determined, Ryan stood in the hall, waiting. This was a vampire house. They walked in the day, they didn't die from the sun, they looked just like other people. He shook his head in consternation.

In other rooms he heard people talking and wondered if they knew he was there.

While he waited, he wondered what he was going to say to Dell to convince her he had to be in her life. He just had to make her understand something had happened between them. He couldn't give her up this way. He couldn't go on with his life as if it were still normal. He was irrevocably changed by her, his life intertwined with hers. He couldn't stop thinking of her. He couldn't live without her, that was the thing.

"Ryan, what are you doing here?"

She stood a few feet away, her hair in disarray, clothes awry. Behind her in the shadows stood her little brother.

"Can I talk to you, Dell? Alone?"

"Why did you tell him?" Eddie asked.

"Leave us alone, Eddie," she said.

"You shouldn't have told him. You know you must never do that."

"Go away, I said!"

"Oh, all right, have it your way. But Mentor's not going to like this."

When they were alone, Ryan reached out his hand for her to take it. "Come outside?"

She took his hand and they went out the door, closing it behind them. Ryan turned to her. He put his hands on her shoulders and looked into her eyes. "I don't care what you are. You're here and I'm here and we belong together. I had to come and tell you that. Ever since you told me, I've been confused and afraid, but I'm not afraid anymore."

"You weren't listening, Ryan. I'm not like you. It's a disease, a mutated disease that affects our whole line, affects us generation after generation. So few of us escape it. I have aunts and uncles, cousins, grandparents, and almost all of them are vampires. It's as if I had some kind of deadly disease, don't you see? Only this doesn't kill me. I wish it would. It makes me live. When I shouldn't be living." She grabbed his hand off her shoulder and pressed it between her breasts. She held his palm hard against her. "I told you my heart doesn't beat. Why can't you understand? I'm an abomination. My whole family's infected. I used to be human; I'm not anymore."

Ryan felt her chest through her shirt, felt the bones, the flesh so cool to his touch. And she was right, there was no movement there, no heartbeat. Something deep in his mind shuddered, but he didn't pull his hand away.

He had to say something. If she'd bared her fangs and gone for his throat, he thought he would have leaned to the side so she could reach the flesh easier. If he couldn't have her, he didn't want anyone.

"I love you, Dell." He was surprised he'd said it, but it was what he'd wanted to say all day.

She slumped against him, her head against his chest. He wrapped his arms around her. "I can't help it, Dell. I love you. I've never felt this way about anyone before. I've had girlfriends and that's all they were. As soon as I transferred here and saw you in class, as soon as I kissed you . . I knew. There's nothing you can tell me that will change what I feel for you."

"This will never work out, Ryan. It causes trouble. It causes all kinds of problems. You need to think about that. I've seen a woman imprisoned on the other side of the world because she loved a man. A mortal. She lost her mind over him. You're mortal, Ryan, I'm not."

"We'll deal with the problems as they come along. That's all we can do, that's all everyone does. You care for me, too, I know it." When she didn't speak, he raised her face from his chest and looked at her closely. "You care for me, too, don't you, Dell?"

"Yes," she whispered.

He leaned down and kissed her, holding her tight to him. He buried his face in her tangled, fragrant hair at the side of her neck. "I don't care about anything," he said, "but loving you."

Dell held onto him for a moment before pulling away. She glowered into the twilight at the street.

"What's wrong?" Ryan asked. He'd never seen that look on her face before.

"Someone's watching us."

He looked across the street at the houses there, but didn't see anyone. "Who?"

"I don't know, but someone. I feel it." She pushed at his chest a little with her fingertips. "You should go."

"All right, but remember what I said. I won't give up on you, Dell."

Her gaze softened and she quickly kissed his lips once more. "We're both crazy," she said.

"You more than me." He smiled.

She pushed him again, more playfully, and he stumbled off the steps. "Okay, okay, I'm going."

As he left, he saw her scanning the street and the houses in the neighborhood, the scowl back on her face.

* * *

"I want you to get him for me," Upton said to George.

They sat in the limo down the street from Dell's house. They had seen the young couple embrace. He and George had followed the girl from one side of town to the other. They had followed her to school and home again. While waiting, making plans, they had seen the boy drive up and park. When the girl came outside with him, Upton knew it was his opportunity. "You have to get him," he repeated. "I don't know if the boy is vampire, but if he isn't, he'll be easier to handle. The girl will do what you say if you get her boyfriend."

"How do I get him, sir?"

"Get out of the car, you idiot, and get over there. When the boy starts to leave, call to him. Ask him for directions or something, I don't care what you do, but get close and get him. Bring him to the car. We're taking him with us."

"Yes, sir."

Upton sat back and watched. He saw George start for the house, saw the boy turn and walk toward his car. George reached the girl's front yard by that time. He saw him gesturing to the boy, luring him down the steps and to the edge of the sidewalk.

It would all be in Upton's control soon. He'd have the power. He'd make the girl turn him into a vampire. He'd threaten her with fire, with decapitation, with harm to her boyfriend, her family, whatever it took. He would have his way or she would die, he meant it. He hadn't come this far and invested this much time and energy in order to fail. He had so little time left. He could feel his disease ravaging him daily. He was nearly to the point of needing a wheelchair. He never slept, aching all through the night. He had more sores that would not heal; they were breaking out now on his back and spreading around his rib cage to his chest. He'd soon get some horrible infection that would kill him long before his disease ever got a chance to.

He needed that girl. He needed the life she could give him.

He'd do whatever it took.

He pressed against the limo window, watching closely. The boy seemed confused. George stepped in close and suddenly took him by the arm, bending it behind his back. He pushed him toward the side-

walk, over the curb, and into the street. As Upton
had predicted, the girl followed. She ran from the
steps and caught up with them close to the car.
Upton had the back door open just before George
pushed the boy inside.

George turned swiftly to the girl.

"What are you doing?" she said. "Let him go."

Upton had a small caliber silver pistol aimed at
the boy. When the girl opened the door, he waved
it at her, making sure it was the first thing she saw.

"Join us," he said, "or your friend is going to have
a hole in him."

She didn't say anything, but the look in her eyes
made Upton think for one second that he'd made a
terrible mistake. "Get in!" he shouted, his sudden
fear causing him to raise his voice. "I'm not very
good with this gun and it might go off."

The girl slid in beside the boy and took his hand.

"Who are you?" the boy asked. "What's this
about?"

"If she's vampire, she can read my mind. Can't
you, girl?"

"He wants to be like me," Dell said. "He's using
you to get what he wants. He's been looking for me
for a long time. He's dying."

George had started the car and pulled from the
curb. Full dark had fallen on the neighborhood now
and lights came on inside the houses as they
passed them.

"I don't understand," Ryan said.

"It doesn't matter what you understand," Upton
said. "Just do what I say and you'll be all right." He
glanced at the back of George's head. "Take us out
of this city. Take us somewhere private, far away
from here."

"You better not do this," the girl warned. "You're
sick and feeble. I can hurt you."

Upton pushed the gun into the boy's ribs until he
grunted. "I'm not playing a game with you," he said,
speaking to Dell. "You'll give me what I want, or

you'll lose this mortal. He'll die a lot sooner than I will—and that's a promise."

All of Upton's fear vanished as he spoke. He saw the girl's resolve waver. She sank into the leather seat, gazing ahead of her, and holding tightly to the boy's hand. She might still be reading his mind. If she were, he wanted her to know just how serious he was.

I wouldn't mind killing everyone in this car, he thought, hoping she could hear him. *You know I'll do it if provoked. Don't try it.*

He relaxed, but kept the gun firmly against the boy's ribs as George drove them from the neighborhood onto a freeway entrance ramp.

For once Upton's frozen smile was genuine. He thought he would smile forever now. Life was only beginning.

24

Mentor and Ross were involved in a deep struggle when they both heard the cry for help from the girl. It was like a screech on the wavelength they both unconsciously monitored every moment of their lives. The wail startled them into rigidity.

Ross, taking advantage of the interruption, threw Mentor off easily. Mentor landed against the wall of Ross' home, striking it so hard his body dented the sheetrock and caused a painting to crash to the floor.

"Stop it," Mentor said, shaking himself off. "We can finish this later."

Ross stood immobile, listening intently to the pleas coming to him from the girl who called herself Dell. "Who is this new one?" he asked. "What makes her interrupt us this way?"

Mentor said, "Dell Cambian. You know the Cambians?"

"Of course I do. I supply them, don't I?"

"Listen," Mentor said, cocking his head, holding one finger aloft to silence Ross.

She was telling them where she was. She was caught, a prisoner of an old crippled man and his chauffeur. They were going to kill her boyfriend if she did not make the old man a vampire. *Help*, she cried. *Mentor! Help!*

"She doesn't want to kill them," Ross said, sneering. "You see how your namby-pamby Naturals handle a crisis? They buckle. They call for help when all they have to do is strike back."

"She's not like you, Ross, you murdering fiend. She's more human. And she loves the boy."

"Look where that got her. Every Natural and every human involved with one ought to be put out of his misery."

"Oh, just shut up, you bastard, and let's go get her."

"Only if I get to take the kidnappers for myself."

"I don't care what you do when we get there," Mentor said with disgust. He had been fighting with Ross for more than an hour, trying to keep him from going to kill Bette and Alan. Ross knew they knew. He knew the woman had thrown off Mentor's memory wipe. He knew they were dangers to vampires as long as they lived.

It didn't matter when Mentor told him he'd extracted a promise from the woman or that he knew she'd keep it, and she'd make Alan keep it. Ross would take no chances, he said. And then he'd landed the first blow, attacking with a fury Mentor had not expected. He had kept the Predator's fangs from sinking into his neck by only centimeters. His own fury rising, he had almost made a determination that Ross was too far out of control to be of use to the clan any longer. He would kill him and train someone else to take his place.

Except . . . he realized suddenly during the struggle that it was his own judgment that had become clouded. Ross was acting as only one who would protect their clan would act. Still, Mentor trusted Bette. She would never bring them harm.

Then they'd both heard the strident call for help from Dell.

He'd let Ross live as long as he didn't say he was going to do harm to Bette Kinyo. No one would ever be allowed that privilege.

The two vampires, Predators both, threw themselves into transformation at the same moment, disappearing from the destroyed living room of Ross' home. Dell was being held in an abandoned old house just outside of Dallas in the suburb town of Ennis, Texas. The house sat on the edge of a newly plowed field that stretched in all directions for hundreds of acres. When the two vampires arrived outside the house, a fierce dark wind was blowing, shaking the boards of the sagging building, lifting shingles and sending them flying. Geese flew past the face of the full moon in the sky.

"This is an ugly place," Ross said with distaste. "But the man's got a car, I can say that for him."

Mentor looked at the limousine. Wealth. Tremendous wealth. This must be the man Alan was going to tell about his discoveries. Obviously, he had told him. And led him back to their dens, their homes. Ross would have even more reason now to kill Alan Star.

Would the complications never cease? Mentor wondered. It was all so out of hand.

"Let's go," he said to Ross. They approached the leaning porch and stepped lightly over the warped boards. It was Ross who pulled the door open, ripping it from rusted hinges and flinging it aside. It clattered and tumbled down the steps and onto the ground.

Wind rushed past them, pushing them into the room, startling the two men there with Dell. They turned in surprise, letting her go. "What the hell?" the old man said.

"Well you may ask," Ross said, eyes flaming as he stepped forward in two long strides and grasped the old man by his throat, hauling him inches into the air off the floor. "What the hell? That's where I'll dispatch your black soul."

"Let's think all this over," Mentor said, moving toward the two men.

Ross let go of Upton, and turned, furious. "We will *not* discuss this. You try to stop me from doing

what's best for our people. I won't stand for it
anymore."

Mentor roared back, "You do what I say, or we'll
continue where we left off before we came here."

"What would you have me do, spare this old
evil one?"

"There might be another way . . ."

"No. No other way. Not this time." Ross advanced
again on the old man.

*   *   *

Dell fell back from George's clutching fingers as
the door to the old house flew open. In the garish
light from the battery operated lantern the two vampires stood as tall as the doorsill, their long shadows
curling over the floor and up onto the opposite wall.
"Mentor," she screamed, so relieved that she went
to her knees.

She hadn't known what to do. The old man was
insane, slobbering, his teeth shining in the lamplight
from stretched tight lips. He was a horror to behold.
Weeping sores oozed on his old wrinkled neck. There
were soiled bandages on his forehead, and other bandages were coming loose from his hands. He could
hardly walk and grimaced all the time, scowling
from thick white brows.

"I have porphyria," he said. "You're going to save
me from it."

"I don't know how to do that," she insisted.

"Yes, you do. You will take my blood, but not
enough to kill me. You'll bring me to the brink of
death and let me return. You'll make me like you."

"You don't understand. We aren't like that. Only
a few of us ever do what you're asking. We're geneti-
cally changed by the same disease you have. In us,
it mutated and caused us to be vampire, and now
it's a gene we carry. We pass it down through generations. But we don't turn one another into vampire
the way you're asking." She was lying. They could

change others if they wished, but she'd never tell him that.

His idea of vampires was very distorted and he could not understand that she was like a vampire child, untried, unlearned, and probably incapable of doing what he wished.

"I'll have George douse you with gasoline from the car and set you afire if you don't do what I want," he threatened. His gaze was as evil and unrelenting as any Predator's. She knew he meant it.

All she could do was to send out a plea for help, for Mentor—either that or kill the old man, and she did not want to kill, ever. Her anger, which sat near the surface all the time, was moving out of control, however, and she feared what she might do to the two men if someone didn't come to her rescue.

She didn't want to do it. She didn't want to hurt them. The old man was desperate and disillusioned. He was pitiful.

And now Ross had him by the throat. She got to her feet and ran forward to pound on Ross' steel-vise arms. "Don't hurt him, don't!" She didn't know what possessed her. She couldn't think about anything but deterring murder in her presence.

"I'll kill him!"

Even as she screamed no and pleaded with Mentor to intervene, Ross swooped low over the old man's neck. Dell reached between them and caught Ross around the neck, hauling him backward. He let go of the old man and knocked her back so hard she flew across the floor, out the door, and all the way across the small broken porch to the bare yard outside.

Inside, Ross sank inch-long fangs into Upton's throat. The old man arched his body, crying out in pain and terror. George ran to him and beat at Ross' face with his fists. Ross swept him aside with his free hand, throwing him to the floor.

As Upton's blood rushed into Ross, he fell into the other man's thoughts and realized with sudden shock how alike they were. The old man said tele-pathically: *Make me like you and I'll give you more power than you've ever dreamed existed. I can help you. Search your soul and see if I'm not telling the truth.*

Mentor stood as if in a trance, then suddenly he moved, rushing outdoors to see about Dell. He lifted her into his arms and tried to get her to her feet.

Inside, using these few seconds alone to make a decision, Ross spoke aloud to Upton. "What can you do for me? Show me." He bent to the old man's bloody neck to take more of his life.

Upton, nearing death, showed Ross all the possibilities. How together they would siphon off from Upton Enterprises all the funds Ross might ever need. When they had enough, they would begin buying corporations, going global, until they owned the largest financial empire in the world. How he'd share all that with Ross, give him anything, give him not only riches, but enough power to do as he pleased about the Cravens and the Naturals. If only he'd make Charles vampire, they could do anything.

Ross paused and removed his lips from the old man's throat. He looked deep into the man's eyes and saw there a kindred spirit, someone so much like himself that it was like seeing a mirror image. "All right," he growled, blood dripping from his lower lip. "I'll give you immortality. And you will give me whatever I ask, forever."

"Yes," Upton whispered hoarsely. "Anything. Everything. Forever."

Ross sank his fangs again for the third time, forcing back the old man's head, bringing him just to the brink of death, feeling his heart beat slower and slower. Then Ross drew back and dropped Upton to the floor. He'd been tempted to kill him anyway, but the thought of what he'd been promised stopped him at the last moment.

When Ross turned, he saw Mentor standing in the open doorway.

"Now what have you done?"

"You want some of this? You're ready to end what we began?" Ross snarled, moving forward.

Mentor took him by the arms and threw him out the door and onto the porch, following in a blur.

Dell, unhurt, entered the house and knelt with George over the old man. He was bleeding profusely from the neck. George tried to cover the wound, but blood welled beneath the palm of his hand and rivered to the floor.

The old man opened his eyes. "I'll be like them," he said. "I'll live forever now. Don't worry, George, don't worry."

Dell looked for Ryan and found him cringing in the corner. She took his hand, lifting him, and pulling him with her to Upton. She stooped down, felt of the old man's heart.

"You shouldn't have come for me," she said, sorry for him now. He was crazy and sick and old and he probably would have killed her—except now she realized she never would have permitted him to do that. With him prostrate on the floor in a pool of his own blood, she could sense the depth of his despair, his terrible longing for life, and she respected that about him. He was human. At least for the moment. He should not die this way.

She heard the sounds of struggle outside the house and left the old man, rushing to the door to see about Mentor. "Stop it!" she screamed. "Ross, stop it!"

Ross had Mentor on the ground, pushing his face in the dirt. Wind whipped Ross' coat jacket away from his body and slicked his hair to his head. He turned to her, teeth bared, eyes like coals, and he growled.

Dell felt all the anger rise within her that had been building ever since she died. It had been lying in wait, crouching within her, eager to spring to the forefront of her consciousness. It came on her in a tremendous wave. It felt red and fiery; it felt slick and red and bloody.

She looked around and saw Ryan watching the

scene, frozen in place. He was caught in a nightmare
that might never end. She must do something to
stop it.

She leaped from the door across the broken porch,
past the steps, and landed on Ross' back. She dug
her hands into his shoulders, clawing at him. Her
fangs locked on the back of his neck where it was
exposed just above his collar.

Ross howled and tried to throw her off. She tasted
blood, warm blood, the first she'd ever tasted and it
filled her with images of great rivers, deep gorges,
endless caves, dark, dark, dark woods where the
moon shone scarlet and the wind carried death on
its feathery wings. She bit down harder, seeking a
vein, hunting for it the way a mole will dig through
earth, making a tunnel toward a tasty root. She
jerked her head this way and that, her eyes closed
tightly, rending the flesh beneath her teeth with a
viciousness that welled straight from her soul.

Ross fell off Mentor and twisted, taking her by the
hair and pulling with all his might. Dell knew nothing, felt nothing but hunger. She felt no pain from
the tearing of her hair from her scalp, no fear of the
huge Predator who was more powerful than any
who might have lived. She meant to kill him and
take his blood. She'd find the vein, she'd bite down
until she reached it, and then he would be hers.

Lightning struck her in the head, or that was what
it felt like, and she was flung across the ground, rolling like a tumbleweed. Mentor stood over her, glaring and pointing. "You stay here," he said. "You are
not to engage in battle."

Blood dripped from her lips and down her chin.
Her tongue snaked out and she licked it clean, then
she smiled. "If he touches you again, I'll be sure to
kill him."

Mentor turned swiftly to Ross. Dell saw he was up
now, a hand to the back of his neck. He was hunched
over. She knew she'd hurt him. If Mentor hadn't in-
tervened, she might not have taken his life, but she

wouldn't have stopped trying. Her arms felt as if
they were made of steel. Her body felt as strong as
stone. Her mind swirled with the aftertaste of his
blood. Though she thought they were all cold and
dead, it wasn't true! His blood had been warm and
alive. It still tingled on her tongue and through her
veins, giving her strength and the desire to take
more.

Ross said, "I ought to kill your little protégée for
that."

"She thought I was in danger."

Ross laughed and it was a terrible sound, compet-
ing with the wind that howled around the eaves of
the old house.

"You can leave now, Ross. I'll handle this." Ross
turned to look through the doorway into the lantern-
lit house.

"You made him vampire. Go now. You've done a
terrible thing."

Ross scowled at Mentor then he looked with new,
bright anger at Dell. "You'd better do something
with her," he said. "If I ever come across her alone,
she's mine."

"Handle your own business, Ross. I am the master
in this region. If I have to, I'll get you replaced."

"You'll try to kill me, you mean. You're nothing
but a weak old man, Mentor. You should never
threaten me."

Ross raised his hands, his coat whipping out behind him, and leaped to the rooftop of the house.
From there he shouted at the sky, "He is Master, he
says! We shall see about that!"

Dell came to her feet, wiping her mouth on the
back of her hand. She watched as Ross rose high into
the sky, not bothering to transform, but flying like a
bird, holding his arms out, his legs together and sailing faster than the human eye could see above the
plowed fields into the starry night.

She turned away and saw Ryan standing on the

old porch. She went to him and took his hand. "I'm sorry you had to see all this," she said.

Mentor patted the boy on the shoulder as he went into the house. He found the servant still hovering over the old man, holding a hand to the wound Ross had made.

"You," Mentor said, standing over the servant. "Get in the car and leave this place."

George looked at him in fear, but as Mentor stood there, George's face grew lax and still, expressionless. Dell watched from the doorway as Mentor performed his magic on the other man's memories, clearing them, making him forget.

George rose, and Mentor took his elbow gently, leading him to the door. He watched until the man opened the car door, got inside, started the motor, and drove away. Then he turned back for the old man.

"What are you going to do with him?" Dell asked. She hunched her shoulders at what Mentor's answer might be. She did not want to have to fight him. Though Ross' blood still gave her the feeling of superhuman power, she knew that she was no match for Mentor.

"I'm going to help him change over. Ross made him one of us. Now . . . I have to help him. Get out of here, Dell. Take your young man. Go wait outside."

Dell watched a moment before leaving. She felt guilty and relieved all at once. She saw Mentor sit down by the body and place his hand on the old man's bandaged forehead.

So that is what he did for me, she thought. *When I died. And now the man is dying, too, and he will be vampire.* Just as he had hoped. Just as he'd wanted.

He has been granted his last wish because of me.

Charles Upton swooned into a dream as the huge vampire snatched him up and sank fangs into his neck. He fought, an instinct he couldn't help, trying to free himself from the vampire's embrace. His mind

screamed out in denial that it was happening.
Though he'd dreamed of it, hunted for it, and lusted
for it the way another man might lust for fame or
fortune or a woman, when it actually began to occur,
he wanted to get away from it. He felt his life leave
him by increments, moving from his old body into
the firm young body of the vampire. He could not
fight him off, could not free himself, couldn't even
cry out for help.

I don't want to die, he thought finally, in the last
seconds of his dying throes. *I want to be like you, like
you, make me like you and together we'll rule the
world. . . .*

And then all was darkness. Someone sat nearby
him and commanded that he rise. He sat, opening
his eyes and looking around. It couldn't be heaven
and his companion was not an angel. He was in a
frightful place that merely resembled Earth but he
knew it was not. It was somewhere he did not want
to be.

"Help me," he cried, turning and clutching the old
man's hand who sat beside him. "Help me, mister.
Who are you?"

"I am Mentor, and I've come to guide you. What
kind of soul do you have?"

"I am a good man . . ."

"You are a cruel, ruthless, sinful man. I suspect
that is your soul showing, but I may be wrong. What
kind of soul do you have, Mr. Upton?"

Upton heard something rustling not far away and
he turned to see. There were bare trees all around
and dark, thick forest debris where he sat. It crawled
with things. He could feel them beneath his skinny
buttocks, could sense them moving and wriggling
through the leaves and decomposed matter, seeking
his flesh. He scrambled to his feet. The rustling he'd
heard strengthened and turned into the roaring
sound of a locomotive. He began to tremble and
clutched Mentor's hand so tightly his fist hurt.
"What's that?" he whispered.

"Look up," Mentor instructed.

Upton looked beyond the stands of bare limbs at the night sky and the full red moon. It began to melt and drip. "Eiiii!"

"You are in the place of the Predator Maker. He is coming for you. Shall we flee? Do you want to stay and wait for him, Mr. Upton? It's up to you. There are other choices, less violent choices."

Upton was immobile, his hand clutched around Mentor's hand. He saw the thing coming now. It bore down on them from the woods, rushing through the trees with a long wailing cry. It was as large as the world. It was taller than trees, greater than the bloody moon. It blocked out the stars and the heavens above. Upton could not move. He could feel its power. He knew he wanted it. He wanted this thing to invade him, to take him to its bosom and whisk him to its home.

"I urge you to flee," Mentor said, gently prying Upton's hand loose so that he could step back. "If you stay, you will be his."

The beast was nearly upon them. It was dressed in layers of black that were more night than cloth. A hood covered its head and from beneath it eyes as large as fists shone yellow bright. Below the eyes all that could be seen were white, glistening teeth, teeth as sharp as razors, rows and rows of them that went back into the horrid head to a pit of darkness.

Upton fell back and threw out his arms. "Go ahead and take me!" he screamed. "I am yours!"

Mentor stood by silently, his head bowed. He would not watch while the Predator took the old man and made him. He had never been able to watch. It had happened to him when he'd first died and he could not watch it when others invited the Predator into their souls.

When it was done—the gurgling and frightful moans, the rattles of death and the susurration of last breath—Mentor watched the corpse for new life. The old man's eyes opened but a slit and within them

was a wicked glint. From out of their depths Mentor
saw the new hunger.

"Come along," Mentor said. "It's over. It's time to
rejoin the world."

The old man opened his eyes in the body on the
floor of the abandoned house. Light from the lantern
reflected off his eyeballs, causing them to appear
milky white. He sat up stiffly, ran his hands up each
arm, down each leg, over his face. Then the fingers
of his right hand slipped into his mouth and he felt
of his teeth, his tongue, the roof of his mouth. He
removed his fingers and looked at Mentor. His voice
was changed, stronger and fearless. "Glory be, I am
like you," he said.

"Not like me," Mentor said, rising from the floor
and going to the door. He turned back. "You will
never be like me. I'm not a monster with my face
turned away from God."

He left him there in his bewilderment and met Dell
and the boy on the steps. "Don't ask," he said. "Let's
go home now. We have done all we could do."

*   *   *

Ross was let into the palatial home of Charles
Upton by his butler, George. He probed the butler's
mind and discovered Upton had tracked the man
down and brought him back to live with him. He
was not vampire, but understood every detail of a
vampire's life. He was handsomely compensated and
felt no compunctions against his employer's lifestyle.
A typical, greedy little human, Ross thought.

"Mr. Upton is waiting, sir."

Ross followed the butler into a dark library where
Upton sat behind a desk and another man, a human,
sat in a Chippendale chair. Upton rose. He looked fit
and lean. There was no evidence of disease or sores
on his body.

"Ross, I want you to meet David, my second-in-
command. I've given him proof of what kind of crea-

ture you've made me. He's scared, as you can see . . ." He gestured to the other man who was hunkered down in the chair, his eyes darting wildly. ". . . but he knows exactly what my plans are and will institute them. Together, the three of us will succeed beyond any of your dreams."

Ross wondered about that, but he didn't dispute Upton. He said instead, "Bringing mortals into your affairs is a very risky endeavor, Upton. I'm not sure I approve. They can betray you at any moment."

"Would you betray me, David?" Upton came around the desk and put a strong hand on David's shoulder. "Would you even dare?"

"No, sir, I'd never do that."

Upton flourished his hands in the air at Ross. "You see? He's totally trustworthy. I've given him visions of what will happen to him, to his wife, and to both of his children if he disappoints me."

Ross shrugged. "I just don't like it," he said. "I thought it was going to be you and me."

"We need David. He can deal with the real world so much better than either of us. That leaves us free to enjoy the bounty."

Ross felt *he* had been betrayed. Upton was a fierce vampire, fueled by desire, ambition, and hate. It was possible Mentor had been right. He'd made a mistake.

"Don't ever think you'll ease me out," Ross said. "I'm going to share equally in your wealth and all your affairs. If I ever discover either of you have cheated me, you'll find me on your doorstep, extracting my revenge."

"Fair enough," Upton said, moving behind the desk again. "Now sit down and let's get on with the meeting. We have a lot to tell David."

Ross sat, fuming and gnawing at worry. A human was involved. That never boded well.

25

For a long time life was nothing if not beautiful in Dell Cambian's eyes. She and Ryan graduated from high school and had a small marriage ceremony in her parents' backyard. Cheyenne was there and Aunt Celia and Carolyn. Grandma and Grandpa sat in the front row of chairs set up on the lawn, beaming at her. Though none of her family thought it the best decision to marry Ryan, they acquiesced to her mounting pleas.

Dell wore a white gown and a veil falling from a small pillbox hat ringed with pearls. She wore an emerald necklace given to her by her parents. It was an emerald cut stone to match the emerald and diamond band Ryan had bought for her wedding ring.

It was a beautiful balmy June day, the crape myrtle bursting with pink blooms. Dell thought she'd never been so happy. Her family surrounded her, the weather was glorious, and Ryan was to be her husband. Nothing might ever be as good again as her wedding day.

Mentor stood far back in the crowd, but he smiled at her as she walked down the aisle created between folding chairs.

After the ceremony Dell asked her mother if she'd be too upset if she and Ryan lived on a ranch a little distance away. Ryan's grandfather had a lot of land

and had given Ryan a generous portion as a wedding gift. It was where he'd always wanted to settle down.

"I'll always be in touch, sweetheart, it's all right with me."

Dell knew her mother meant they'd communicate telepathically and could visit very easily.

Dell and Ryan discussed college and decided to take courses over the Internet. For a couple of years, Ryan could take the basic credits and later go to A & M for more advanced courses to finish a degree so that he could be a vet. Every night they took turns at the computer in a corner of their bedroom, downloading course work and uploading finished assignments. It was a perfect arrangement.

For a while Dell missed her parents and Eddie, and she missed Mentor and even her friends and teachers. But the longer she was away and with Ryan, the less she missed her old life.

Sometimes her family visited, and the visits always cheered Dell. In the first spring of her life on the ranch, she watched Aunt Celia drive up in her old Toyota Camry. She waved her inside and got iced tea. They sat at the dining table while Ryan worked on his old truck in the garage.

"It's a nice place you have here," Celia said. "I like it."

"Me too. I think I was cut out to be a country girl. I'm really glad you came, Aunt Celia. Where's Carolyn?"

Celia grinned. "Well, she has a boyfriend and they spend a lot of time together. It seems she doesn't have much time left over for her old mom."

Dell understood that. Once she'd fallen in love with Ryan she couldn't think of anyone else.

"What I came for was to tell you about something I've been reading," Celia said, taking up her glass of tea to sip.

"Yes? Is it about vampires?" Aunt Celia had been researching physics for years trying to find a clue about vampire existence. Though she had never become one, her daughter might face the ordeal one day, and like the clan's researchers in Houston, Celia hoped to find a way to prevent it.

"In a way it might be about vampires," Celia said. "It's a book by Dr. Kaku, one of the top seven physicists in the States. It's called *Hyperspace*."

"What's a hyperspace?"

"It's not a what, actually, it's a where and I think its existence is the reason vampires can dematerialize and reassemble themselves. Here's how Kaku explains it.

"He was contemplating a small pool of goldfish one day. They swam in no more than three or four inches of water, hiding under lily pads. He got his face right down to the water's surface, but the fish didn't respond, not knowing he was there. He said that's how we are, in our third dimension, unaware of the fourth dimension, hyperspace.

"You see the goldfish can move back and forth and side to side, but beyond the surface of the water they don't have any conception of 'up.' Up to them doesn't exist and everything above the surface of their world would be another dimension to them."

"Oh, yeah, I see," Dell said, interested in the little goldfish world.

"Well, Kaku postulates this theory and it made some sense to me because I think you and the others go into that hyperspace realm when you disappear. Kaku said if you pick up a goldfish from the pool, the other goldfish think it simply disappeared. If you put it back, they think it appeared, out of thin nothingness. They don't know we exist up above them in our own dimension. But if a wind comes along to ripple the surface of the water, or if raindrops pound it, they begin to sense an outside force, you see? From another dimension. It's affecting their world. Kaku explains that light beams aren't straight, they ripple, too, it's been discovered."

"They do? Wow."

"And light ripples because it's acted on by another

dimension—what Kaku calls hyperspace. So like the fish, we're feeling the effects of that fourth dimension, though we can't see it and most of the time, to us, it doesn't even exist."

"Gee, I'm going to have to read about that, Aunt Celia. It makes sense to me. Maybe we're all part of that fourth dimension, we act within it at times . . . vampires, I mean."

"That's exactly what I was thinking! If some of you could try to harness that space or dimension or explore it and the power there, there's no telling what we could discover."

Dell sat silently, thinking about what her aunt had said. Hyperspace. A fourth dimension. The place that allowed vampires to disappear and reappear back into human form.

"It's part of the Unified Field Theory," Celia was saying. "There's speculation that there might even be ten dimensions, eleven, who knows yet how many. I find that just amazing."

After her Aunt Celia left, Dell went to the bedroom where the computer sat and did a search on the Internet for hyperspace and Dr. Kaku. She wanted to know more, she wanted to try to understand it better.

Ryan found her there and asked, "How was Celia?"

Dell turned from the monitor, "Oh, she's fine, just fine. I'll tell you all about it later."

That night she discussed it with him and saw he wasn't quite as excited as she had been. "What if he's wrong?" Ryan asked. "Has it been proved scientifically?"

"I'm trying to find out. It just opens up a whole new thought for us, Ryan, all of us, not just vampires, but for the human race. If there are dimensions beyond the reality we know, then the existence of creatures such as ourselves isn't so strange, is it? In other dimensions, why . . . there might be all sorts of worlds and creatures, but they're just beyond our notice, like our world is to the goldfish."

"Well," he admitted, "since there are vampires and I know that's real, I guess nothing should surprise me."

She boxed him on the ear and laughed. "Funny guy," she said, hugging him close.

Later that night as they sat studying in the living room, Dell let her mind wander over their new life together. They lived outside a small town south of Dallas where she could still buy supplies from Ross' worker bees. They had a hundred acres, a small house, and a barn for Lightning. The old horse was showing his age, but he still didn't mind a little trail riding now and again. Ryan bought a roan gelding for himself and most weekends found them riding across their land, talking and laughing.

Ryan had taken work on a local ranch, breaking horses and training them for cattle roundups. Dell worked at the town library, spending her days reading everything on the shelves when she wasn't arranging story parties for area children or checking out a book for the occasional reader who wandered in.

Life was calm, quiet, routine even, and as wonderful as Dell might ever have imagined. The brightest element in her universe was Ryan. He was all she needed. He loved her fully and without restraint. She loved him back with every ounce of her being. When they'd married, she knew her destiny was sealed to Ryan and that, yes, she would suffer a thousand deaths when he grew old and died. But she also knew without him she might have wasted away, or given in to her baser instincts and become a heartless machine, a taker of blood, a killer.

She never let him see her take the blood they kept in the refrigerator and she never told him how sometimes when they were making love she wanted nothing more than to lick and nip at the skin just at the juncture of his strong, smooth jaw. Mentor had not told her she would fight forever the urge to drink even from the one she loved.

One evening, days after Aunt Celia's visit, as Dell sat poring over an assignment in math, she felt something move in her abdomen. It was nothing more than a slight flutter, but it was undeniably something unusual. Growing stiff, she sat straighter on the sofa and glanced at Ryan. He was watching a football game and eating from a can of cashew nuts.

She moved into her own thoughts and began to probe her body. She let her consciousness move from her mind to her chest and then lower, to her abdomen. She sought out her reproductive organs, ovaries, tubes, and finally, her womb.

She was pregnant! It was unmistakable. Though she did not have monthly periods and therefore never thought about impregnation, it had happened to her. To *them*. A baby.

A child of their own.

Would it carry her disease and be vampire like her one day? Would it be human like Ryan? Oh, dear God, what had they done? Her mother had told her of a child called a dhampir came from the union of human and vampire. She had said sometimes such a child grew up and turned on its parent. Her world seemed to tumble down around her ankles. They had been so happy, two people with a secret life, living far from the city and the humans. They worked at jobs they liked, kept the little farmhouse secure and snug, went for rides on their horses, studied college subjects together. They'd created a world unto themselves.

After a while they planned to buy a few calves and begin a small herd of cattle. They led such a serene and rich life together. It never occurred to them that they could procreate. Why hadn't she listened to her mother?

A baby. What did it mean? Would it even live? She had to talk to her mother about it again, she had to contact Mentor. She needed advice. Or was it too late?

"Ryan?"

He turned at the sound of her puzzled voice. "What? Is something wrong?"

He saw it in her face. She could never keep anything from him. "I don't know if it's wrong or not, but something's changed."

That night they went to bed and held each other. She cried a little and he patted her back. "What will we do?" she asked, despondent.

"We'll love it," he said.

"But what if . . .?"

He touched her lips with his finger. "It'll be fine. He'll be a boy, a big strong boy, and we'll name him Sean."

"Sean?"

"Or Tom. Or Joshua."

She laughed and snuggled close. "I love you so much. You're crazy as a doodlebug and I still love you."

"That's why it's going to be all right, Dell. This baby comes out of our love. It's pure and good and a new creation."

"But it might be . . ."

"It won't. He won't."

"*She* might be . . ."

"I won't have it," he said. "He'll be like me. He'll have a way with horses. He'll love animals and the ranch. He'll grow up and turn this hundred acres into a thousand, build our herd to hundreds. I'll teach him how to work on my old truck to keep it running. He'll be respected and honorable, and he'll be ours."

"You won't love her if she's like me?"

He leaned back to look into her eyes. "I'll love him more!"

"Her."

"Him."

They laughed and they cried and they held onto one another in the darkness, thinking their own individual thoughts, both afraid as they could be.

* * *

Having gained his heart's desire, Charles Upton reveled in his new life. He had moved his operations to Dallas to be near a supply of blood. However, lately he'd been preying, trying it for the first time when he had been shopping at a downtown jewelry store for a bauble for one of his women. They flocked to him now, the women, despite his age. He was rich, and becoming vampire had done away with all the terrible symptoms of porphyria. His skin was smooth, his eyesight sharp, and his mind as brilliant as it had been when he was a young man.

He had been in the store, looking over a velvet tray of diamond bracelets when the manager came from the back to help the clerk with Upton's purchases. The manager was in his twenties, well-muscled, with a full head of thick, shining brown hair. Upton felt a hunger for him suddenly. He felt his fangs growing and determinedly retracted them before anyone could see.

He paid for the bracelet, a gaudy, much too expensive five-carat tennis bracelet, tucked the box into his coat pocket and left the store. But he did not go far. He told George to leave, take the car home. He'd be along shortly. He had no need of the car and only used it for trips that entailed being seen by humans.

He would not be seen doing what he wanted to do now. It was dark, the store about to close. He waited patiently for the employees to drift out the door and leave. He stood at the end of the building, hiding behind the corner, watching and scheming. When the last of the employees had gone, Upton returned to the store and knocked gently at the glass with his knuckles.

The manager looked up from an accountant's book spread out on the counter and, seeing him, smiled. He came to the door and said, "We're closed, I'm sorry."

Upton said in his most polite voice, "I know, I hate to bother you. I just have one question about the guarantee on the bracelet."

The manager's smile dissipated, but he took a set of keys from his pocket and unlocked the door. "Come in, I'll be happy to help."

The moment he turned his back, Upton flew through the air and knocked the camera to smithereens from a corner of the room. Then he turned, snarling at the shopkeeper. "Come to me," he said. "Come give yourself."

The killing was not swift or neat. Upton had never killed before and had no practice at it. He made a bloody mess of the man before dropping him to the carpeted floor and stepping back, satiated.

For a brief moment Upton panicked. If he were caught in the store with the dead man, it would be found out he was not human. He also had to find the video made by the camera he'd destroyed. He hurried to a back room and found the machine, crashing a fist through it. Back in the store, he flung open the glass front door and ran. When he reached the next building and found an alley, he lifted into the sky and flew to his home.

George saw the blood covering his face and shirt when he entered. He did not flinch. George was paid more than any corporate executive to be discreet and to keep his mouth shut. He said simply, "How can I help you, sir?"

Upton waved him away and washed in the guest bath on the first floor. Spasms coursed through his body, causing him to tremble. These lasted for an hour after the kill. He was as elated as he had been when he first looked in a mirror and saw that the ravages of his disease had vanished.

This was the true joy of being immortal and vampire. No one had told him how exquisite warm, fresh blood could be. They had failed to instruct him in making clean kills, assuming he would always buy their plasma bags, but he thought that occasionally

he would take a human. Maybe more than occasionally. He felt more powerful than ever. He was
indomitable.

He could be king.

The phrase slipped into his mind and stayed. *He
could be king.* He was already higher than any man.
If he wanted, he could rule over the vampires, take
over Ross' control, do away with Mentor, and lead
the rest into the future as they did his bidding. Why
shouldn't he?

He stripped off his clothes, throwing the boxed
diamond bracelet onto the top of his dresser. One of
his women was coming over tonight. This was her
gift. She'd do anything for diamonds.

Upton stood naked before a full-length mirror and
felt both love and loathing for his body. It was hard
and strong. His teeth were his own and were white
as bone. But it was his skin, the unblemished skin,
that sent him into ecstasy. God, he had yearned for
years to be free of the sores. But his body was old,
so old. He was skinny-legged and his buttocks
drooped. His face was wrinkled and he hadn't much
hair left, the remaining sprigs a shade of yellowing
white.

He wondered if he would be trapped in this old
body forever. He got women because he was rich
and because he could use his power to lure them.
He could make them believe he was handsomer than
he was.

Why were there so many drawbacks to his new
immortality?

As he showered, he pondered the question of his
aging form and what he might do about it. Surely
there was a solution. Look at Ross, he was a beautiful
immortal. He didn't walk around in an aging body,
trapped within it. He'd have to ask Ross what he
might do about his age, find out if it could be reversed or something.

As he dried off, he relived the murder of the jewelry store manager, losing himself in how won-

drously exhilarating it had felt to drink the man's blood.

When the woman arrived and George showed her to Upton's bedroom, he handed her the box. He listened while she gushed over the beauty of the bracelet, but all he could think about was sinking his fangs into her beautiful, swanlike throat.

He made up his mind. Before she was able to leave tonight after their lovemaking, he would kill her.

He would kill whomever he wanted, whenever he wanted to. He had a whole world full of victims to prey upon.

No one could stop him.

*　　*　　*

Ross brought the problem to Mentor's attention. "I should have killed that old bastard."

"For once I'm inclined to agree."

Charles Upton was totally out of hand. He had sold out his business and the twin-tower building he owned in Houston and moved his operations to Dallas in order to be in the midst of his kind. He was no longer ill, but strong and growing braver and more wicked each day. "Nothing and no one can stop me," he was heard to say often when thwarted in business affairs. "Either get out of my way or I roll over you."

He wanted the Strand-Catel operation, and he wanted to ease Ross out of his position. He had not done one thing to increase Ross' power. He'd reneged on his deal, forgetting what he owed his maker. In fact, Upton took it upon himself to announce he was the only Predator with the business acumen to bring all the clans together and help them infiltrate and gain control over industry in the Southwest. Then they'd move out to the West, the North, and the East. His plan was national and in years to come would evolve into international.

"We don't live in the dark anymore," Upton proclaimed to anyone who would listen. "It's time we came out into the light and made this world our world. For those of us who don't have the guts for it, the Cravens, and the weak beasts—they need to be cut off from the tree."

"Although I agree with Upton in principles—I've been saying the same thing for years—he's a megalomaniac," Ross said. "And I'm here to tell you he needs putting down."

"If you hadn't made him like us . . ."

"I know. For the first time I trusted a mortal. It won't happen again."

Mentor said he would take care of it, as he always did. Without spilled blood, without rancor and riot.

"I don't know why I keep listening to you," Ross said. "I wish you'd just take him out and let me help you burn him."

"We won't do that unless we have to," Mentor said.

He walked with Mentor through Bette Kinyo's neighborhood. It was twilight, and children were being called indoors. As the lights came on and the cars turned into the driveways, they passed by Bette's house. "Here, for instance," Ross said, pointing at the front door. "So far she's kept her promise, but she's human, Mentor. She's prey to vanity and ambition, morals and laws. I don't trust her."

"She's never brought us harm. You must never come here without me." As they walked by, Mentor glanced longingly at the house.

Ross flung his head and his long hair fell back on his neck. "I don't know how we've kept things going here the way you let everyone do as he pleases. Upton's going crazy, just crazier every day. That woman in there and her man, they could bring us down anytime they feel like it. And Dell. Running off with that boy, turning her back on the rest of us, breaking every code we ever taught her."

"You're intolerant, Ross. It must make your life miserable to see so many things you want to put to

rights and they're all out of your reach. Dell's doing
fine. She's gone away on her own and living the life
she was meant to live."

"I don't think she should have done it. And none
of these people are out of my reach, Mentor. You
know better than that."

It was true things had changed, but they always
did. It was the only certainty, Mentor realized. The
world turned and change came and they adjusted.
He had no worries about Bette or Alan, but he did
keep a mental watch on Dell and he was in constant
surveillance of Charles Upton.

Though he knew Dell was pregnant, which pre-
sented a whole new set of problems, it was Upton
he must do something about right now. Immediately.
He was one of the most powerful Predators who had
ever been made since Ross, perhaps since Mentor
himself, and that made him a great danger. Mentor
was going to have to go to him, to reason with him.
If it didn't work . . .

"It won't," Ross said, reading Mentor's thoughts.
"He has to be put down."

"All you ever want to do is kill."

Ross stepped close to a hedge growing at sidewalk's edge, reached down quickly, and came up
with a silky, long-haired white cat. It spit and clawed
at him, instinctively knowing it had been trapped
and now was prey. "I don't kill for fun," Ross said,
slipping one hand around the cat's head to break its
neck. "Just for the blood of it."

Mentor reached out and held Ross' wrist. "Let it
go. You're just testing me. It's tiresome."

Ross looked him in the eye and loosened his fist.
The cat fell to its feet and scampered away like a
flash of silver in the darkness. "You're no fun at all.
You're the prissiest Predator who was ever made."

Mentor laughed, his laughter booming out from
deep in his chest, and it made him feel almost
human. "Prissy, am I?" He laughed more, laughed
so hard it brought a smile to Ross' full, red lips.

"And not only that, but you're old and incredibly wrinkled and look like a sack of bones. When are you going to drop that suit of flesh and get one that won't scare birds from the trees?"

When Mentor left him, Ross headed into a violent Fort Worth barrio where gangs drew blood every night of the week. He would prey there, taking some young buck and draining him dry before dropping him into a dumpster or a ditch. "I hate that stuff we call blood in the blood bank," he said, leaving Mentor. "It's colored water compared to the real thing. You ought to try it again sometime. Maybe you wouldn't act so grouchy."

Mentor shook his head and went on his way into the heart of Dallas, moving slowly toward Charles Upton. Work to do, always there was work to do.

*   *   *

George answered the door. He bowed his head and led Mentor inside to wait in a comfortable room overflowing with rich gilt, ornate cornices, a hammered tin ceiling, and a dead fireplace filled with a vase of lilacs. Where Charles had found lilacs Mentor could not fathom. They must have been trucked in from some northern clime where the heat did not kill them.

"Hello, and how are you?" Charles asked, bustling into the room like a man half his age. "I don't have much time, I have a phone call coming in a few minutes."

"We have to talk, Charles. Forget the business." He noticed a faint smear of blood on the old man's cheek. He wondered about it, but dared not probe the other vampire's mind just yet.

"We have nothing to talk about. You do your job, and I'll do mine. Now if you'll excuse me . . ." He turned to leave, dismissing Mentor.

"Come back here." Mentor did not raise his voice,

but his command could not be disobeyed when he sent it with the power of his mind.

Charles turned slowly. "I don't like you coming here," he said. "I didn't like you with me when I died, and I haven't liked you any better since. You shouldn't even be allowed to call yourself vampire. All you want to do is help people. It's a weakness I really despise."

"You and several others," Mentor said, thinking of Ross. At least Ross could be made to listen to reason—either with talk or with battle—but he feared Upton could not.

"All right, all right, what do you want? You're wasting my time."

"What do you plan to do, Upton? Take over the world? And what's that blood doing on your face? Have you been killing?"

Upon squinted his eyes. All his sores had healed, strength returned to his muscles, and even his face had relaxed, though his lips had long since forgotten how to smile with genuine feeling. He stalked closer, his fists balled at his sides. "I kill when I want to. You can't stop me. I'll take over the world if I want, too. Do you hear me, Mentor? When it's time and when everything is in place, I will indeed rule this world. It may take me years, decades, even a century, but it will be mine. Is that what you wanted to hear? Is that what you feared in the dark dream when I was made, when I embraced the Predator's life? That one day I would rule over even you?"

"I don't think that will ever happen."

"Won't it?" Upton turned on his heel, but before he reached the doorway Mentor was at his side. He had him by the arm, staying him.

"Upton, I tried to talk to you. I've tried to understand the agony you suffered in your human form and believed you could get over it now that you have a second chance. But you nurse the past, don't you? You blame the universe. You blame God."

"God!" Upton spat out the word. "Never speak to

me of a god. One who let me shrivel up and break out in sores. One who lets children get run over, molested, and mauled and mutilated. One who lets the world suffer floods and fires and winds and pestilence. What God?"

Mentor sighed. He dropped his hand from Upton's arm. "I'm sorry, Charles, that you feel that way. You have to come with me now."

"With you? I'm not going anywhere with you. I'm not spending another minute on you."

Mentor moved as fast as light, wrapping his arms around the old man, holding him to his chest, his face in Upton's, so that his words would not be mistaken. "We're going away, Upton. To a place where you'll be safe and the world will be safe from you."

"I will not. Let me go."

George ran down the hall and stopped at the doorway, where the two men were locked together. "Mr. Upton?"

Mentor turned his head and looked at George. "Stay here as long as you wish. Say good-bye to Mr. Upton. This time it's forever. If you ever speak of this, I'll come for you."

"George, get him off me!"

"Let's go, Upton. It's time to go."

Mentor whisked his charge from the house, through the door that he opened by the force of his mind. Once outside, he took Upton with him straight up through the Dallas night sky. They sped faster than any machine man had ever devised until they were high above the Earth, watching it turn. The last time Mentor had done this had been with Dell. It was at least a year ago on another summer night in the endless stream of summer nights that were to come.

Upton turned and twisted, bit and spat and cried. Mentor hung onto him. They sailed down, down, dropping with dizzying speed toward Thailand. Toward the only safe place for Charles Upton, the vampire who possessed no control, no soul, no feeling for the human race from whence he'd been born.

The monks wrestled Upton into chains. Mentor knew he would one day realize his power and try to leave, but he'd not get far.

"I'll get you for this," Upton shouted. "You can't do this to me."

"We have to do it, Charles."

"I'll . . . I'll stop killing, is that what you want? I only did it twice!"

"That's only part of it. And you'll never stop killing. What I want is for you to be a creature who understands consequences. And either you do and don't care, or you don't possess the capacity to understand. You must stay here until we find out if you'll ever change. The only other alternative is to kill you."

"If you leave me here, I'll make you pay, Mentor. I swear it."

Mentor paused at the prison cell door and stared at the old man. He shuddered inside. He had tapped Upton's mind and knew he not only meant it, but he would work every single second of his existence to make it true.

"You can try," Mentor said finally. "But I would advise against that route. Stay here and listen to the monks, Charles. Learn from them. Maybe one day you can be free." Even as he said it, Mentor knew he was wrong. Upton could never be free.

Upton spat at his captors as they padlocked his chains to the damp, smelly wall. "I will never speak to these mothers of monsters again," he shouted, twisting away from them. "I'll kill them the first chance I get."

Mentor thought he would never get that chance.

Walking down the corridor, he glanced in on Madeline and took her abuse before leaving her to her papers and her writing. In the chapel, while red candles burned and the subtle scent of incense wafted through the air, Mentor knelt on the hard stone floor and hung his head. There was no evidence of a crucifix or any other religious artifact in the monastery, but Mentor knew it didn't matter. Prayers had been said here for hundreds of years. Maybe the God Upton didn't believe in would hear Mentor's pleas.

Being vampire was no easier than being human. It was harder. It was always a hard-fought battle between evil desire and higher morality, no matter what type of vampire you became, Natural, Craven, or Predator.

Do you hear me? Mentor cried out silently. *Have you ever heard any of us and have you any mercy for us in the end?*

After his meditation, Mentor rose and left the monastery. In his mind he could hear Upton calling after him, threatening, weeping, begging. He would probably have to remain in his cell until the end of time. Mentor did not believe Predators such as he ever reformed. He was a human born bad, with evil in his heart, and there it remained. While Madeline grieved through a thousand years, Upton would plan and scheme, rant and rave. Let him. If he ever devised an escape, they would all track him down and set him on fire, scattering his being to the wind.

*   *   *

Ross sat in the office waiting for the acting president of Upton Enterprises. David would do as he said. He had no choice.

Ross did not bother to rise when David entered the room. He immediately took over his mind, leading him to sit in a chair opposite. He put suggestions and commands into the other man's brain so that he would do as instructed, the way someone would who has been successfully hypnotized. Mentor called it mesmerizing. Ross just called it control.

I will supply a body, he said telepathically, *from people I have in a Houston hospital. They will contact you when it's ready. There will be a closed casket funeral for*

*Charles Upton. You will arrange the funeral and return
to take over the company. Your press release will say what
the death certificate says: Upton died of his disease. From
that day forward, you will report to me only. I am your
boss, your master. All profits will be put into my account
in Switzerland. You will run things for me, handle all
daily affairs, and you will never question either your for-
mer employer's death or my command. Do you
understand?*

David nodded mechanically.

"That's fine, then," Ross said, standing and speaking aloud. "Tomorrow you will send out word Charles
Upton is dead. He is dead. You understand?"

"Yes, sir."

Ross patted the man on the back and left the office.
Upton Towers in Houston would have been dwarfed
by the new building they'd bought in Dallas. It rose
in gold glass from the center of the Dallas financial
district, towering over lesser buildings. And it was
all his with Upton out of the way. Sometimes Mentor
did him great favors without even realizing it.

Ross smiled and punched the elevator button for
the lobby. He hoped Upton was enjoying his sojourn
in prison. He never should have betrayed a business
partner that way. It had been his undoing.

* * *

Charles leaned against the cold stone in his cell
concentrating on moving his mind beyond the monastery's walls. He could not reach either Ross or
Mentor, but after several attempts, he was able to
connect with David.

He tried to converse with him, but it was as if he
were roaming a vacant bank vault. Finally, he settled
for reading the memories in David's mind. When he
got to a recent memory involving Ross, Upton halted,
biting down on his tongue until it bled into his
mouth.

He was going to be reported dead. No one would

look for him. They were going to supply a body, a
death certificate, and tell the press the wealthy fi-
nancier had been killed by his disease. No one would
ever question it since it was public knowledge he
had suffered from a terminal illness.

Upton struggled against his chains, screaming out
vocally. A monk passed his cell, paused, looked in,
and moved on.

Upton tried to reach David's mind again, suc-
ceeded after much effort, and searched his memory
for all the details.

Ross was taking over.

Mentor had put him away so that Ross could
take over.

Together they'd found a way to make him disappear so they could cheat him and use his power.

This time Upton howled so loud and so long several monk guards came to his door and shushed him.
He roared into their faces, throwing himself this way
and that around the cell his chains rattling like
thunder.

Seeing they would not subdue him, the monks left
again, just as if he were no threat. No one could hear
him beyond the monastery enclave. No one would
ever search for him. He had been outwitted and
imprisoned.

Well! He would find a way to extract his revenge
on both the old Predator vampires who had done
this to him. If it took a thousand years, he would
find satisfaction.

He stopped fighting and sat back quietly to think.
His considerable intelligence would save him.

All he had to do was think his way out of this. He
had all the time in the world at his disposal to put
a plan into motion.

*　　*　　*

Mentor was alerted when Upton went crazy. He
kept a very minor watch on the vampire, but even

if he hadn't, the monks would have sent word. He knew Upton planned escape some way, some day. He'd have to watch him closer now.

It did not surprise him to discover Ross had taken over Upton's enterprises. He cared little about that, feeling Ross would always be pliable to some extent. He was no Upton.

Mentor sat in the backyard of Bette's house. Inside, she slept in the arms of her husband. Outside, the trees rustled and the moon went in and out of cloud cover.

Mentor's thoughts moved to Dell. He gently probed the fetus she carried, touching it with his consciousness. She would give birth to a dhampir, half vampire, half human, and the half-breed would grow to loathe his mother's clan. It would want to eradicate them from the Earth. She didn't yet know these things, not truly know them, but she would learn when it was too late.

But no matter, no matter, the world would go on. God might listen, or He might have gone on a vacation. Ross would continue being rambunctious and often deadly, his power growing as Upton's billions burgeoned. Bette would love Alan, and she would be loved in turn throughout all the days of her life. Upton would rage and plot, his heart growing ever darker.

And the world would continue to turn. That was all Mentor knew with any certainty.

He looked around once more at the peaceful Japanese garden before sailing above the Earth where he paused, looking down upon it. He then looked up, into the vast reaches of dark, endless, cold space where the universe twirled. None of them had ever tried to go farther out than where he was now. What if they tried? What if there was another habitable planet they could migrate to? But they would just die there, cut off from mankind.

He sighed and looked down again at the blue,

swirling globe of his home, the prison where human and vampire were caught in a timeless struggle.

If he must have solace, then this was it.

The world would go on, whatever happened to him and his kind. It cared little for the affairs of the creatures living upon it as it spun through space and time.

It would always go on, with or without him, through all the risings of all the red moons.